WITHOUT THE STAR

A JACK SAGE WESTERN - BOOK 2

DONALD L. ROBERTSON

COPYRIGHT

Without The Star

Copyright © 2023 Donald L. Robertson
CM Publishing

All rights reserved. No part of this publication may be reproduced, distributed or transmitted in any form or by any means, including photocopying, recording, or other electronic or mechanical methods, without the prior written permission of the publisher, except in the case of brief quotations embodied in critical reviews and certain other noncommercial uses permitted by copyright law.

Publisher's Note: This is a work of fiction. Names, characters, and incidents are a product of the author's imagination. Locales and public names are sometimes used for atmospheric purposes. Any resemblance to actual people, living or dead, or to businesses, companies, or events, is completely coincidental. For information contact:

Books@DonaldLRobertson.com

Without The Star

ISBN: 979-8-9855100-5-8

❋ Created with Vellum

1

Jack, his horse Smokey, and his mule Stonewall were tired and wet. It had started raining the second day out of Cherry Creek, and Jack was soaked. He looked down on the log cabin at the bottom of the hill and watched the smoke rise from the chimney. There was a protective lean-to and corral with at least twenty horses in it a short distance from the house, farther from the creek.

"Would you boys like to be dry tonight?" Jack asked his animals. Neither, with heads hanging low and turned away from the driving wind, showed any interest in him or his question.

"I'll take that for a yes." Jack clucked a couple of times, and Smokey started forward. Stonewall followed close, his head bobbing next to Jack's leg. Reaching the hitching rail in front of the house, Jack called, "Hallo the house." In the dwindling light of the evening, the glow shining through the curtains had grown brighter even as they descended the hill.

Jack, rain pounding on his soaked and drooping Stetson, sat hunched over on Smokey's back, hoping the owner of the cabin would respond. Sure enough, after about ten beats of his heart, the door opened, and a woman called through the crack, "What do you want?"

What the blue blazes does she think I want sitting here drenched in this rain? Jack thought. "Ma'am, my name's Jack Sage. I hate to trouble you, but me and my animals would sure appreciate a mite of cover from this rain, and I'd be eternally obliged for a hot cup of coffee."

The woman's response was silence. After another ten heartbeats, she asked softly, "Are you alone?"

"Yes, ma'am. I truly am. Alone, wet, and hungry."

The muzzle of the business end of a ten-gauge shotgun poked out the door, followed by the woman. Through the rain it was impossible to determine her age. She examined him and must have made up her mind. "We've room for your animals in the barn. When you're finished with them, come on in. Supper's about ready. We'll wait."

Jack touched his hat. "Thank you, ma'am. I'll make it quick."

He bumped Smokey and guided him to the lean-to. Stonewall pushed out ahead. Jack eased slack in the lead rope, allowing his mule to hurry into the makeshift barn. Once they were all three protected, Jack dismounted and looked around.

Whoever had built the lean-to had done a good job. It was solid, and there was no leaking. It faced to the east, providing good protection, and was deep. However, the horses in the corral had no protection. There looked to be about twenty or twenty-five. They were bunched up on the east side, with their tails turned to the southwesterly wind.

There were two horses already stabled at the back of the barn, and they stood watching the new arrivals. Stonewall marched over and greeted them while Jack stripped the saddle, wet blanket, bridle, and gear from Smokey's back. Straw covered the floor, and there was a pile of hay at one end of the building, protected from the wind and the rain. He picked up straw and dried Smokey as best he could. The water trough was outside, running from an aboveground rock cistern that itself was running over around the top, flooding the corral. Jack looked around, found a bucket and walked to the edge of the lean-to. He leaned out into the rain and dipped a bucketful of water from the trough and brought it back for his horse.

He admired the animal, a grulla. Some people called it a gray dun. The big horse was gray with a black mane, tail, and legs. His legs had gray stripes in the black markings, and he had a white face. Jack patted him on the neck as the animal drank. "You're a fine horse. You'd have to be to carry me." Around most men, Jack looked like a giant. He was six feet three and a half inches tall, before he put his boots on, and weighed a solid two hundred and five pounds. He needed a big horse.

Stonewall, his mule, had returned from his socializing. Smokey finished drinking, and the mule took over. While he drank, Jack stripped the pack and pad from the animal's back and started drying him with straw. He worked quickly, and both animals were soon as dry as they were going to get. He led each into a stall, tied them, and forked hay into the bin. Then from the pack Stonewall had been carrying, he dumped some corn for each.

He pulled his Spencer from the boot and, along with his saddlebags, headed for the house. He intentionally made plenty of noise as he stepped onto the front porch and knocked loudly. He didn't want to surprise anyone who had a ten-gauge shotgun at their disposal.

"Come on in," a child's voice called.

He pulled the latch and pushed the door open. Two women were at the fireplace, cooking, and there were three children staring at him, eyes big.

He removed his Stetson, leaned his Spencer against the wall, and lifted the poncho over his head.

The older woman said, "You can hang your poncho on the peg by the door."

"Thanks, ma'am, I want you folks to know I surely appreciate your hospitality. It's wet and nasty out there, and it doesn't look like there's much hope it'll stop anytime soon."

The woman had bent back over the skillet. She raised up, pushing gray hair back from her face, and said, "I suspect you're right, Mr. Sage. This here is Texas, and it's no tellin' how long it'll rain now it's started." She pointed at the younger woman. "That's Scarlet, and I'm Amelia." She smiled at the kids. "Those are Ellie, Buster, and Zach. They're good kids, but they've been cooped up in here for three days."

"Call me Jack, ma'am. I'm pleased to meet you."

The house had two more rooms at the back, separated from the front by quilts sliding on a rope for curtains. A low moan drifted in from one of the other rooms.

Amelia turned to Scarlet. "Go check on your pa."

Scarlet stepped to the quilt, pulled it aside, and moved inside the room, allowing the curtain to fall closed behind her.

Amelia turned to Jack. "That's my husband, Jesse. A horse threw him in the creek. He got caught under a tree root. When me and Scarlet and Buster finally got him out, I figgered he was dead, but we got the water out of him, and he came to life. He ain't come all the way back to us though. That's been over three months ago, and he ain't said nary a word. He just occasionally moans." She looked at Jack and the kids. "I'm talkin' too much. You sit down. Scarlet will join us when she's done. Kids."

The three children ran to their chairs and jumped onto them. The youngest, Jack figured he was about eight, reached for a biscuit. Ellie, who looked to be fifteen, said, "Zach, we need to wait for Mama to say grace."

The brown arm jerked back, but Zack kept his eyes on the biscuits.

"Mr. Sage, Jack," Amelia said, "go ahead and sit at the head of the table." She looked at the children watching her. "Your pa won't mind." Her head turned to Jack. "We say grace before eating."

"Yes, ma'am. That's fine with me."

Amelia moved to the table and sat at the opposite end. "Ellie, it's your turn."

Everyone bowed their heads. "Heavenly Father, we thank thee for this food and ask thee to bless it. We ask thee to please help Pa. In the name of Jesus Christ, amen."

Zach's hand shot out for a biscuit.

"Wait for our guest, Zach," Amelia said. "Ellie, pass the biscuits to Mr. Sage."

"Thank you, ma'am," Jack said, "but I'd be obliged if these young folks went ahead and ate."

She nodded to the kids. "Go ahead."

As Jack ate, he asked, "You say your husband has been laid up for over three months?"

"That's right. We've all pitched in around the ranch, but it's hard without a man around to do man work."

Jack nodded. "I can certainly understand. How about tomorrow I work off this fine meal. You can tell me what needs to be done, or I can just look around."

Jack thought the woman was going to cry. The children stopped eating, and all of their big-eyed faces turned toward their ma, watching, waiting. She controlled herself. "Jack, that would be wonderful. We do so need some help. In fact, if you could check the horses, and farther down the creek Jesse has gathered our cattle. He's gonna try to sell them. We need the money. Mr. Jorgensen has a roundup going on, and Jesse thought he might buy them." She shook her head. "I don't. He has so many cattle already . . . but it would be nice. We could use the money."

Scarlet came to the table. She saw her ma's expectant look. With sad eyes, she gave a slight shake of her head. Then she turned to Jack. "Where are you from, Mr. Sage?"

Her ma's hand shot out and gripped her daughter's forearm. "You know we don't ask people that, Scarlet. It's not polite."

Jack shook his head. "Doesn't bother me at all, ma'am." He turned to Scarlet, whom he estimated to be about seventeen. "Miss Scarlet, I'm originally from Virginia, and now I'm in Texas. I spent some time in Laredo and some in Cherry Creek. Right now I'm headed north."

Jack finished eating, had two more cups of coffee, and stood. "Mrs. Amelia, I thank you for your hospitality. If you wouldn't mind, I'd like to sleep with my animals. After doing whatever needs to be done, I'll be on my way tomorrow."

"I'll not hear of it. If you don't mind sleeping on the floor, we'll make you a bed by the fireplace with the boys. It'll be warm and dry."

"That's mighty generous of you. I sure won't turn down the opportunity to stay dry tonight."

The children picked up the dishes, scraped them into a bucket, and washed them in another. They stacked them on the counter for the next morning. Amelia and Scarlet made pallets for the boys and Jack, next to the fire. Within half an hour, everyone was in bed, lamps were out, and Jack was stretched out on a pallet on the wooden floor. It felt great. He was dry.

JACK WOKE to the sound of rain beating against the house. He lay still for a few seconds, appraising the situation. The smell of coffee in the warm cabin grabbed his attention. He threw his quilt back, sat up, and looked around. Amelia Massey was busy at the fireplace. The big coffeepot was steaming.

"Good morning, Jack. Sleep well?"

"I did, ma'am, thanks." He pulled his boots on, stood, placed his hands at his sides, and leaned his head and shoulders back. It felt good to stretch and, listening to the rain pound against the house, reminded him how good it also felt to be dry.

"Coffee?"

"For sure, thanks."

Amelia poured him a cup and handed it to him over Buster and Zach, who were still sound asleep. She shook her head. "Those boys could sleep through a war."

Jack looked down at the innocent faces. "Ma'am, it isn't any of my business, but they'll live a lot longer if they start learning to sleep light. This can be dangerous country. Aware of what's going on around a person could save his life."

Amelia gave Jack a sweet smile at the reprimand. "You mean like you were while I was getting the fire going and making coffee, Mr. Sage?"

Self-conscious and embarrassed, Jack looked at her sweet smile, rubbed his chin, and shook his head. "Amelia, you have me there." He grinned at her. "I reckon that comes under the heading of do what I say, not what I do."

"Ahh." She gave a couple of wise nods. "Spoken like a true parent. Do you have any children, Jack?"

A momentary darkness spread over the big man's countenance. "No, ma'am, I don't." He could see Amelia catch the change, but was thankful she didn't pursue it with a question. "Before I give you any more *sage* advice, I'm going to step outside and check the animals. Your corral is getting mighty wet. Those horses shouldn't be left standing in that mud and water. Plus they need to get fed. I'll take care of that, too. You know if your husband has any other corrals built on higher ground?"

"Yes, he does. He has one on the hill behind the house. It's about a half mile."

"Thanks for the coffee, ma'am. I'll go have a look."

Jack buckled on his gun belt. He slipped the poncho over his head, making sure the .36-caliber Remington New Model Police was protected, and pulled his Stetson down tight. He picked up his Spencer, opened the door, and slipped out.

The first thing to get his attention was the roar of Comanche Creek over the sound of the heavy rain. The cutbanks of the creek, though a hundred yards away, would normally be visible across the cleared pasture. This morning no banks were in sight, and all that could be seen was swirling water as close as fifty yards from the house.

The creek had jumped its banks and was climbing the slope. With the rain continuing, it would climb higher and higher. *Will it make it up to the house?* Jack thought. *Could I throw up some kind of dam between the house and the rising water?* He looked in the opposite direction, past the corral and up the hill. *Why didn't Jesse build his house higher? People don't realize how far water can spread once it's out of its banks.*

Head down, he trudged across the muddy ground toward the creek. As he neared, the creek rumbled ominously in his ears. The water, out of the banks, was swirling around the bend and, with the force of the creek, spreading up the shallow sloping ground. He spun around and hurried back to the house, throwing open the door and charging in.

"The creek's on the rise. It's already made it halfway to the house and is still climbing. You folks had better start packing everything you need to survive. You'll also have to get your husband out. Do you have a wagon?"

Amelia's hand flew to her mouth. After a wide-eyed moment of fear, she calmed and removed her hand. "Mr. Mica Jenkins borrowed it last week before the rain started, but he hasn't returned it."

Jack could feel anger rising toward this Jenkins. How could a man take a helpless family's only means of transportation and keep it for a week? "Where does he live? I'll go get it."

Amelia shook her head. "You can't. He lives across the creek.

It started rising before the rain started, and hasn't stopped. He hasn't been able to return it."

Jack nodded, realizing the man hadn't been an inconsiderate neighbor, he'd just gotten caught by circumstances. "Can everybody here ride? I don't mean ride a nice calm horse on a picnic, I mean ride. It's rough weather out there, and those horses won't be in the best of moods, forgetting all about the muddy terrain."

"Mr. Sage," Amelia said, "Jesse has been a wrangler for many a year. He taught every one of his kids to ride before they could walk. If we have to, there will be no problem riding."

"Good," Jack said, "that's one less thing we'll have to worry about. You have any of the horses broken to packsaddles?"

The kids had been silent. Now Buster spoke up. "Mr. Sage, both Billy and Ranger are good pack animals. Pa has two packs stored with the tack in the barn. I can show you where."

Jack looked at the determined face of the thirteen-year-old boy. He had a good face, a strong chin and wide brow. His gray eyes gazed at Jack with confidence. "Alright, boy. You have a slicker or poncho?"

"Yes, sir." The boy ran to one of the pegs by the door and pulled a beat-up hat and slicker from the nearest. He shrugged into the slicker and pulled the hat low and tight. "I'll show you."

"Good." Turning to Amelia, Jack said, "Is there any place you folks can stay until the water starts receding?"

"Yes. East of here a few miles is the Jorgensen place. They're good friends. Their home is large. They will most certainly let us stay with them until this storm is over."

Jack nodded. "Come on, Buster. Let's get those animals ready. I don't know how long it'll take for that water to get up here. I'm thinking we don't have more than an hour or two."

The boy charged out the front door, with Jack right behind him. Jack looked to his left. The water was closer. A small mesquite that was no more than forty yards from the house was bent over, with water whipping around it. He turned and jogged after Buster.

Entering the barn lean-to, he was relieved to see Smokey and Stonewall standing peacefully in their stalls. He hurried to the other two horses.

"This pinto is Ranger," Buster said, patting the horse on his neck. "The black is Billy. They're both good horses."

Jack looked around and spotted the pads and pack frames. "Let's get them saddled up. Then we'll have to rope five to ride."

The boy's young face wrinkled with worry. "What about Pa?"

Jack had forgotten about the injured man. "I'll carry him with me on Smokey. That horse won't even notice his weight." The rain beat on the lean-to.

Jack looked out at the corral. Water was running through it from up the hill and from the overflowing cistern and trough. The horses stood in mud and at least two inches of water. "Buster, we need to get your five best out of the corral and then release the others. We'll close the gate behind them. We don't want any of them back in the corral until it dries. Hopefully their feet aren't already swelling."

Buster grabbed a rope from the tack area of the barn and headed into the corral. He made a loop, walked up to a bay gelding, and slipped it over the horse's neck. He led him through the corral gate and into the lean-to. The animal was anxious to get out of the rain.

Jack grabbed a pad and pack frame. Both he and Buster worked quickly. While they readied the horses, the rest of the family packed their belongings and what foodstuffs they could take without it spoiling in the rain. As Amelia and Scarlet brought the items out, Jack packed them in the packs. Between loads, he stepped around the edge of the barn to look west toward the house and the creek. The water was closer, and even the shallow water was moving faster.

2

They needed to leave and soon. Jack had managed to saddle Smokey and Stonewall between saddling and loading the packs for Billy and Ranger.

Buster worked steadily, bringing horses into the barn and saddling them. Jack glanced at the boy. Slogging in the mud, saddling the horses, nothing seemed to slow him down. *That's a boy any pa can be proud of,* Jack thought.

Buster finished the last animal and looked at Jack, who was slipping the pack into the pack frame. "That's it, Mr. Sage. They're all ready to go."

"Alright, Buster. You've done a fine job. That was a lot of work, and you didn't slow down a bit. We only have one more thing to do."

"Get the horses out of the corral?"

"You're exactly right. Let's drive 'em out and close the gate so they can't get back in." Jack swung up on Smokey, and Buster mounted a little bay. In no time, they had the corral empty. The horses milled around the lean-to.

"They're hungry, Mr. Sage."

"Fork 'em out some hay onto dry ground under the overhang.

That'll have to do until we get back. I'm gonna take a look at the water and see about your pa."

The boy jumped off his horse, looped the reins around a post, and went to work with the pitchfork. Jack left Smokey under the lean-to with Stonewall, stepped out into the driving rain, and slogged back to the house. He lifted his head high enough to see the creek. The slope from the little mesquite tree to the house was gradual, almost level. The creek's overflow had spread rapidly, now within five feet of the house. He pushed the door open and stepped inside.

"Everyone about ready?" He looked around the house. Everything that could be moved on top of a counter, bench or chair had been. The quilts that were acting as curtains had been laid across their support ropes so they were well clear of the floor, providing Jack his first look at Jesse. Amelia and Scarlet sat with him. They had dressed him, even with his slicker coat and his hat lying next to him. Zack and Ellie stood at the end of the bed, solemnly watching their father.

Jack strode to the bedside. "Get your slickers on. We've got to get out of here." He bent and lifted Jesse in his arms. It was like lifting an oversized rag doll. The man's head lolled back, and his mouth fell open. Amelia jumped forward, but before she could reach her husband, Jack had repositioned the man's head against his massive shoulder. *Jesse can't weigh more than two sacks of grain,* Jack thought, *maybe a hundred pounds. I was more right than I realized when I told Buster Smokey wouldn't even notice the extra weight.*

Amelia and the three children were donning slickers and hats. All of them wrapped bandannas over the tops of their hats and tied the ends beneath their chins. Amelia did the same for Jesse.

"You all ready?" Jack asked. He watched Amelia look around the house one last time before she answered.

Then she nodded. "Yes."

"Then let's get out of here." Jack had noticed water starting to seep under the logs on the creek side of the house, and across the floor. They were cutting it close.

He followed the woman and her three children into the driving rain and took one final glance toward the creek. The water swirled at the front corner of the house. He knew the house and everything inside would be gone when they returned.

The family ran to the barn, with Jack clutching Jesse close in his big arms. Buster had the horses ready, and everyone mounted. Momentarily, Jack laid Jesse across a wide shoulder, grasped Smokey's reins, stuck his left foot in his stirrup, and lifted the combined weight with his left leg. It was all one fluid motion. As he reached the top, his right leg swung over Smokey's back as both arms grasped Jesse close, keeping his head from lolling around, just like a mother would a newborn infant. He settled into the saddle. He needed Jesse astride the saddle, and the unconscious man's body was draped over the left side of Smokey like he was trying to ride sidesaddle.

Jack looked up to ask for help, but he needn't. Buster and Amelia were there. He lifted Jesse high, and Buster, almost as tall as his ma, pushed his pa's leg up, flexing the calf and thigh. He held the booted foot, thrusting it across the saddle to his ma on the opposite side. Once Jesse was astride the saddle, Jack settled him into the front, making him as comfortable as possible. *I'm glad this is a short ride,* he thought. *Hang in there, Jesse. You'll be out of this saddle in no time.* But another, more ominous thought slipped across his mind. *Will this be the last time Jesse forks a horse? He's as close to dead as a man can be without dying.*

"Somebody lead the way. Let's get out of here," Jack said.

Amelia was in the lead with a packhorse trailing her. Next came Ellie with another pack horse, then Zack, Scarlet, and Buster leading Stonewall. Jack brought up the rear with Jesse. As they came out from under the protection of the barn, each person turned to look back at the house and creek. When it was Jack's turn, he did as the others had, and was amazed at the sight.

The water had traveled the entire width of the house and was piling against the front. The door was still closed, but Jack knew water was filling the inside of the home. It was sad to see, but folks had to learn. This was the hard way. At least no one had drowned. Then he thought of the weight of his passenger. Comanche Creek had claimed a victim, even though it was before the flood.

Jack pulled his eyes from the sight and watched the folks ahead of him, all bent low against the driving rain. He felt Jesse's head roll off his shoulder. He simultaneously lifted his right shoulder and grabbed the man's head with his right hand, gently moving it back against his chest. With the man this close, Jack could smell him, not the strong male odor of exertion, horse sweat, and hay, but the smell of a clean child, the scent of soap.

When Jesse had been stretched out on the bed, Jack had gotten a close look at him, a good-looking man, as men go. Sharp cheekbones, sharper now that he'd gone three months in bed, wide-set eyes and a solid chin. Buster looked a lot like him. He must've been a strong man, for his son had surely been taught his ways, and the boy wasn't afraid of hard work. He'd make a good man. Jesse had that legacy. His sons were all alive.

Jack pulled himself back to the present. Smokey was slowly making his way up the trail behind the other horses. Jack could tell the grulla didn't like following. He was a leader and expected to be in front. "If you're gonna be a good leader, boy, you've also got to know how to follow." He thought about what he had said, and added, "And who to follow." The gray horse shook his head. Though Jack felt sure he was shaking away the rain, he laughed. Maybe the big horse was disagreeing with him.

They rode on. The roar of the creek faded. The only sound was the beating of the rain against his hat and poncho. The skies were low. Clouds rushed across the sky, seeming at times close enough to reach up and touch. They had left the timber and the house behind. They rode across hilly pastureland, normally dry and dusty, but now muddy with rivulets and small streams cut into the slopes and filled with running, splashing water. Patches of trees were scattered across the land, some oak, some mesquite, all green from the rain. The rain would sweeten the grass. At least that would be good. It would also fill the creeks and leave ponds of water across the normally dry countryside, making for a trail drive without concerns for the next waterhole.

Jack thought about the trip ahead. Would he be able to tie up with a herd? If he did, would they be heading to Abilene? Maybe the rails had made it farther west? Farther west would keep him closer to the mountains where he'd like to end up. His own ranch. His dream for a long time. *But,* he thought, *I'm getting ahead of myself. I don't have any cattle. Maybe I should just hire on with a drive? No. If I'm going to buy cattle, here's the place, where they're ten times cheaper.*

He rode on, following, occasionally holding Smokey back while making plans. There would be no drives until the countryside dried out, and there would be no drying out until the rain stopped.

They had ridden for an hour when Jack saw a chimney above the next rise. Buster turned in the saddle, grinned, and pointed. Jack nodded, tossing the boy a faint grin. It would be good to be out of the rain.

Topping the rise, he saw the ranch and yard. Amelia was right. It was much bigger. They had a large barn with a corral and a bunkhouse. The main house had a whitewashed picket fence surrounding it, with a gate only large enough for a person to walk through. To the side of the gate was a long hitching rail. Scarlet pulled out of line and galloped ahead. Water and mud flew from the heels of her horse as she rode. Smokey looked up. Jack could feel his muscles quiver. "Easy, boy, no running for you today." The horse's muscles jumped for a few seconds more and settled down. Jack leaned forward, keeping Jesse in position, and patted Smokey on the neck.

Scarlet had no sooner pulled up to the hitching rail than a man stepped out of the main house and stared toward them. Jack saw the man's mouth open and felt sure he shouted, but could hear nothing over the heavy rain. Moments later men burst from the bunkhouse, and, from inside the main house, someone handed the man a slicker. He slipped it on quickly and stepped into the downpour, marching toward the gate. He arrived as they did.

Two men came to Jack's aid. Jesse was carefully slipped from Jack's arms. Under Amelia's close supervision, and the man who appeared to be the ranch owner, they placed arms around Jesse's waist, while she held his head straight, and carried him to the main house. Jack swung down as another cowhand came up to take Smokey's reins.

Jack shook his head. "No, thanks. If you'll just show me where I can go to get him some food and water and a good wipe-down, I'll take care of it." He pointed at Stonewall. "The mule too."

"Sure thing. We're taking all the animals into the barn. There's plenty of room."

Buster followed Jack's example. The other women and kids made it toward the house as fast as they could. A ranch hand had rolled the big barn door open just wide enough to let the men and horses into the barn. Once everyone was inside, he pushed it closed again.

The rain beat on the tall wooden roof. Jack looked up and was pleased to see no leaks, even after days of continuous heavy rain.

The ranch hand watched him look, and unbuttoned his slicker. "Mighty nice, huh? No leaks. Mr. Jorgensen likes a tight building. Means a little more work, but it sure is nice on days like this." He extended his hand. "Name's Gideon Marsh. That's tough about Jesse. He was a heck of a wrangler. You never had to worry about a piece of horseflesh that feller broke. They was all good." Gideon shook his head and kept on talking. "Mighty strange. He ends up gettin' throwed by a horse and danged near drowns. Probably woulda been better if he had."

A saddle was pulled from a horse and dropped onto a rail. Gideon and Jack turned at the sound. Buster was standing by the rail, staring at Gideon.

The puncher shook his head and kicked some horse apples. "Dang, boy, I didn't know you was there. I'm mighty sorry you heard that. Sometimes I talk too much."

In three long strides Jack was by the boy's side. "Let's get these animals unloaded and dried off."

Buster nodded his head and stared at Gideon a moment longer. "It wouldn't have been better if he had died, Mr. Marsh. He'll be getting well. You'll see."

"I hope he does, Buster," Marsh said, "and I'm sure sorry about my loose mouth."

One of the crew Jack hadn't met yelled at Gideon, "You oughta be. Why don't you stop talkin' and get to work."

Gideon nodded like he thought it was a good idea and pitched in unloading the horses and rubbing them down. Jack worked steadily unloading Stonewall and Smokey. He talked to them as he worked. "Don't you boys get too spoiled. It'll be a long time before you get this kind of hotel living again."

One of the other hands pointed to two wide bins with tops that lifted. "There's corn in the one on the left, and oats on the right. You help yourself. Mr. Jorgensen said to take good care of you. Seems you was a big help to Mrs. Amelia."

"Thank you. I'm sure these two fellas will enjoy your hospitality."

"When you're done, Mr. Jorgensen said to tell you to come on in to the main house. He'd like to meet you."

Jack nodded. "Obliged." He looked at Buster finishing up a rubdown on Ranger. "You about done?"

"Yes, sir. I sure am."

"You look hungry. Why don't you come with me. I bet they

can find something to eat inside that big house for a hardworking gent like you."

Buster grinned up at Jack. "That'd be real fine."

Jack put a hand on the boy's slickered shoulder. "Then let's go." He looked around at the other punchers standing around. "Thanks, boys. Me and my animals owe you."

He picked up his rifle and saddlebags and followed Buster through the door of the barn into the incessant rain. They lowered their heads in unison and made their way in the mud, through the gate, and onto the porch. The two of them took several minutes scraping the sticky globs of rock-infested clay from their boots. Once cleaned, Jack knocked, and a voice boomed from inside, "Come on in." Jack pulled the latch and opened the door, allowing Buster to go in ahead of him. He stopped when he stepped inside.

It had been a while since he had been inside such a warm and inviting home. There was a long leather couch to the right, where Amelia, Scarlet, Ellie, and a lady he did not know, presumably Mrs. Jorgensen, sat. The lady rose as he and Buster came in.

"Mr. Sage," she said, advancing from the leather sofa with her hand extended, "I'm Cathleen Jorgensen. Please call me Cathy. After hearing of you from Amelia, and from all that I've read, I'm exceedingly happy to meet you."

Jack leaned his rifle against the wall and dropped his saddlebags. He removed his hat, inclined his head, and took her hand. It was cool, dry, and small inside his massive paw. He grasped it firmly but gently. "Ma'am, any other gent would have done the same thing, and as far as reading, those writers get paid to print tall tales. That's how they sell papers."

"Well, Mr. Sage, Christopher tells me he knows the doctor in Cherry Creek, and he speaks highly of you."

"Dr. Cook is a fine man. I appreciate any good words he sends my way."

"Cathleen, can't you see you're embarrassing the man,"

Christopher Jorgensen said. He stepped forward and offered his hand to Jack. "But I must say, Mr. Sage, that was a fine thing you did for the Masseys."

Jack took the man's hand, but threw his left arm around Buster. "Thanks, Mr. Jorgensen, but here's the man who got us out of there so fast. He roped and saddled five horses in that downpour all by his lonesome. We wouldn't have made it in time if it weren't for him."

Jorgensen stepped to Buster and extended his hand. "Hi, Buster. I always knew you'd grow up strong, just like your father." He released the boy's hand and placed both of his on Buster's shoulders and looked him over. "I'd say you look like a hungry man to me." He turned toward the kitchen. "Rita?"

A muscular woman appeared in the doorway of the kitchen. Her sleeves were rolled up midway on thick forearms. "Yes, sir?"

"I've got a young man here who is hungry. Do you think you could round up something for him and the rest of his family?"

She smiled at Buster. "I'm sure I can, Mr. Jorgensen. Come on in here, Buster. Zach is wrapped around a donut and a glass of buttermilk. Maybe you can join him while I whip up some stick-to-your-ribs food."

Amelia jumped up. "Thank you for your hospitality, but I can help while we're here."

Mrs. Jorgensen turned to Amelia. "That won't be necessary."

"But it is, Cathy. I'll not be a burden. Come along, Scarlet."

Cathy also turned for the kitchen. "In that case, we can all pitch in. Many hands make light work."

"My dear," Jorgensen said, "I'd like to talk to Mr. Sage. Can you have someone bring him something to eat in the office along with coffee for both of us?"

"I'll see right to it." She wheeled into the kitchen behind the others.

Jorgensen spoke as he started toward his office. "Call me Christopher. May I call you Jack?"

"Certainly," Jack said. He followed the ranch owner into his office. The man had an average-sized desk with a comfortable chair behind it. Two equally thick-cushioned chairs sat in front. Christopher sat and signaled to Jack, who pulled a chair closer to the desk and sat. It felt good to relax. *Don't get used to it,* Jack thought. *You still have a long way to go before you have a place like this.*

3

Rita brought in a tray with a big bowl of chili and a stack of cornbread. To one side were two pieces of apple pie and two cups of coffee.

"Thanks," Jack said.

Rita nodded to Jack and spoke to Christopher. "I'll bring more coffee."

"Thank you, Rita."

Jack watched the woman until she had pulled the office door closed. "She looks tough."

Christopher nodded. "She is. She lost her family to rustlers, but she shot two of them and beat another one till he was begging for the sheriff to arrest him. I gave her a job afterward. She's a great cook, and the hands don't give her any guff."

He leaned across to the tray, took a cup of the coffee and a piece of pie. "Rita knows apple pie is my weakness." With the fork, he sliced off a bite and slid it into his mouth. He chewed patiently, swallowed, took a sip of his coffee, and asked, "So what brings you to this part of the country?"

Jack had eaten several bites of his chili. He stopped and raised his head to look at Christopher. "I really hadn't planned to stop, except to get out of the rain and hopefully get a cup of coffee. Then Amelia invited me to stay the night. I did. The creek got up, and here I am. Just one big coincidence."

"I'm not much on coincidences. I believe most things happen for a reason. Say you hadn't stopped in at the Masseys' last night. They may have gotten washed down the creek today. We both know their home is gone. Jesse knew better. I tried to tell him, but he just laughed it off and said he'd build higher later. He was always like that, a cheerful guy who could break the wildest horse you've ever seen. He had the touch. But he couldn't plan his way to the outhouse." He stopped, stared out the window, and shook his head. "I'll miss him, though. So will his family."

Jack finished chewing and swallowed a bite of cornbread. "Do they have anywhere to go?"

Worry lines creased Jorgensen's wide face. He gazed out the window at the sheeting rain. "Jesse was an orphan. He has no one. I believe Amelia has family in Austin, but I don't think she'll go back. Buster's getting big enough to work, and I think the neighbors will pitch in and help them build a new house. It'll be a sight farther up the hill this time. Amelia's a solid woman. She doesn't have a lot of back-up in her."

Jack finished the chili and cornbread and took a long sip of his coffee. "That's mighty good food." He slid the chili bowl out of his way, pulled the pie to him, and took a bite.

Christopher grinned at Jack's pleased expression. "Good, isn't it?"

Jack nodded while chewing, waiting till he swallowed to speak. "About the best I've tasted."

While Jack finished the pie, Christopher mused, "As soon as this rain stops and the country dries out, we'll be rounding up for a drive to Ellsworth. You familiar with it?"

Jack shook his head. "Not much. I know it's a ways west of Abilene, but that's about it."

"This'll be our first drive there. For the past few years, we've been heading up to Abilene, but since they've opened Ellsworth, it'll shorten the trip by a few days."

Jack noticed something was different. He looked out the window. The rain had slowed to a drizzle. He glanced back at Christopher. The ranch owner was also gazing through the window.

Christopher watched a few more seconds. "As much as we always need rain, I'll be happy to see it stop, and it does look like it has slowed. Hopefully it's close to over."

"Yeah," Jack said, "dust might not be such a bad thing for a while."

"You're speaking the truth, Jack. Although I'd say any cowhand riding drag might disagree with you."

Jack chuckled. The rain had completely stopped, and shafts of sunlight were shooting across the floor. "Would you be open to taking any cattle besides yours on the drive?"

Jorgensen grew serious. "Where are you planning on coming up with stock? Most of the cattle around here are owned. You'd have to go a hundred miles west to get into the wild stuff."

"I've got a little extra money. Figured on buying a few. No more than four or five hundred head. With the difference in price between here and Kansas, a man could make a tidy profit."

"Have you talked to Amelia? I know Jesse put together a nice little herd of about four or five hundred. With all that's going on, I'm sure she's in the market to sell at least part of the herd, and I know of several other folks who have a few head to sell."

Jack shook his head. "I haven't talked to her. Things happened pretty fast since last night. There hasn't been an appropriate time."

"You should, but I have to be honest with you. If it were up to me, I'd tell you to come on, but it isn't. I've never taken a herd north. I use a trail boss. He'll be putting a herd together of several ranchers around here. He would've already been here, except for the rain. He'll be showing up anytime. I'll have about a thousand head. There's two other ranchers, who together should bring in another fifteen hundred, more or less. He won't take more than three thousand. I'll be glad to recommend he take you, but it'll be up to him. His name's Carson Bryant. He's a fair man, but hard."

Christopher looked out the window. "With the sun out, I'd say he'll be arriving in three or four days. I'd recommend you have a herd ready when he gets here. As wet as it is now, the ground should be dry enough to start work tomorrow. We'll begin gathering. Once he gets here, he'll be pushing the herd north in no more than a week."

Jack stood. "Thanks for the hospitality, Mr. Jorgensen. I'd be obliged if I could rent a horse from you and leave my horse and mule for a few days. They need to rest up."

Christopher rose to his feet. "Don't think about renting. I'll have Gideon pick you out a good mount, and your animals will be fine here. They'll be well taken care of. One other thing, you'll need a string of ten or twelve horses for the trip. When you're looking for cattle to purchase, you might keep that in mind."

Jack nodded. "I think I've got an idea of where to find horses."

Christopher stepped to his office door and pulled it open. "Good. You mind if I ask where?"

"I figured Amelia might want to sell some of her animals. With just Buster and Zack, that's a mighty large number of horses."

Christopher chuckled and shook his head. "That's a smart move. I was planning on buying some of Jesse's stock, but there'll still be plenty left when you're done." He looked Jack up and down. "And I won't be needing the size animals you will."

"Yeah, that can be a problem, finding good horses strong enough to carry my load."

They stepped back into the main room. Amelia could be heard in the kitchen, along with Cathy, Rita, and the kids. Jack's boots clunked and his spurs jingled as he walked across the room to the kitchen door and leaned in. Amelia was busy washing dishes, and Cathy was drying. Rita was mixing a big bowl of dough and talking to Scarlet. Buster, Ellie, and Zack were working on what looked like their second donut.

"Amelia," Jack said, "could I speak to you?"

"Certainly." She glanced at Cathy. "I'll be right back to finish these." She dried her hands and followed Jack to the front porch.

Once outside, Jack wasted no time. "How many head of cattle do you own?"

She thought for a moment. "Jesse said he'd gathered four hundred head, but before the rain, Buster counted only three hundred."

Jack's eyebrows rose. "Why the difference?"

"All the smaller places are seeing their cattle disappear. We're starting to suspect rustlers. Rita had that bunch who killed her family. Maybe there's more."

"That's not good. Of course, it could be Indians. Have there been any reports to the law or concerted effort from the ranchers?"

She shook her head. "Not that I know of."

Jack thought on it. "I'll talk to Christopher, but for now, are you interested in selling any of them?"

Amelia clasped her hands at chest level, her eyes wide with hope. "Oh my goodness, yes, Jack."

"Now think about my next question before you answer. What do you want for them?"

Jack knew the very best she could hope to get at the local market was three dollars a head, and probably no more than two. In 1871, cattle were still almost as thick as jackrabbits in Texas.

Finally she looked up at the big man standing in front of her with hope in her eyes. "Would two dollars a head be too much?"

If they made it to market with all of her cattle, Jack knew the least he could make was over ten thousand dollars and possibly fifteen or more. He couldn't bring himself to give her only two dollars a head.

"I can't do that deal." He saw hope disappear from her eyes, and her head dropped. He felt a twinge of guilt for teasing her. "I won't give you a penny less than three dollars a head."

A wide smile spread across her face, and tears filled her eyes. She placed her hand on his forearm. "Are you sure?"

He nodded his head.

"Oh, thank you, Jack. Thank you. This is going to help us so much."

"Do you think Jesse's count of four hundred was accurate?"

Amelia's eyes tightened, and her face became grim. "Oh, yes. Jesse grew up around cattle. He would never exaggerate numbers. If he said there were four hundred head, you could take that to the bank, and I'll tell you something else. A hundred head did not wander off. He had them on good feed, and they had water. On their own, they wouldn't have gone anywhere."

"You suspect anyone?"

Amelia's frown deepened. "You understand, I have no proof, but there is a family who settled several miles down the creek from us. I'm suspicious of them. When Jesse was still alive, we rode down in the wagon, to welcome them, but they didn't even invite us in. We had taken some bread and several pies. They were extremely surly, even the mother. At least I suspect she was the mother. She was hard and spoke as roughly to the kids as her husband, and when I say kids, I'd guess they were all over twenty. They took our gifts and stood there, no thank you, nothing, just waiting for us to leave. It was extremely awkward. Jesse was mad, but I persuaded him not to say anything. They had several grown boys, all armed, sitting on the porch." Then she shuddered.

Jack asked, "You all right?"

Amelia nodded. "Yes. They were extremely intimidating. I didn't like them or their place. The house looked like a shack they had thrown up in a day. I feel kind of guilty about our barn, you know, the lean-to? But theirs was even worse, and I saw no stock and no farming. They were just . . ." Amanda looked out at the barn and corral. "They were just there, like they weren't planning on making a go of it, temporary."

"Armed?"

Amelia gave a single emphatic nod. "Yes. Everyone. The youngest looked to be nineteen or so. He was wearing a gun belt. Even the mother had one on like they were expecting a Comanche attack or something."

Jack thought about the family, if that was what they were. They could be rustling cattle and moving them south. On the other hand, they could have had a rough go of it since the war. He put thoughts of them out of his mind. He didn't need any trouble and wanted to stay away from it if he could. Right now, he needed cattle and horses. "Amelia, if it's all right with you, here's what I'll do. Why don't you draw out a bill of sale for three hundred head of cattle and twelve horses."

"You're buying horses, too?"

"If you're selling 'em."

"Yes, of course I am. What price?"

He grinned at her, his mouth spread wide, showing white, even teeth. "That's my question. You give me a price."

He could see her switch modes and start thinking. Cattle were one thing, but good horses were something else completely. *This is going to cost me,* he thought.

"Jack, I want to give you a good deal. You've been so helpful. Jesse broke and trained all those horses, and he was the best there ever was at his job. I guarantee they won't give you a bit of trouble."

Jack nodded. "All right, how much?"

"You say you need twelve? Why do you need so many?"

Jack could tell she knew exactly what he needed them for. She was horse trading. "Like I'm sure you've guessed, I'm driving the cattle north to sell. I'll need a string for the drive."

"Yes, of course, and you'll want good horses. Horses you can trust, like you can trust Smokey." Before he could answer, she continued, "And you'll need strong horses. Horses that can carry your weight, are fast, and have bottom. Am I right?"

"Yes, ma'am. You hit all the points."

"Normally, Jesse wouldn't let one of his animals go for less than two hundred dollars."

Jack slid his hat to the back of his head. "Now, just wait, I—"

She interrupted him. "But you've saved our lives and are buying our cattle."

"And maybe more than three hundred head, if I can find them."

She pursed her lips and gazed at him, like she would at a child who had interrupted her. "Yes, maybe more." She stared at the barn. "Those horses are our last source of income until Buster is old enough to start breaking and training them. If you take twelve, that's almost a third of our herd." She blew out a breath, as if she'd come to a conclusion. "I can let you have all twelve, fine animals, that you can pick out, for only two thousand dollars."

Jack took a deep breath, looked to his right, off the porch and down, and then shook his head. "Amelia, that's way too much for horses."

"Think about it, Jack. You're going to sell them wherever the herd ends up. You'll get your money back. We'll never see them again. This is our only chance to make money on the work Jesse did."

"That's true, but that's gonna happen no matter who you sell them to." He thought, *If I can get them at one hundred and forty dollars a head, that'll be a good deal for both of us,* and figured in his head for a moment. "Tell you what I'll do. I'll give you fifteen hundred dollars for the twelve, and I get to pick them out, with Buster's help."

Amelia shook her head and looked at Jack like he was losing his mind. "Jack, there's no way I can let you have twelve of those fine horses for fifteen hundred dollars. Jesse would haunt me forever."

Jack watched the clear sky through the breaking clouds and turned back to Amelia. "I've got to have expense money. Since my herd will be included in the drive, I won't be getting paid for my time, and I'll have expenses. Don't you have any room to deal?"

Jack could see the iron in the woman as she bargained for her horses. He almost felt guilty for haggling with her. If he'd had the money, he would've paid her price, but anything over one fifty a head would be biting into his cattle money.

There was silence on the porch. The door opened, and Zach stepped out. "Ma?"

She turned and said sternly, "Not now, Zach. I'll be in shortly."

The boy recognized the tone of his ma's voice, said nothing more, and quietly stepped back into the house, closing the door.

She looked up at Jack. "For you, I will lower the price to eighteen hundred dollars for twelve. You will have your choice of horses and Buster's help. Jack, that is the lowest I will go. Take it or leave it."

Perfect, Jack thought. He thrust out his hand. "You're a tough horse trader, but you've got a deal."

Her hand disappeared in his, and Jack watched the woman wilt. "Oh, thank goodness. Thank you, Jack. I hated to be so adamant, but those horses are really important to us."

"I know they are. You were as good as any horse trader I've ever dealt with."

She smiled at him. "Why, thank you. I think."

The two of them walked back into the house. Christopher had been sitting in his office when they came in. He rose and entered the parlor. "Business completed?"

"Yes," Amelia said. "Mr. Sage has been quite generous. I need to draw up a contract for our animals, and we will be done."

Christopher motioned to his desk. "Please, you can use my

desk. There is paper in the middle top drawer. You'll find a pen on the desk."

Jack grabbed his saddlebags and followed Amelia into the office. Once there, he drew out a thick, brown leather pouch. It had a long flap, which was held in position by a leather tie. He counted out eighteen hundred dollars and laid it neatly in a stack in front of Amelia.

She stared at the money, her mouth open.

Then he closed and tied the pouch, dropped it back into his saddlebags, fastened that side of the bags, and opened the other. From this one he drew out a heavy leather bag tied with a leather drawstring. He opened the bag, tilted it, and dumped eighteen fifty-dollar gold pieces, slugs, into his big hand. He closed the bag and set it on the desk, the bag obviously much lighter. Then he divided the eighteen slugs into two stacks of nine and set them on top of the neatly stacked bills. He looked at Amelia.

She sat motionless, eyes wide and mouth open. Christopher had stepped into the room and pulled the door closed when he saw the first pouch come out of the saddlebags.

Jack cleared his throat. At the sound, Amelia gave a small jerk. Her eyes blinked, and her mouth closed. She looked at Jack, then Christopher, and then back at Jack. "I don't think I've ever seen that much money in my entire life."

"I have a safe in my office," Christopher said. "We can keep it there until you decide what you would like to do with it."

She turned to him. "Oh, thank you. I will rest so much easier. Keeping that kind of money on me would make me horribly uncomfortable." She looked back at Jack. "I didn't realize just how much that would be. Thank you again."

Jack nodded. "You drove a hard bargain on those horses. You deserve it."

Christopher spoke up. "Jack, do you have a brand registered?"

Jack nodded again. "I do. It's the J Bar S. The bar's in the middle, not touching either the *J* or the *S*."

"Good. You have a branding iron with you?"

"Two." Jack looked down at Amelia, still working on the contract. "What's the name of those folks you were telling me about?"

Without looking up, she said, "Mould. Father's name is Eli, and the mother's name is Isabel. I saw at least four sons, all grown, but I don't know their names. We weren't welcome there, so we didn't stay."

Jack looked at Christopher. "Two questions, do you know these Moulds, and have you or anyone you know been losing cattle?"

4

The next morning Jack rode out on a wide-shouldered buckskin. Gideon had said it was a steady horse. *However steady it is,* Jack thought, *it's a smooth-riding animal.* For some reason the horse's name was Adam.

Buster rode at his side on a little chestnut gelding. His name made a little more sense, Red. Jack glanced to his right and watched the boy ride. Buster took to riding like he'd been born to it. In the boy's rifle scabbard, a Winchester 1866 .44-caliber rifle rested under his right leg. The stock faced forward within easy reach. The Winchester was also called a Yellow Boy, for its yellow brass receiver. Jack could see the pride in the boy's face for being trusted with the weapon. His mother hadn't been so excited about it, but common sense won out over motherly concern, especially after Jack's assurances he would keep the boy out of trouble. *I sure hope I can,* Jack thought.

Fortunately, Jesse, Buster's pa, had trained the boy well, and he respected the business end of the rifle. They rode along quietly, Buster acting as guide. Christopher had told Jack he expected his trail boss to be there in three days. A week to get all the cattle branded with the road brand, and they'd be on their way. Jack had enough remaining funds to buy another two hundred head. He'd buy them from Amelia if he could find her cattle, otherwise, he'd stop at several of the homesteaders'. He felt sure he could find enough animals to hit five hundred.

Jack liked Buster. He could tell the boy had spent time around men. He didn't talk much. He was quiet but observant. There was little that missed his eye. He could stand more training, but for thirteen, the lad was alert and competent. That was more than Jack could say for many adults.

They had ridden for several hours when Buster pulled up and pointed to a low mesa ahead. "Mr. Sage, around that hill we'll find our herd. Pa has them set up on good grass, and they have plenty of water, especially now. No reason for them to leave."

"Sounds good, Buster. Let me take the lead. I'm gonna ease around the south side of the mesa and hang in the mesquites. I don't expect any trouble, but a man can never be too careful. Why don't you unlimber that Yellow Boy and make sure it has a full belly."

The boy leaned forward, pulled up and away, and the Winchester slid smoothly from its scabbard. Making sure the muzzle wasn't pointed at Jack, he eased the lever down just far enough to open the breech. He could see a cartridge in it, so he eased the lever back up, locking the breech. The rifle was ready to fire.

Jack pulled his Spencer from the scabbard, checked it, and returned it to its leather. He tapped Adam on the neck with the reins, and the big horse stepped forward with the chestnut following. The white, gray, and red rocks lay fractured around the base of the mesa. There were numerous bunches of mesquite and quite a few oak. But the two types of trees were both outnumbered with prickly pear. It was everywhere. The two riders couldn't ride in a straight line for more than fifty feet without having to detour around a patch. Each leaf was covered with fruit ranging from yellow to a deep purple. Jack had been introduced to the fruit in Laredo. It was delicious, as long as you removed the hairy little spines all around the outside. His friend had called it tuna. When they took a break, he'd pick a few, and they'd have a treat.

The loose rock rolled under the horses' feet as they made their way around the base of the mesa. The large patch of mesquite was close. Jack motioned for Buster to wait, slipped off Adam, and handed Adam's bridle to the boy. He slipped his Spencer out of the scabbard and moved toward the mesquite patch.

It was thicker than he had expected. He moved cautiously through the thorny limbs until he was in position to see the herd. His brow wrinkled in consternation as he examined the cattle. There weren't three hundred there. He'd be surprised to find two hundred.

The cattle were about four hundred yards from him. He pulled up his binoculars and examined them closely. There was no sign of a disturbance. They fed peacefully. Several had bedded down, and others chewed their cud. Occasionally one would low, but not in fear or concern, more in contentment. Jack made a quick count through the binoculars. He came up with two hundred and twenty-five. That was a far distance from three hundred and especially four hundred. He had just about made up his mind to get the cattle moving to the holding area, when three whitetails burst from out of the treeline on the other side of the cattle.

Hitting the open area, the deer didn't slow. They raced across the little valley in front of the stock. While the cows calmly watched them race past, Jack swung his binoculars back to where the deer had first become visible. He waited. In a short time three men rode nonchalantly out of the same treeline and toward the cattle. The cows paid them no mind. It was obvious the cattle weren't threatened, so this had happened before. Jack watched, seething. This was going to embroil him in a fight, and though he didn't mind fighting, in fact there were times he welcomed it, this was not one of those times. Time was in short supply. He had to have his cattle ready and accepted by Bryant, or he'd have to drive them north by himself or find another drive to hook up with. To make matters worse, he had a young boy along with him, and he'd promised Buster's ma he would keep him safe.

As the men reached the cattle, Jack examined them closely with the binoculars, one really young, and two not much older. He felt sure he knew where these people had come from, and he was boiling at the old man sending his youngest boys out to rustle cattle and possibly stretch rope. The ranchers would want to hang them, and cattle rustling was a hanging offense. He watched as the men cut out twenty-five head and turned them south, the direction they had come from.

Jack waited until they were out of sight, and eased back to Buster. The boy had dismounted and was holding both sets of reins, watching him approach. "See anything, Mr. Sage?"

"I did, Buster. I saw our rustlers at work. They cut out about twenty-five head from the remaining two hundred."

"Only two hundred? We've got to go get 'em. They're ours."

"You're right about everything except the we. I'm going to get them."

Buster started to protest.

"Listen to me, son. This is what I do. I have a lot of experience at this. I want you to ride back to the ranch and tell them what's happening. Tell them I believe it is the Mould family, and ask Mr. Jorgensen if he can spare two or three men. Tell them to meet me at the Mould ranch. I'll probably have them in custody by the time they get there. How long do you think it'll take?"

"It'll be at least six hours before they can get back here. Then you've got to add another hour from here to the Mould place, so it'll be a long time. Are you sure you don't need me to stay and help you out?"

Jack clapped the boy on the shoulder. "Buster, if we didn't

need more people to drive the cattle, I think you and I could take care of these fellas. But I need to get these cattle, and I'm hoping to find the rest of them, driven to the roundup. I'll need extra men for that, and if I'm late, I'll never get my herd out with Mr. Jorgensen's."

Buster nodded, understanding the importance of Jack making it to the roundup. He gave Adam's reins to Jack and swung up onto Red's back.

"I'm counting on you, but be careful of your horse, and tell whoever you bring they don't need to push it. Save your horses. I'll be fine."

"Don't you worry, Mr. Sage." Buster swung Red around and dashed the way they had come, disappearing down the slope and through the mesquites.

Relieved, Jack pulled his extra .36-caliber Remington Police Model from the saddlebags, checked the loads, and slipped it behind his waistband. He made sure the thong holding the matching weapon in its holster was free. He stepped around to the left side of the buckskin, placed his foot in the stirrup, and swung up. "Let's go, Adam. We've got a long day ahead."

Jack watched the sun. They were turning further south, away from where he would expect the Mould ranch to be. Following their trail was not difficult. Twenty-five head of cattle plus three horses cut a wide swath through the countryside. He felt little concern for being spotted. He had eased forward a couple of times and watched them. They were riding like they didn't have a care in the world, never checking their back trail. These were undoubtedly the stupidest rustlers he had ever followed.

The country opened up more, and Jack dropped farther back. He could hit them now, and they'd never know what happened, but he wanted to find where they were hiding the remainder of the stock. If they hadn't moved them out and sold them already, he just might get lucky.

Jack kept noting the sun as it drifted lower and lower in the sky. The hands from the ranch had a long way to come, but they'd be coming hard, so they'd make up ground pretty fast. He felt a warmer than usual breeze brush over him, and on it the smell of cattle, a lot of cattle. He could feel the heat coming from the animals and hear their lowing and the rattling of hooves against rocky ground. He pulled up in a small patch of oaks and listened.

There were a lot of cows close. This must be where the old man was hanging out with his other sons. They'd need them to keep the cattle calmed down. Grass was sparse here, not like the grassy area where Jesse had left them. Grass was scattered here, and it wasn't as thick or as sweet. He could hear the discontent in the cattle's restless movement and constant mooing. The rustlers were going to have to do something with their prizes soon, or they'd start losing them, if they weren't already.

The sun gradually disappeared in the west. Only a few clouds remained to reflect the orange light that was no longer visible at ground level. Jack squatted next to Adam and chewed on a piece of jerky. There were still puddles of water everywhere, but the ground had already lost its glue-like consistency. Walking still caused depressions in the mud, but it no longer stuck to boots. Tomorrow the ground would be dry except in lower areas.

Keeping the patch of oaks between him and the herd, Jack mounted and slowly rode Adam back the way he had come. After about a mile, he found a knoll that gave him a good view of the herd and his back trail. He removed his binoculars from the saddlebags and, in the remaining light, examined as far as he could see to the north. Nothing.

I can't wait, he thought. He turned Adam back toward the herd as the light changed from pale to dark gray and then dark. Now he could see the campfire clearly. He tied his horse in the oaks and pulled his rifle from the boot.

He preferred his Spencer over the Winchester for most circumstances. The Spencer fired a heavier bullet, three hundred and fifty grains versus the Winchester's two hundred and sixteen. It also pushed the hunk of lead with almost twice the amount of powder, forty-five grains against the Winchester's twenty-five, and he'd seen the results on both men and animals. The Spencer would put a man down, while with the Winchester, he'd keep moving. Granted, he wouldn't be feeling too good with the Winchester's two-hundred-grain slug in him, but if he was determined, he had a better chance of getting a shot off. Plus Jack's Spencer reached out farther.

Unfortunately, his Spencer had one drawback, and it was an important one, especially in the situation awaiting him, speed of fire. With the Spencer, a man fired, worked the lever, pulled back the hammer, and squeezed the trigger. It was fast when compared with a Springfield or a muzzle loader. But on speed, the Winchester had his Spencer beat going away. With the Winchester, the shooter fired, worked the lever, which also cocked the hammer, and pulled the trigger—much faster.

He could be facing multiple shooters today, and there was no way he'd be able to get more than one shot fired from his Spencer in the melee that might ensue. *I'll use the Spencer like a pistol and follow up with my Remingtons,* he thought. *I'd best not do much missing. With the rifle and revolvers, I'll have eleven rounds, more than enough if I don't miss or have to blast several of them more than once.*

The darkness cloaking him, he worked his way toward the camp, carefully moving from prickly pear to mesquite to prickly pear to oak. He eased close enough to listen to their conversation.

"When we gonna sell these cows, Pa? Somebody might come along. I sure wouldn't want any of us to get our necks stretched."

"Don't you worry about it, boy. Nobody knows nothing. Why, that Massey feller's done gone and drowned hisself, and his kids ain't old enough to do a thing. We can sell every single one of his cows. We skin 'em out and git a dollar a hide. Shoot, with all of 'em, we'll have nigh on to five hundred dollars." Jack heard a yelping laugh that sounded more like a turkey than a man. When it stopped, the voice continued, "Once we git them cows taken care of, we'll git those horses. They'll fetch a pretty penny. I'm bettin' we can sell 'em for at least fifty apiece. She's got maybe forty horses, could be more. We can make a thousand dollars off 'em. Think of it, a thousand dollars plus the five hunnert for the cows. Boys, we'll be in high cotton."

Inside the patch of scrub oak, Jack bumped against a small boulder. He felt it—just the right height for a temporary seat. The reflected light of the fire aided him. He eased to the front of the boulder, scattered trees still stood between him and the rustlers, and settled onto the smooth surface, relaxed, and listened.

A younger voice spoke up. "Pa, what we gonna do after we sell them horses? Ma says she ain't movin' again."

"Shoot, boy. Yore ma has said that mostly ever time we've settled anywhere. Time comes to move along, she'll be fine with it. She might bless me out for a while, but she'll git over it. Anyway, I'm thinkin' we might move south. You know, head down close to San Antone. No tellin' what we might find down that way, with all that money. Why, boy, we'll be pert near as rich as old man Jorgensen."

Jack's leg cramped, and he straightened it. His foot rubbed through dry oak leaves, causing a faint crunch. Conversation ceased at the camp.

An older voice, not the old man's, said, "You hear that, Pa?"

Jack knew he had to make a move. If they scattered into the night and decided to come after him, he could be in trouble. He had a good view of the fire and the men circled around it. Counting the old man, there were five. He didn't want to shoot the old man, but it wouldn't break his heart. However, he for sure did not want to shoot the two youngest. The year before, a young fella had called him out, drawing on him. Not one of his finest moments. He'd had to shoot the boy. It had added to his regrets. He didn't want to add any others.

He stood and, while rising, pulled the Spencer's hammer to

full cock with his left thumb, and the Remington's with his right. The metallic ratcheting of weapons cocking and the Remington's cylinder turning filled the darkness.

His voice was cold and authoritative. "Sit very still. One move, one twitch, and I'll shoot you where you sit."

None of the five budged. Their eyes were locked on their pa, as if waiting for direction. Eli Mould, the patriarch, was positioned perfectly for Jack to see the man's expression in the firelight. His eyes were wide and his mouth open as if his words simply froze between his lips, preventing him from closing his jaws. The only things moving were his eyes, and they were darting across the darkened landscape, attempting the impossible, to see Jack, who looked like another tree trunk, although a very large one. Because the men had been staring into the fire, their night vision was ruined. Now, trying to penetrate the darkness, the only thing they could see was the lasting impression of the leaping flames. Their night vision would come back if they kept their eyes off the fire, but not soon enough.

5

Jack's voice cut through the night again. "Unfasten those gun belts, nice and easy, and drop them as far behind you as you can stretch." He watched as each began unfastening his gun belt. The oldest of the sons, Jack didn't know his name, looked around cautiously while he unfastened his belt. Jack eased the muzzle of the Spencer to where it was covering the man. This one wasn't dressed in homespun and flop hats like his pa and brothers. He wore a black shirt and pants, a black vest, and a black Stetson. The leather of his gun belt glistened in the firelight, as did the butt of his Colt.

"Easy does it, gunfighter," Jack said. "You pull that six-shooter and I'll put a hole in you big enough for one of your brothers to pass through."

Black Stetson jerked his right hand away from his body, unfastened the gun belt with his left, and turned so he could place the belt and gun gently on the ground behind him. It looked as if everyone was complying.

"Good. Now you fellas sit nice and still while I pick up those weapons." Jack stepped from the oaks and slowly walked forward. He picked up each gun belt and rifle, moving them to a pile well away from the rustlers. Once all the weapons were collected, he asked, "Who's in charge?"

No one answered, but he saw all eyes turned toward the old man, Eli Mould. Jack laid his Spencer on the ground, squatted, and picked up the kid's cup. He tossed the coffee out, set the cup back on the ground, and extended his left arm for the coffeepot. Black Hat's eyes narrowed, and Jack could see the muscles tensing in his exposed forearms.

Jack glanced toward Black Hat. "Not a good idea, fella. This Remington may not leave as big a hole as my Spencer, but it'll leave you just as dead. You sit nice and relaxed. Tell me your name."

"Harley Mould. You may have heard of me."

Jack raised the cup to his lips, took a sip, swallowed, and shook his head. "Nope, can't say as I have." He turned back to the old man and jerked his head toward the lowing cattle. "Whose stock?"

Mould finally found his voice. "They be ours, mister."

"What about the twenty-five head I followed your boys driving from the Masseys' herd?"

Mould nodded, feigning relief. "Mister, we can straighten this out real quick. We bought those from Jesse afore he was drowned. Yessiree, Jesse was a good friend. It's a blamed shame about him drowning, but we figgered we'd help him out. Times being so tough and all for 'em."

"Really. That's mighty interesting. I'm betting Buster'll know all about your dealings and verify what you're telling me. He should be along any minute."

Mould's eyes again started searching the darkness. "You by yourself, mister?"

Jack smiled. "I am, Mr. Mould, but I won't be for long. We should have a few Jorgensen hands arriving anytime, along with Buster. That should give you some relief."

Sweat had started slipping out from under Eli Mould's hat

and was slowly running down his forehead. "Why, that'll be fine, just fine. I didn't catch your name."

"Name's Jack Sage, Mr. Mould."

Harley's head jerked up, and he looked at Jack more closely. "You from Cherry Creek?"

"I've been through there."

"Pa, the marshal who cleaned up Laredo and Cherry Creek was named Jack Sage. He killed several folks doing it. I heard he beat a man to death afore cutting his heart out."

Stories, Jack thought. *But sometimes they come in handy.* "He shouldn't have pulled a knife on me. Now you boys sit peaceful like, and we'll all get along fine. If you don't . . ."

The youngest boy heard them first. His head came up, and he craned toward the north.

"Hoofbeats," Jack said. "I think the days of rustling for you boys are about to come to an end." He could see the fear in each Mould's face. This was Texas cattle country, and most rustlers ended up as buzzard bait at the end of a rope.

Jack had expected Buster plus two maybe three men, but the hoofbeats told a different story. There were at least six men, and they were riding hard. They rode into the firelight, and Jack recognized Buster, Gideon, and one other Jorgensen hand, but he didn't recognize the other three. He looked at the horses, at Buster, and then at Gideon. "Looks like you rode those horses mighty hard. There was no call to." He looked at the boy. "Buster, didn't you tell them there was no need to push?"

The oldest of the three strangers spoke up. "He told us. I'm Carson Bryant, and cattle are my business. Cattle rustlers are also my business." He looked at the white faces of the Mould family. "The only way to make a cattle rustler honest is to stretch his neck, and that's just what I aim to do." He turned to the other two men. "Get their horses, and find trees for this bunch. We'll hang them before daylight, and we can get back to our business." He turned to Jack. "You. You keep them covered until we get their horses ready. If any one of them moves, shoot him."

The two riders turned their horses toward the Moulds' animals.

"Hold it, boys," Jack said in a normal voice.

The riders pulled up and turned hard faces toward Jack. Carson Bryant's face reflected surprise and anger in the firelight. "What do you mean, 'hold it'? I gave an order, and when I give an order, I want it carried out."

Jack's cold eyes locked on Bryant's. "I want to sleep in a feather bed tonight, but I figure there's about as much chance of that happening as you hanging anyone. Now, stand down. These fellas are getting a trial. If it's decided they hang, then that's what will happen, but not before, and not by any of you."

"You're Jack Sage," Bryant said.

"Guilty as charged."

"Christopher Jorgensen said you'd be wanting to add some of your stock to our drive."

"I had hoped to, but I'm sensing a veto coming up."

"You can be sure. If you don't get out of my way, you'll make no drive with me or anyone else I know. Do you understand me?"

Jack nodded. "I understand you're a small man who enjoys punishing people for disagreeing with you. I understand that."

Bryant turned to his two men. "Montana, you and Bronco get those horses saddled and these men in their saddles. Do it now."

Jack looked the two over. They were tough-looking older cowhands and wore their guns like they knew how to use them. Montana was taller than the average hand, almost six feet, and built like an upside-down triangle. Wide shoulders with a thick neck, deep chest, and narrow waist. A bullet had left a scar on his right cheek as it burned its way past him, leaving him with a forever reminder. They could almost have been twins. Bronco was shorter, maybe five eight, but with the same wide shoulders, deep chest, and narrow hips. They both looked to be hardworking and hard-fighting men who had little back-up in them. He didn't want to hurt them, and he knew they'd deliver some pain before it was over, but he would do what was necessary.

In the same low tone, Jack said, "Montana, Bronco, that's an order you don't want to follow. It could get you killed."

The two men turned their horses so their gun hands were toward Jack. He could see the leather thongs that held the revolvers in their holsters were loosed. Each man's hand hung relaxed at his side.

Montana, no fear in his voice, said, "Mr. Bryant, I don't think this is worth killing over. These men will get their due. We don't need to hang them."

Bronco nodded in agreement. "Monty's right. This here Jack Sage is known. He's an honest man. Why don't we just go along with what he's saying."

Carson Bryant looked first at Montana and then Bronco. "How many herds have we taken north together?"

Montana thought, his eyes never leaving Jack's. "Thirty?"

Bronco nodded, also keeping a close watch on Jack. "Close. I'm thinkin' thirty-two."

Bryant nodded. "Bronco's right. Thirty-two herds, through all the trouble and Indian fighting a man could imagine." Bryant sat erect to his full height, and his chin lifted. "But if you two don't do what I say, there will not be a thirty-three for you. You have your orders, now carry them out."

Jack had assessed the character of the two cowhands he faced. He took his eyes from them and turned to Carson Bryant. "Mr. Bryant, including the American Civil War, I have fought in wars on two different continents, occasionally under leaders like yourself. These were leaders who were willing to put their men and equipment in harm's way with no concern for anyone's welfare but their own. They were the worst and least effective men I have known. I am amazed that Christopher Jorgensen would hire the likes of you. But let's put that aside, and let me make you a promise. If either of your men draw against me, my first shot will not be for them, but for you. You are the one ordering my killing, and therefore, I will calmly blow you out of that saddle you are so pompously sittin' on."

Buster and the Jorgensen men had been left completely out of the altercation. Now, Jack turned to Gideon. "Gideon, you and your cowhand take Buster and move out of the line of fire. I wouldn't want any of you harmed."

Without a word, Gideon and the other man moved their horses back and away from the coming gunfight.

Buster said, "Mr. Sage, I'll stand with you. I have my rifle. I can shoot. You're just one man—"

Jack cut him off. "Buster, do like I say. Think of your ma. What do you think it would do to her if she lost both you and your pa. You move back with Gideon."

The boy thought for a moment and nodded his head. "I understand, but I don't like it." Then he turned to Bryant. "Mr. Bryant, I heard you're a hard man, but that's not true. You're a mean man, and you'll never be hired to drive one single head of stock that belongs to my ma or me." With that, he yanked his horse around to stand with Gideon.

Jack glanced at Gideon. "Keep an eye on the rustlers. I don't want them taking advantage of the situation, and watch the one in black. He fancies himself a gunfighter."

Gideon, whose Winchester rested across his saddle and already covered the thieves, gave a slow nod.

Jack dropped his Remington back into its holster and turned to Montana and Bronco. "Alright, boys. It's time to fish or cut bait."

Montana pushed his hat to the back of his head and leaned forward, crossing his arms across his saddle horn. "Bronco, I'm about to be without a job. How 'bout you?"

Bronco grinned at his partner. "Monty, it won't be the first time, and I reckon it sure won't be the last."

Jack nodded to the two men and turned back to Carson Bryant. "Bryant, you can count yourself a lucky man. If either of your men had twitched, I would have blown you out of your saddle, so turn your horse around and count your blessings on the way back to the ranch. Get out of here."

Bryant's head swiveled like an owl. He looked at his two previous employees, at Jack, at the rustlers, at Jorgensen's crew, and back at Jack. "I can't go back tonight. My horse is exhausted."

"You should've thought of that before you rode him so hard. I'd suggest you stop on the way and let him rest up. Now, get out of here!" Jack stepped up and slapped Bryant's horse on the rump. It jumped as Bryant was laying the reins over, and raced into the night.

Jack looked at Montana and Bronco. "Thanks, gents. I'm too tired for a gunfight." All the men laughed. "I'm Jack Sage."

The two men swung out of their saddles and stepped forward to Jack, hands extended. The first said, "Montana Huff, my friends call me Monty. Glad to meet ya."

"I'm Bronco Fenn." He looked all six feet and four inches of Jack up and down. "Don't think I've ever seen as big a target as you. I'd sure hate to be yore horse."

Monty grinned at his friend. "And he's as wild as his name. Shoot, I thought he might draw just to see what would happen."

Jack laughed. "I'm glad you didn't. That sure wasn't a reason to die over."

Monty's face turned serious. "We've worked for Mr. Bryant for several years. He's always been a hard man, but his wife died a couple of years back, and he's taken to drinking. When he drinks, he turns into one of those mean drunks, and he's always slipping a swig or two. One of these days it's gonna catch up with him."

Bronco pulled his bandanna from his neck, removed his hat, and started wiping out his hatband while looking at Jack. "This might sober him up. Hopefully, when he cools down, he'll realize how close he came to joining his wife tonight." He looked at the coffeepot next to the fire. "Any coffee in that danged thing?"

Jethro, the youngest of the Mould bunch, said, "Yes, sir, I just made it 'bout an hour ago. A little before Mr. Sage here rode in."

Harley, the gunfighter Mould, said, "Shut your mouth, Jethro. Ain't no reason to be suckin' up to the likes of them."

Bronco opened one side of his saddlebags and extracted a cup. He pulled his gloves from where they had been hanging across his gun belt, slipped them on, and picked up the pot and sloshed it around. "Thank you, boy." He looked around at the Jorgensen riders, Jack, and Buster. "Pot's near full." He poured half a cup, stood, and looked at Harley. "You've got a big mouth, feller. You might try being friendlier." He tossed the half-cup of hot coffee in the rustler's lap.

Harley let out a yelp, leaped to his feet, and began dancing around, frantically wiping at his steaming pants. Bronco ignored the commotion and turned back to get another cup of coffee.

Jack, watching the proceedings, was having a hard time suppressing a grin. He thought, *You'd think a man as old as Harley Mould would learn when it's in his best interest to keep his mouth shut.* The thought had no sooner hit him than Harley started cussing Bronco.

Harley addressed Bronco's lineage with the inclusion of the word old, mentioned several times. Bronco straightened, his full coffee cup in his right hand, turned, and looked at the no longer steaming, but still cussing rustler.

Monty spoke up. "Don't waste the coffee, Bronco. There's others who'd like some."

Bronco nodded, walked three steps around the fire until he stood directly in front of Harley. Watching the cowhand approach, the rustler fell silent. Bronco said nothing.

Jack watched the uppercut start from Bronco's hip. The two men were about the same height, and the blow traveled no more than twenty inches, but it packed the power of strong, hardworking shoulders and arms. Jack noticed Bronco threw the punch flatfooted, without putting any body into it, no pushing off, no leverage. On top of that, he used his left hand because his right hand was occupied with the cup of coffee. The gloved fist hit the rustler on the right jawbone, between the point of his narrow chin and where the jawbone joined his head below his left ear.

Jack also heard the loud clack of Harley's teeth slamming together. A good reason to keep your mouth closed. Jack thought again, *If that didn't break any teeth, Harley Mould has some strong ones, which I doubt.* He had seen the father's teeth when he was grinning at him, and all he could see were either brown, jagged, or black.

The blow lifted Harley to his tiptoes. His head slammed back, and his arms dropped and hung at his sides, like they were no longer receiving any instructions from his brain. He made a quarter turn to his left and fell, stretching full length across the rocky ground.

Bronco turned away from the unconscious man and walked to his horse, drinking his coffee.

Monty shook his head. "Bronco's been called everything Harley was calling him. Shoot, I've probably called him that more than once, but a man steps over the line when he calls him old. That'll do it every time." He had retrieved his cup. He squatted by the fire, lifted the pot, shook it, poured a cup, and held the pot up. "Anybody care for a cup? Still plenty here."

Jack nodded at Gideon and Buster and the other cowhand to step down, and pulled his cup from his saddlebags, and with a grin filling his face, said, "Think I will. Remind me to never call Bronco old."

Bronco looked at Jack. "It ain't the old, so much . . . I just cain't stand disrespect of anyone." Then a wry grin turned one edge of the thick mustache up. "I don't much like being called old, either. Especially from some young whippersnapper rustler."

Monty spoke up. "You did throw hot coffee all over his family jewels."

Bronco's grin widened. "I did, didn't I. Guess I forgot about that. Maybe I'll apologize when he wakes up." He took a long sip of his cooling coffee, stared up at the stars, and after appearing to think about it, said, "Naw, don't reckon I will."

6

Jack was up well before there was any stirring in the camp. His first thought was the rustlers. They had left them tied and set guards to watch them. There had been enough men, so they'd set four watches of two hours each. That would allow plenty of sleep for everyone and offer no chance of anyone falling asleep, or so he had thought.

He glanced over to where the guard sat, and jerked upright. The guard, Troy Eustis, who was the other cowhand with Gideon, wasn't there. He was gone, along with all of the rustlers. Jack slapped his hat on, grabbed his gun belt, and reached for his boots. They were in trouble. Hopefully the rustlers wouldn't kill Eustis, but if they did, it was almost a certainty they would stretch hemp.

He kicked Gideon. "Wake up. Everyone wake up."

All three men and the boy jerked upright, blinking in the fading dark.

"Rustlers are gone, along with Eustis. It looks like they left our horses."

Bronco said, "That's about the stupidest thing they could do, besides rustling."

Jack nodded, picked up his saddle, blanket, and saddlebags, and headed for Adam. "Seems stupid, but if they were trying to get out of here without waking us, they succeeded. It's near daylight, and I don't see Eustis's body around or any signs of a struggle."

He glanced over at Gideon, who was saddling his horse. "Could Eustis have done this?"

Gideon shook his head. "Don't know, Jack. He's been with us less than a month. Came in riding the grub line, and Mr. Jorgensen gave him a job. I don't know nothin' about him. You know how it goes. A man's not asked many questions, and if he don't answer the ones he's asked, there ain't much thought of it."

Monty asked Jack, "You think he could've been in cahoots with the Mould bunch?"

Jack watched Buster saddling his horse right along with the rest of them, and shook his head. "I haven't the slightest idea. Maybe. Maybe they offered him something to let them go. Your guess is as good as mine." He went back to where he had slept and picked up his rifle, then moved to the fire. There was still coffee in the pot. He kicked at the fire and saw a few live coals remaining. He slowly poured the half-full pot over the coals. Then he kicked dirt over the fire and shook the pot out. "Anybody need a coffeepot?"

Bronco spoke up. "I'll take it. Ours is getting pretty beat up."

Jack tossed it to him, and the man tied it to his saddlebags. Then Jack stepped into the stirrup and swung astride the saddle. He looked over at Buster. "I promised your ma I'd keep you safe. If we catch up with them, I want you to hang back. Don't get involved in the shooting."

Buster looked down at his saddle horn and didn't answer.

"Buster, look at me."

The boy looked up.

"I mean it. I don't want you hurt. Do you hear what I'm telling you?"

The boy nodded. "Yes, sir. I'll hang back."

"Good." He looked around. "This is really no one's fight but my own. If any of you boys want to take your own trail, feel free to do so. There'll be no hard feelings."

Bronco didn't even look at Monty. "We'll be ridin' with you. Neither of us care for rustlers."

"Goes for me, too," Gideon said.

Jack looked at Buster. "You know the way. You can go home if you like. In fact, that would probably be the smart move."

Buster sat as tall in the saddle as his thirteen years would allow, and held the butt of his Winchester on his left thigh, so the muzzle jutted toward the sky. "I'm ready, Mr. Sage. Anyway, I'll be fourteen in August."

Monty grinned and winked at the boy, while Gideon said, "Them Masseys always did come with the bark on."

Buster sat a little straighter in the saddle and grinned back at Monty.

Jack didn't laugh. He gave Buster a flinty look. "Just remember what I told you. Stay behind."

The four men and a boy headed southeast, following the trail of the rustlers.

Jack nodded at the tracks. "They aren't making any effort to hide their trail."

Bronco pointed ahead, where the distance between the impressions grew wider. "No, but they ain't hangin' around in this country either. Looks like they figured they was far enough away from camp and cut loose. Notice there are six horses. It don't look like that Eustis feller is being forced too hard."

Gideon shook his head. "Mr. Jorgensen shore ain't gonna be pleased about this."

Buster looked at the cattle as they rode past. "What about the cattle? They're hungry. They'll start scattering 'cause the grass is all but gone."

Jack replied, "We won't be gone long. We'll follow these fellas for a while. If we don't come up on them, we'll just count them off as being lucky. We know who they are, so I imagine the ranchers in the area will contribute to a reward. I'd bet they'll be in jail within a month unless they completely leave the country."

Jack scanned the area ahead. The rolling hills were dotted with green, and the rain had greened up the patchy grass. The mesquites had thinned, and now the dark green of the clumps of oak competed with the only slightly lighter green of cedar and the occasional desert willow. But in the open portions of the rolling hills, no rustlers were visible. Only cattle, deer, and a lonesome coyote occupied the grassland, and he wasn't in sight for long.

They rode in silence for an hour. Approaching a rise, Jack pulled Adam to a stop. The others did the same, remaining beneath the top of the rise.

Jack pointed to the tracks. "They're splitting up, and there's more of them than us. I'd say chalk it up to experience, and let them battle with the marshals, sheriffs, and bounty hunters who'll be looking for them. I'm going to head back to the herd and get 'em moving."

Monty gave a single nod. "Could you use some help?"

"Sure I could. It looked like there's close to six hundred head back there. It'll be a lot easier with you two fellas pitching in."

"You got it," Bronco said.

They turned the horses and headed back to the cattle. Monty eased up beside Jack. "What you planning on doing with them cows?"

"I'm buying the Masseys' part. We'll drive them all to the roundup. I'm sure other folks have cattle in there. They'll probably be joining Bryant for the drive north. I'll wait for the next drive or move them along behind him. I might run into another bunch who'll let my cattle join up."

"You're dreaming," Bronco said from the other side of Monty. "They'll have their herds made up and the number of cowhands they need for it. The cattle will have settled down on the trail. Nobody'll take more cows. Ain't gonna happen."

Jack said nothing. They continued toward the waiting cattle.

After topping another rise, they watched a herd of whitetail deer watch them, then go back to feeding. Every few moments a head or two would pop up from the herd, watch, then drop back down to feed, replaced by another one or two or more.

"I guess I could drive them to Kansas myself."

This time it was Monty who answered as their horses walked slowly past the deer. "You ever make the trip?"

"No, can't say as I have."

Bronco said, "Experience helps."

Jack turned in the saddle to look at Monty and Bronco. "Yep. I know that's the truth. But the only way I'm going to get experience is to do it."

Monty gave Bronco a questioning look.

Bronco answered with a small incline of his head.

Monty, without looking at Jack, said, "We've made the trip a bunch of times."

Jack nodded. "Sounds like you have experience."

"Yep, we do. We could go with you."

Jack pulled Adam to a stop. The horse nodded its head several times, then reached to the ground and started pulling at a stand of bunchgrass. "Are you serious?"

"Sure we are. How many head do you think you'll have?"

Jack figured for a moment. "I'll have to see how many belong to the Masseys in that rustled bunch, then I'll know exactly. I'm thinking somewhere around four hundred."

Bronco added, "We might mosey west of here and pick us up another two, three hundred head. Might even make a little money for the first time."

"Sounds good to me. That'd give us close to a thousand head. A reasonable herd."

"We'll have to come up with a road brand," Monty said.

Buster chimed in, "How about double arrow on the left shoulder?"

Bronco looked at the boy and then at Monty. "I like it. You know if any other trail drive uses that?"

Monty shook his head. "I don't, and I like it, too." He turned in the saddle to Buster. "That's a fine idea, boy. I think we'll use it."

Jack thought for a moment and turned to Monty. "What does Bryant charge for being trail boss?"

"Bryant's been around for a long time and has a well-deserved reputation. With him, a rancher or ranchers feel pretty certain their herd will make it to market. He pulls down about a hundred and forty a month, plus a dollar a head for every cow that makes it." He turned to Bronco. "You wanta be the trail boss?"

Bronco looked at his friend and turned loose a long string of expletives.

"I'll take that for no. Reckon that means I'm elected." Monty turned back to Jack. "But since you're involved in putting this here drive together, and we'll have cattle in the drive, there'll be no monthly charges. If it's agreeable to you, there'll only be one dollar for every head that makes it to the market."

"Sounds fair to me. How many men do you think we'll need?"

Monty started figuring. He turned to Bronco. "With three thousand head, we had a trail boss, twelve drovers, two wranglers, and a cook. What do you think we'll need for a thousand?"

Bronco looped his horse's reins around the saddle horn, letting the animal walk forward with the group, and started figuring on his fingers. After several minutes he turned to Monty. "What do you think?"

Monty didn't crack a smile. "The trail boss is taken care of and two drovers." He glanced at Bronco and Jack. "I'd say, with two wranglers for the horses, and a cook, and only a thousand head, we could get by with five more drovers."

Bronco shook his head. "That ain't much for fightin' and protectin' the herd. I'd think about adding maybe two more drovers. That'd be more than enough for the cattle, with a little extra for the fightin' should we need 'em."

Monty rode on, quiet, thinking.

After a few minutes, he said, "Look, Bronco, I know what you're saying, but those two drovers would cost an additional two hundred and forty dollars for the trip and leave no room for a bonus. If we're gonna do this as a business, we've got to get the cattle there, but we need to have the men frothing at the mouth to work for us. What do ya think of making it an even six drovers?"

Bronco nodded. "It may be a little thin, but I'd be willin' to try it."

Jack had been following along with the two men as they discussed their needs. If he was figuring right, they had the trail boss and two drovers, he and Bronco. That would leave them six drovers, two wranglers, and a cook to pay. He looked at Monty. "What's the pay for a cook and wranglers?"

Bronco spoke up. "Cook's the most expensive besides the trail boss. He's around a hundred a month. The wrangler will run a little cheaper than the drover. He'll be about thirty a month, where the drover is forty."

"Thanks," Jack replied, and started figuring. For a three-month drive, it would be three hundred for the cook, three-sixty for the two wranglers, and seven hundred and twenty for the drovers.

"You mentioned a bonus," Jack said to Monty.

"Yeah. Not everyone pays it. It depends on what you're getting per head from the buyer. If you have a successful drive and arrive with the majority of the animals still in your possession, and fat, the drovers could get paid a bonus. On a herd of a thousand, I'd recommend two dollars a head divided evenly among everyone. Course, the three of us will own a portion of the herd, so we wouldn't be included." He tossed Jack a wry grin. "We'll be paying. That'd leave a total of nine on the receivin' end. Nine divided into two thousand would be a little more than two hundred for each man. They'd like that."

Jack nodded. "I'd be willing if all of the conditions are met." He could hear the lowing of cattle ahead. "But we can't spend the money until we make it, and we have a long way to go. Let's get those animals moving."

~

JACK SAT a tired Adam and looked across the sloping ground where once the Massey home had stood. Nothing of the home remained. Everything had been washed down the creek. Jack glanced at Buster.

The boy's face showed no emotion while he looked over the space where his home had stood. He turned and looked up at Jack. "I'd never have thought a little creek could have done that. We were really lucky you came along."

"I'm just glad I did. Now we'd better get those horses some feed." They swung down and led their horses to the trough. The animals wasted no time in thrusting their thirsty mouths into the water. Jack looked over their two additional days of riding.

The corral held forty-four head of prime horseflesh. He had to acknowledge Jesse Massey knew what he was doing when he broke horses. While they had been rounding them up, and Buster had been a huge help, he had picked out the animals he wanted. They were all bigger. They had to be to carry his weight, but they were quick and, according to Buster, were stayers.

Jack heard Buster in the lean-to barn, forking hay into the corral. The ground had completely dried and so had most of the horses' hooves. There were still a few whose hooves were swollen, but their swelling was coming down quickly. "You have anything besides hay?"

"Yes, sir, we've got some corn and oats, but I hate to spread it on the ground. They'll be nipping and kicking trying to get to it. One of 'em might get hurt."

"You're right," Jack said. "We'll save it for later."

The boy called from inside the barn, "You think those Moulds could be a problem when Ma and the kids come back down here?"

"Buster, I can promise you the Moulds are gone. I don't know which direction, but I can assure you, now that they are known rustlers, they will disappear from this part of the country. You can stop worrying about them."

The sound of a bouncing, rattling wagon drew Jack's eyes toward the creek, which was already down to a shallow little stream meandering around the many rocks. The wagon bounced across the stream, made it up the steep washed-out bank, and stopped in front of where the Massey house had stood. A tall man and a boy sat in the wagon, staring at the vacant land.

Jack walked out from inside the lean-to. "Howdy."

The man jumped in surprise, recovered, and drove the wagon to where Jack stood. By the time he pulled to a stop, Buster was standing next to Jack.

"Hi, Mr. Jenkins, Dud."

"Hello, Buster," Jenkins replied. "Is your family all right?"

"Yes, sir, they are. Everyone's at Mr. Jorgensen's. This here is Mr. Jack Sage. He saved us."

Jenkins's forehead wrinkled. "Sage? You from down Cherry Creek way?"

"I've been there."

The man's eyes widened. "Howdy, Mr. Sage. I'm Mica Jenkins. This here is my boy Dudley. We just call him Dud. Masseys are lucky you came along."

Jack nodded to the man. "Buster gives me too much credit. The water rose slowly. They would've probably recognized the problem and evacuated safely."

"Yes, well, I brought Mrs. Massey's wagon back. If you'd tell her I'm real sorry. I tried to get it back over here, but the water rose too fast."

Jack had been ready to condemn the man for taking the family's wagon, but there was no indication he was lying about his attempt to get it back. "I'll tell her." He turned to Buster. "Where do you want him to put the wagon?"

Buster pointed to a spot by the corral. "Can you put it over there, Mr. Jenkins?"

"I sure can, boy."

Jenkins pulled the wagon next to the corral. Dud leaped out, stepped up on the bottom rung of the corral, and rested his arms across the top. "Mighty pretty bunch of horses, Buster. Your pa did good work."

Buster stepped up beside the larger boy. "Thanks, Dud. He sure did. I helped him with a bunch of 'em." He pointed to a big, slick strawberry roan. "See him?"

Dudley nodded.

Buster gave a long slow whistle. The horse stopped eating and looked up, strands of hay sticking from its mouth. It turned, walked over to Buster, and stretched its neck. The big brown eyes were even with Buster's head.

Jack watched.

The boy reached forward, rubbed the horse's nose, and scratched behind its left ear, all the while speaking softly to it. Then the boy said something, and the horse went back to the pile of hay and resumed eating.

Dud said, "Anybody can whistle up a horse, Buster."

Jenkins had walked up beside Jack and was watching.

"Alright," Buster said, and gave a low intermittent whistle. This time a dapple gray turned from the hay and walked to Buster, who repeated the scratching and petting before sending the horse back to the hay.

"How many can you do that with?" Dud asked.

"Most of them. Some of the whistles Pa showed me I haven't gotten right yet, but I'm workin' on them."

Jenkins shook his head. "That boy's pa had a real touch with horses. It looks like he's inherited it."

Jack nodded. "It does, doesn't it."

"You know if the Masseys need any help rebuilding?"

Jack shoved his hat back and turned to the man. Jenkins wasn't a small man. He had obviously been born to hard work. His shoulders were wide and forearms thick. He was about average height, so Jack towered over him, but he was thick in the chest, probably from swinging an axe since he was a boy.

"I imagine she will. Since it's drying out, they should be coming back soon." Jack slapped at a mosquito sucking on the back of his hand.

"Tell her I'll pass the word. We'll get her a place up in no time once we know where she wants it. I imagine she'll be movin' to higher ground."

"I'll tell her. You sound like you think she'll be back."

Jenkins gave an emphatic nod. "You can bet next week's pay she'll be back. That lady doesn't have a quit bone in her body. Just let her know."

Jack nodded and watched the man pull a blanket and one of the saddles from the back of the wagon.

"Come on, Dud," Jenkins called. "I unhitched 'em, but don't expect me to saddle yore horse for you."

Dud jumped down from the fence. "Yes, Pa." He turned to Buster. "Glad you're all right, Buster. I'll see you when we come back to help with your place. Maybe we can go fishing."

"I'd like that, Dud."

Dudley ran to the back of the wagon, grabbed the other blanket and saddle, and carried it to the remaining horse. He laid the blanket across the horse's back, smoothed it out, and swung up the saddle. Once fastened, he hurried to mount. His pa sat waiting for him.

Buster jogged over to the homesteader. "Mr. Jenkins, would you mind lookin' after the horses until I get back? It'll just be a few days. I'd sure appreciate it."

The man looked down at the youngster and nodded. "Be glad to. You take care of yourself."

"Thanks."

Jenkins clucked to his horse and headed for the creek, Dud right behind him. He raised his hand as they rode by. "Nice to meet you, Mr. Sage."

"Likewise."

Buster and Dud waved to each other, and the man and boy rode across the creek, up the opposite side, and soon disappeared behind the scattered mesquite.

"How long have you been working with your pa and the horses?"

Buster took his flop hat off and scratched at his thick, jet-black hair. "I dunno, Mr. Sage. As far back as I can remember. Some of my first memories are listening to Pa and walking amongst the horses. Near as I can tell, since I could walk."

Jack's eyes moved continuously across the landscape, checking bush and tree. "Did you ever break any?"

"Well, sir, Pa didn't like to call it breaking them. He always said we was training them to trust us and follow our commands. You know, friendly like."

"I know, Buster, but did you ever have to ride rough stock?"

"Oh, I see what you mean. Yes, sir, most every day. They don't trust you right off, but Pa never made 'em buck." Buster's forehead wrinkled and his eyelids tightened as he thought. "He never made 'em bleed from spurs and such is what I mean. Don't get me wrong, he'd use spurs on a horse if he had to, like getting away from Indians, but never when he was training . . . uh . . . breaking them."

"You get thrown much?"

Buster grinned. "Yes, sir. Pa used to laugh and say I bounced like a fresh-caught catfish thrown out on the bank." Jack could see the boy enjoyed the momentary thought of his pa. Then he watched as the youth grew serious again.

Jack slapped another mosquito. They were getting thicker.

Buster said to no one in particular, "They're gonna get a lot worse before they get better."

7

Jack and Buster returned with Jack's horses, dropping them in a corral near the edge of Christopher Jorgensen's property. Jack wasn't sure what kind of welcome he was going to get from Jorgensen after he had warned Bryant he would be the first to die if his men drew against him.

They rode straight to the barn. Gideon, who had brought the cattle to an area near the horse corral, with the help of Monty and Bronco, walked out from inside the barn. He watched Jack swing down from Adam's back. "You might not be gettin' the most pleasant welcome. Seems Bryant got back and filled Mr. Jorgensen with all sorts of lies. There for a while, I thought they wuz gonna get the Rangers after you, but Amelia and Mrs. Jorgensen got them calmed down."

Jack turned to Buster. "I'll take care of your horse. Why don't you go around to the side door into the kitchen. You don't want to be caught up in this."

Jack watched Buster's lips purse and his forehead wrinkle. "Mr. Sage, it ain't right, Mr. Jorgensen believing Bryant. That's just not fair."

"Listen, Buster. It's not about fair. It just is. Your ma needs the

Jorgensens' help, so you don't want to be involved in this. Take the rifle, clean it up, and return it to Mr. Jorgensen later."

Defensively, Buster said, "I'm not gonna lie."

"I'm not asking you to lie. You say whatever you want to say, but keep your ma in mind." Jack extended his hand to the youngster. "Thanks for your help. You're an excellent horseman."

The boy took Jack's hand and grinned up at him. "Thanks, Mr. Sage."

The door slammed on the front porch of the big house, and multiple sets of boots could be heard coming down the front steps.

"Now go on, get out of here."

Buster turned and walked off, never glancing at Jorgensen, who was accompanied by Bryant.

Jack opened one side of his saddlebags and drew out a leather sack, which was getting much lighter. He dropped six fifty-dollar gold pieces into his hand, closed the bag, returned it, and fastened the saddlebags before turning to Gideon. "You'd better take the horses. I'll be along to help, shortly." He slipped the gold into his vest pocket and turned to face the two approaching men.

"Jack," Jorgensen said, "I hear you had some problems."

Jack turned his head to Bryant, stared at the pompous angry man, and turned his head back to Jorgensen. "Did you talk to Montana Huff and Bronco Fenn?"

Bryant spoke up. "We did not. I fired them. They were thrown off this ranch, as is about to happen to you."

Jack never took his eyes from Jorgensen's face. "So, Bryant controls who comes and goes on this ranch?"

Jorgensen's face flushed red, and he turned to Bryant. "Carson, this is my ranch. I'll determine who is not welcome on it. Do you understand?"

Bryant at once capitulated. "Of course, of course, Christopher. I'm sorry. I let my emotions overcome me. I do apologize."

Jorgensen gave the trail boss a nod. "Thank you." He turned back to Jack. "Do you have anything to say for yourself?"

"Only what I've previously asked you. Did you talk to Montana and Bronco?"

Jorgensen gave his head a short shake. "Only for a moment. When they began to malign my friend Mr. Bryant, I did as he indicated. I asked them to leave and not return."

"So you're telling me you didn't hear their side?"

"As I said, I will not listen to malicious gossip, not from them or you."

Jack's face hardened at the suggestion he would lie about any man. "I'm going to ignore the suggestion that you expect me to lie. I need to speak to Mrs. Massey to settle up with her. Once we've completed our business, I'll be on my way."

Confused, Jorgensen's face took on a look of puzzlement. "Aren't you going to explain what happened?"

"If I explain what happened, you won't like it. I wouldn't want you making the mistake of calling me a liar, so, once again, may I conduct my business with Mrs. Massey?"

Jorgensen's face hardened. "Yes, but when you are finished, leave my ranch."

"I plan to. I'll talk to her in the kitchen."

Bryant opened his mouth to speak. Jack's gray eyes, flint-like with anger, locked on the trail boss and held him in their gaze for a long moment. Bryant said nothing.

Jack was seething. He knew what kind of man Bryant had become, and Jorgensen's herd would be completely in the man's hands. Jack, as he climbed the steps to the kitchen, shook his head and thought, *I wish them luck, but I sure don't hold out much hope for the success of their trail drive. Not with a drunk at the helm.* He opened the door and walked in.

Amelia and Cathleen stood at the kitchen door to greet him. Cathleen spoke first. "I am so sorry, Mr. Sage. I have no idea what has gotten into Christopher. I can't believe he ran off those two good men, and now you." She shook her head. "I'm afraid he will regret this."

Jack nodded to the two women. "You may be right, Mrs. Jorgensen. When Bryant found Buster and me, he ordered Monty and Bronco to shoot me down because I wouldn't allow him to hang the rustlers. I'm glad they could see what was happening and decided against drawing on me. If they would've drawn, Bryant would be dead, and I'm guessing several more." He turned to Amelia. "Sorry about the problems. I imagine Buster has already told you it was the Moulds doing the rustling. Unfortunately, they escaped. You won't be seeing them again. If they show their faces around here, any rancher will hang them. You don't ever have to worry about them again."

Amelia rubbed her forehead. "That is such a relief to know they're gone. I'm glad they weren't hanged. The youngest, I think his name is Jethro, is a fine young man. I hope he can get away from that bunch before he turns rotten, too."

"Ma'am, I don't mean to rush you, but we've got business and need to take care of it so I can get out of here. If any of the cowhands come in while I'm here, there's liable to be a ruckus."

"Yes, of course, but I do need to tell you something." She took a deep breath. Her face paled before she spoke. Jack watched firm jaws clamp in determination. She exhaled and took another breath. Color began to return to her face. "Jesse died."

Jack knew the feeling of despair and loss. His voice softened. "I'm mighty sorry, ma'am."

"Yes, thank you. Your buying Jesse's cattle and horses has made all the difference for us. I can't thank you enough."

Jack could think of nothing to say, so he remained quiet.

Amelia managed a weak smile. "So what do we need to do?"

They stepped toward the table. Ruth was at the counter, preparing dinner. She reached to the stove, picked up the coffeepot, and, while looking at Jack, held it up. He nodded. She pulled a large mug from the cabinet, marched over to him, set the mug down, and filled it with coffee. Jack picked up the cup. "Thank you, ma'am."

Amelia and Cathleen sat. Jack joined them on the opposite side of the table. Amelia pulled out the papers she had previously completed from a dress pocket and laid them on the table.

Jack removed the six fifty-dollar gold pieces from his pocket and placed them in front of her. "Your husband's count was exact, just like you said. We picked up another hundred head of Massey stock, plus some that belong to a few other ranches."

She shifted the papers and marked out the three hundred number, filling in four hundred above it, and signed her name adjacent to the amount and at the bottom of the page. She signed the other document, which was a bill of sale for the horses. After waving both papers in the air to hasten the drying of the ink, she handed them to Jack.

He took them, laid them side by side on the table, and took a long sip of coffee. "Mrs. Massey, I know this is a hard time for you, with the loss of your home and your husband, but I've got another serious question for you. I'd like you to think it over before you answer. It's important for me and for Buster."

"For Buster? I don't understand."

"Ma'am, that boy's already one of the best I've seen with horses. They take to him. He was telling me he'll be fourteen in August. I'd like to hire him as a wrangler. He'll make thirty a month, plus a possible bonus, depending on our success upon arrival in Ellsworth. It'll be great experience for him."

She started shaking her head. "No. I can't. His father just died. How could I allow him to go on a cattle drive at his age? I can't. I won't."

Jack leaned toward the mother. "Think about it, Amelia. Something could happen to him right here at home. He'll be with strong men. He'll have to pull his weight, but I've seen over the past days, he's a hardworking boy. He won't have any trouble, and we'll never find a wrangler who can handle horses the way that boy does. What he doesn't know now, he'll know when he gets back home."

She turned to Cathleen. "What do you think?"

Her friend shook her head. "Oh, no. I'll not contribute to this decision. This one has to be all yours."

She turned to Jack. "Will you take care of my boy?"

Jack's eyes were on Amelia's. "When we left here after the rustled cattle, I promised I'd look after him and make sure he comes back in good shape. I can't make that promise again. If he stayed home, you couldn't make such a promise. Sometimes things happen. What I will promise you is that I will do my best to see him back safely to you."

"You'll be coming back?"

"If you had asked me a week ago, I would have said no, for I want to start a ranch in Colorado. However, my perspective has changed. I plan on coming back and making another drive, but with more cattle. My answer is yes, I'll be coming back, and I'll bring him back with me."

"Jack, are you talking about driving a herd up yourself?"

He shook his head. "No, Monty and Bronco have made the trip with Bryant almost as much as he has. Monty will be the trail boss, and we're going to drive our own cattle north."

"Oh, my goodness," Cathleen said, "do you think you can make it?"

Jack nodded. "I wouldn't do if I didn't think we could. Monty and Bronco are good men. They know good men we can hire. I may not have made this drive before, but I've seen many trails. We'll make it. My biggest concern is for Mr. Jorgensen's herd. I don't think Bryant has a chance of completing the drive with the herd intact."

Cathleen's brow wrinkled in concern. "Why would you say that, Jack? He's made that drive many times for us before. Surely he can make it again."

"I don't think he can. That's all I can say."

"All you can say about what?" Christopher Jorgensen demanded as he and Bryant walked from the parlor into the kitchen.

Cathleen spun around and glared at her husband. "Christopher, have you been eavesdropping on our conversation?"

Jorgensen's face turned red. "I have not. But this is my house. I can listen to whatever and whoever I desire to inside these walls."

Jack nodded to the women, folded the papers, and slipped them into his inside vest pocket. "It's good doing business with you, Amelia. Think about what I said." Without acknowledging the presence of either Jorgensen or Bryant, he marched out of the kitchen, closing the door gently.

Walking across the porch, he heard Jorgensen demanding to know what had been discussed. Cathleen's strong voice sounded clearly. "It concerned Amelia's business and is none of yours!" He smiled. *Backbone isn't just in the men of this country.*

His thoughts continued, *Now the work begins. Fortunately, we have no cattle mixed in with Jorgensen's, but we still have a great deal to do. There's hiring to be done, a chuckwagon to buy and fill, and Monty and Bronco still need to come up with a herd of their own.* He continued to the barn, anxious to be on his way north.

∽

TWO WEEKS HAD PASSED since Jack had left the Jorgensen place. He was whipped. Every day he was up before the sun and could barely keep his eyes open in the evening to eat before falling into his bedroll, only to do it over again the next morning. *How can I be so tired,* he thought, *and we haven't even started up the trail?*

And the mosquitos. In his travels, Jack had seen bad mosquitos, but he'd never seen them this bad. Since the rain, they were around all day, but in the evening, they'd rise up in clouds. The stock caught the worst of it. Cattle lowed plaintively throughout the night. It was necessary to keep a double guard on the cattle, as restless as they were. Daytime made it easier, but, though fewer, the mosquitoes were still out and biting. The rain had been a great boon as far as water was concerned, but the mosquitos were everywhere. Even though the ground had dried, there were waterholes, and where there was water, there were mosquitos. He knew they would eventually disappear as the water holes dried up, but he didn't want to wish the waterholes away.

He glanced up from stomping on his boots, to see Buster and Dale, the other wrangler, gathering horses. Jack smiled to himself. Bringing Buster on had been a great decision. He swung his gun belt around his waist, fastened it, and walked to the chuckwagon to grab a cup. Monty and Bronco were both drinking coffee by the fire.

Jack joined them. "We getting close?"

Monty nodded. "Another two days, and we'll be pullin' out. We got lucky finding Hamm. He's one of the best cooks in the country. Glad he was available."

Jack nodded. From his experience, he knew if the men were kept fed with good food, you had the battle more than half won. "How do you like our group?"

Bronco chimed in, "All in all, we did pretty good. We wuz lucky to find most of them boys." He looked over at one of the men slowly crawling out of his bedroll. "Though I have to admit, I'm already gettin' tired of that Gil Forest. He's always shootin' his mouth off about hisself. He ain't old enough to have done even half of what he claims."

Jack took a careful sip of the hot coffee and swallowed quickly. "How do you think Buster's working out?"

Monty answered the question. "He's one good kid, hard working. You'd never expect a boy of that age to have the skills with horses he does. Mighty impressive."

"Yep," Bronco said, "lot more impressive than a cowhand who cain't rope."

Monty said nothing. Jack knew Bronco was baiting him, but

couldn't resist commenting. "I've never had the need for roping. It never occurred to me to rope a guy who was trying to kill me. I just shot him. Wish you'd been there to show me, Bronco."

"Me too. I don't think I've ever seen a hand who does so poorly with a rope. I reckon it may not be possible for you to learn. You know, Jack, some people just ain't cut out to be a cowhand."

Jack was about to respond when Roger Hamm stepped to the front of his chuckwagon and started beating on a washbasin with a thick iron rod. "Come get it afore I throw it out."

The men still in their bedrolls cursed Hamm and his heritage, but rolled out and started pulling on their boots.

One of the bigger cowhands, Vern Kitchen, called to Monty, "Hey, boss, back home if we had a noisy rooster, we'd just kill it and eat it. What do you think?"

Monty glanced over at Hamm. "I reckon he might be a little tough to eat. I'm thinkin' if you boys was nicer to him, you might get tastier food. How does that sound to you, Roger?"

The cook stopped beating the basin long enough to say, "Sounds good to me, boss. You'd think they'd learn." Hamm placed the basin and rod on the chuckwagon counter, walked to the fire, and stirred a bubbling pot.

Jack had to admit it did smell good. "What kind of stew is that, Roger?"

The man smiled at Jack. "That is armadillo stew, Mr. Sage, and it's mighty tasty. Try a bowl."

"What's wrong with bacon and biscuit?" Gil Forest asked in a surly tone.

"Not a danged thing," Hamm responded. "Only I didn't kill a pig this morning. I killed an armadillo, hence armadillo stew." He gave the basin a couple more half-hearted beats and walked back to the chuckwagon.

Jack got a metal plate and filled it with stew. He picked up a couple of biscuits and returned to where he had been sitting. In no time, the stew was gone, with the accusers begging for more.

"I got more, but it's for the wranglers, not you cowpunchers." At the mention of wranglers, Jack looked across at the horses being readied, and saw Buster look up and grin. He could see the satisfaction on the boy's face and thought, *You deserve a few compliments. Both you fellas have been doing a good job.* Jack heard Dale tell Buster to go ahead and get something to eat. He had everything under control. Buster made his way to the chuckwagon. He ladled a portion onto his plate, picked up a couple of biscuits, and headed over to sit by Jack.

Jack turned his head, watching the boy, a smile on his face until he saw Gil stick his booted foot out as Buster walked by. Buster's foot hit Gil's, who let out a yelp. Buster pitched forward, hitting the rocky ground. At the jolt, his plate of stew shot across the ground, and his biscuits rolled away in the dirt. His face slammed against the ground, with his nose driving into a jagged rock. Blood spurted everywhere. Jack sat, thinking, *Come on, Buster. Get up and ignore the worthless jackass.*

Buster jumped to his feet, blood running down his chin and dripping onto his new shirt. He spun around and, without uttering a sound, hit Gil with a roundhouse right.

The young cowhand, at least six years older than Buster and filled out with muscle, didn't expect such a violent, rapid response and was caught off guard. He fell backward off the log he had been sitting on and spilled his stew and biscuit. Buster's blow had caught Gil just above his left eye, leaving a shallow gash, but one deep enough to bleed profusely.

Gil jumped to his feet, his face livid with anger, blood streaming into his left eye. His right arm bowed out, hand hovering above his Colt. "Kid, I'll kill you for that."

8

Bronco grabbed Jack's arm as he started to rise. He leaned close and said, "Leave it to Monty. He's the trail boss. He'll take care of it."

Monty had started moving the moment Buster tripped. He grabbed Gil's gun arm and spun the cowhand to face him. He leaned into Gil so his face was scant inches from the angry man.

"Pack your gear. You're finished."

Jack could see Gil's eyes bugging out as he stared at Monty. His lips pulled back, and his right arm gave a small quiver.

"Don't try to draw that gun, boy, or I'll take it away from you and make you eat it."

"He hit me."

Monty moved his face closer. "No discussion. Pack up."

"You'll regret this."

Monty spoke in a cool, conversational voice. "I already regret hiring you. I won't tell you again."

Gil held Monty's glare for only a moment, then turned away and reached for his bedroll, blanket, saddle, and rifle. He picked them up and looked for Buster. Hamm, the cook, had already wiped the blood from the boy's face and given him a cloth to hold against his nose. "I'll see you again."

For the first time, Jack spoke. "Bad idea, Forest. You see him again, you're going to see me. When I hit you, you'll have more than a cut over your eye."

Buster shot Jack an angry look, while Gil Forest turned toward the remuda. Dale, the other wrangler, had the man's pinto cut out and ready.

Monty turned to the rest of the crew. "Show's over. Eat up and mount up. We've got a lot of work to get done today. I want to be moving out day after tomorrow. Make sure you get all those longhorns branded so they'll be ready."

Buster, still angry, cradling his nose with the bloody rag, walked straight to Jack. "I can fight my own fights."

Jack nodded. "I know, but you're no gunfighter, not yet. I was just trying to help." Jack knew he had injured Buster's pride by stepping in. He also knew he probably shouldn't have done it, but he felt sure Buster's father would have done the same thing. Gil Forest was a man making man threats. Buster couldn't handle him yet, either with a gun or his fists.

"If you want to help, then teach me how to shoot. I'm pretty fair with a rifle, but I've hardly ever fired a handgun."

Monty stepped back to the fire. "How you feeling, Buster?"

"I'm alright, Mr. Huff. It's not like I haven't had a bloody nose before."

"Good. Get back to the remuda. See to those horses."

"Yes, sir." Buster ran past the chuckwagon, tossing the rag on the corner. The cook stopped him. When the boy pulled up, Hamm gave him two biscuits. Jack could see they had been broken in half. Butter and jelly dripped from between the halves.

"Thanks," Buster said softly, a big grin on his face.

"Get to them horses, boy. We're burnin' daylight," Monty yelled.

Buster took off running, and Hamm gave Monty a dirty look.

When Buster was gone, he said, "You don't have to be so hard on the boy. He missed breakfast."

Monty shook a finger at Hamm. "Don't you go babying that boy. He works and earns his pay just like everybody else." He turned and looked at Jack and Bronco. "What's with you two? You think you're privileged just because you own a couple of them cows? Get out there and get to work. Bronco, I'm expecting you to teach Jack how to dab a loop. Now git."

Bronco grumbled just loud enough for Jack to hear it, "Ain't no chance of that."

∼

JACK HAD his bandanna pulled up to cover his nose and mouth. The dust was thick enough to chew. The only breeze he felt was that caused by his horse's slow walk. Though still spring, it was a hot Texas day, made hotter from the heat pouring off the cattle. His face would have been covered with sweat if it weren't for the dust. Now it was caked with mud.

They had been on the move since before daylight, to take advantage of the cooler part of the day. Now the sun was high and so was the heat. *How did I get back here?* Jack thought. *I could be riding up front with Bronco, on point, but no, I wanted to be fair. I should know better than to listen to Bronco. He made the comment, "New guys always ride drag," and I leaped on it like a hungry chicken on a grasshopper, and here I am.*

He glanced at the other drag rider, who was working his way toward him. Porter Odell. Port sidled up, and Jack looked at the man, who laughed at him. "You're a sight. I've never seen a mud pie as big as you, and riding a horse."

"Get out a mirror," Jack said, and coughed. Port's face looked like he had been playing in the mud and smeared it all over his face. Everything else had the reddish tan color of dirt in this part of Texas.

"How you takin' to being a cowpoke?"

"I've had more fun elsewhere," Jack said. He had no desire to be talking to anyone, especially not in the dust and heat.

"We'll get a break pretty soon. Dinnertime comin' up."

"Yeah." They rode on in silence for a ways, and Odell drifted slowly back to his side of the drive. Jack looked toward the front of the herd. He couldn't see it because of the dust, and the herd was strung out for at least a mile, maybe two. Odell was right. Dinner break would be coming up soon. He'd never been so excited about eating. Anything to get him out of this dust. He'd had to put up with it in Algeria, but it was more sand than dust. This was hanging in the air everywhere the cattle had been.

He noticed the cattle slowing, and the flank rider signaling. Dinnertime. He swung to the right and picked up the flank rider on his way. Being to the side of the dust made life much more pleasant. Jack slipped his finger inside his bandanna and pulled it off. Jasper Gibson was riding right flank. He looked at Jack and grinned. Jack silently congratulated the man for not laughing. He could just imagine what he must look like, all white from the bridge of his nose down, and mud from there to the line of his hat.

"Not the most pleasant of jobs, riding drag," Jasper said.

"No, I have to admit I've had few worse."

"Yep, I think if most cowhands had to ride drag all the time, they might find themselves another line of work."

They rode on in silence to the now visible chuckwagon at the front and left side of the herd. Finally Jasper spoke again. "Never known an owner to ride drag."

"May be my first and last."

"That'd be my decision, though I think the boys respect you for doing it."

Jack laughed. "I don't need respect that bad."

This time they were both laughing when they rode up to the camp.

Jack swung down from the big roan.

Buster walked over. "You wanta switch to Smokey?"

"Sure," Jack said. "Since I'm having to eat dust, he might as well get his share."

Buster grinned at Jack's face and tossed a thumb over his shoulder. "Creek's running a little. You might want to get some mud off."

Jack listened. Sure enough, he could hear water gurgling around rocks.

"Great idea, Buster. Would you mind wiping this fella's nose out? I've done it twice, but I think he's picked up another load of dust."

"Sure, I was planning on it."

Jack walked over to the creek. It was like many he had seen, wide, deep cutbanks, with a trickle of water filling scattered deep holes. He examined the edge and found a steep deer trail. Holding to a bush, he stepped into the trail and slid halfway down, his boot heels digging into the soft dirt. A pecan tree root lay exposed, and he grabbed it, sliding the rest of the way to the rocky bottom. His spurs jingled against the creek bed as he walked to the flowing water. He knelt and, using his left hand, began to dip water and wash the mud from his face. The flowing water was clear, cool, and refreshing. He lifted a handful and drank. It was sweet and cooling to his lips and throat. He went back to washing his face.

Stopping for a moment, he raised his head, thinking he might have heard something. No more than forty feet from him stood a coyote. He wasn't big, no larger than a medium-sized dog, but he acted funny. The animal watched him while its head swayed back and forth. Spittle dripped from its lips. Occasionally its tongue lolled out to one side. It sat down for a moment. *It looks tired,* Jack thought. He slipped the leather thong from his revolver and slowly stood.

The coyote followed him with its eyes, its head still lolling right and left, spittle continuing to drip. When Jack was erect, the coyote stood and started to walk toward him. "Shoo," he said, waving his arms.

It kept coming. Now its gait changed from a walk to a trot, its head still doing the crazy lolling. Jack waved his arms again, trying to scare the animal away. He had no desire to shoot it. When it reached ten feet, its lips slid back, and deep from within its throat came a low, menacing growl. That was enough. Jack yanked out his .36-caliber Remington and shot the animal in the chest. He heard cursing from the camp and running feet. Then the running feet were combined with running horses and the lowing of cattle.

Monty was the first to appear above him at the creek's edge. "What's going on, Jack? Don't you know you could have stampeded the cattle, firing that gun?"

"Come down here, Monty. I want you to look at something."

Monty slid down the bank using the same trail Jack had. He walked over to the coyote, bent, examined him, and backed away. "How'd he act?"

"I've never seen the like. I was washing this dirt and mud from my face. When I raised up, there he was, about forty feet away, staring at me. He was producing so much saliva, it almost looked like he was foaming from the mouth, and his head was swaying back and forth. I tried to shoo him away, but he kept coming, so I shot him."

Monty nodded. "Good thing. You don't want anything to do with that animal. It appears to be he's got hydrophobia. He was mad, Jack. He's still dangerous, even dead. I'll get Bronco to drag him off and bury him. We don't want any other animals eating him, or they could get it, too."

"I've heard of that. It can affect anything, man or animal. People die from it."

Monty kicked a rock into the stream. "Horrible death. I seen men bitten. They look just like the way you described that coyote. The funny thing is they hate water, won't drink it. It's a wonder he was here in the creek. Guess he saw you and planned on adding you to his list. No telling how many other things he's bit." Monty turned back to the bank. "Let's get out of here. How 'bout you give Bronco a hand burying it. Then you can eat. Port can handle the drag until you get back there."

They turned and headed back to camp.

After telling what had happened, everyone had a story to tell about mad dogs and skunks and squirrels and anything else a man could think of. Jack considered himself fortunate that he and Bronco were headed off to bury the animal. They found a way into the creek and followed it to the coyote.

Bronco said, "Jack, don't try to rope him. Get down, and pull a loop over his hind legs, low. When you get that done, we'll drag him up the bank and find a good place to bury him, deep."

Jack did as he was instructed, being careful to touch the coyote only with a gloved hand, and they dragged him to a spot that Bronco deemed perfect.

Jack had brought a shovel from the chuckwagon and began to dig. Bronco sat his horse, watching. Jack could feel the sweat running between his shoulder blades. The ground was hard and rocky. Only his size and strength allowed him to dig a hole deep enough.

After he had been digging for thirty minutes, Bronco stood in his stirrups so he could see better into the hole. "Looks good, Jack. Drag him in and cover him up. I'm hungry."

Jack, his Stetson pulled low over his eyes, tilted his head so he could see his friend. "Thanks for helping."

Bronco nodded several times as if he didn't notice the sarcasm dripping from each of Jack's words. "Don't mention it."

Jack finished filling the hole, and dragged several large rocks over the grave. When he felt sure nothing could get to the dead animal, he coiled his rope and swung into the saddle. He laid the reins against Smokey's neck. The horse turned and started back to camp.

Bronco joined him. "Whew. That digging sure builds an appetite, don't it?"

Jack looked at the older man, who was grinning at him. "Bronco, if I didn't know better, I'd say you're hoorahing me."

Bronco laughed. "I'd never do that to a man with a reputation like you've got, Jack. I'd be a plain fool." He laughed again, and they rode back to camp.

Upon arrival, Jack saw a stranger talking to Monty, away from the camp. When Monty saw them, he motioned for Jack and Bronco to join him. When they neared the two men, Jack could see the badge under the left side of the stranger's vest.

"Howdy, Bill," Bronco said, shaking the man's hand.

Monty turned to Jack. "Bill, this is Jack Sage. Jack, Sheriff Bill Stanton."

Jack said, "Sheriff Stanton, nice to meet you."

"Call me Bill. Hear you're the Laredo and Cherry Creek Sage."

"I've been there. You can call me Jack."

"Bill's got some not-so-good news for us."

"Monty's right. The Moulds, Eli Mould and his sons, are now wanted for a killing in Austin. Seems they got crossways with a Texas congressman in a local saloon and shot him so full of holes he looked like a rag doll." He pulled out a wanted poster and handed it to Jack.

Jack let out a whistle. "Lot of money, and they didn't waste any time getting this circular out. It's only been about three weeks since I had my little run-in with them."

"Most of that five thousand dollars is federal money. They don't mind spending it when someone kills a U.S. congressman."

Monty pointed at Bronco. "You mind gettin' 'em moving. You know what to do. I'll catch up with you in a bit."

Bronco gave Monty a nod and touched his hat. "Good to see you, Bill. Luck to you." Jack watched him swing by the chuckwagon, and Hamm tossed him a couple of biscuits. Hamm saw

Jack looking and signaled he had a couple for him. Jack gave the cook a wave and turned to the sheriff.

"I wish you luck, Sheriff. Be careful with that bunch. They come across as pretty low on the smart scale, but they know tracking, stalking, and killing. They rate pretty high in those categories. Watch out for 'em."

The sheriff looked at Monty and then Jack. "I thought you might join me for a couple of days. I'd deputize you, and we could split the reward. Heard they might be headed up into this part of the country."

Jack shook his head. "Sorry, Sheriff. I've got a herd to take care of. Every dime I have is tied up in these steers."

The sheriff raised his boot, placed it gently on a pill bug that had rolled up into a ball, rolled him around, and then smashed the bug. He looked up at Jack. "Reward would help. Only need you for a couple of days."

"Not this time. You get in a bind, I'll try to break loose. But for now, I need to stay here."

"Come on, Sage. Just a couple of days, and that could earn you twenty-five hundred bucks. Not bad for two days' work."

Jack could feel his anger rising. He didn't like pushy men, especially if they wore a badge. He turned to Monty. "I'm getting back to work." Jack wheeled around, shoved his foot in the stirrup, and swung into the saddle. He bumped Smokey lightly with his spurs and turned toward the chuckwagon, leaving the sheriff staring after him.

Hamm saw him coming and handed him up two biscuits with jelly and butter between them.

Jack raised them in a salute to the cook. "Thanks." Smokey broke into a lope, and Jack wolfed down the biscuits. Plum. The taste of the biscuits and consideration of the cook helped cool him down. Upon reaching his drag position, he was ready for the heat and dust. He pulled the bandanna up over his nose and joined Port behind the cattle.

A breeze had begun out of the west, keeping a good part of the dust off the drag riders. He could see the cattle stretching north in a long line. Almost half of them were his. If the Moulds stayed away, and he didn't have any lawman problems, and if they made it to Ellsworth, and if the prices were high, and if, and if... He shook his head. He had to admit, those were a lot of ifs. But if it happened, he'd have the start of a stake. Not enough yet to do what he'd like, but a good start, and one more drive should do it, if he was lucky, and he'd always been lucky. At least after leaving Algiers and the Legion.

9

The longhorns had been in a fractious mood all night. The cowhands weren't much better. Six days earlier, Monty had ridden with the sheriff to town, if you could call it that, and hired two more men. It had been alright with Jack, if Monty figured they needed them, and both men fit in well, though neither was very experienced with cattle. Bronco and Bo Dawson got stuck with showing them the ropes, and the ropes included riding drag. Since the new men had been hired, Jack had graduated to riding right flank, which was alright with him, less dust. However, Bo and Bronco, who rotated with the new men on drag, now were eating dust, and neither of the more experienced men were happy.

Jack rode along, thankful to be away from Porter, not a bad guy but talky. All Jack had to do was keep the steers from quitting the herd, and so far, it hadn't been a tough job. The southeast wind kept most of the heat generated by the cattle blowing away from him, as well as the dust.

A young, solid brown steer broke from the herd and trotted toward the mesquite thicket on Jack's right. He bumped the pinto, laying the reins across its neck. The horse had already spotted the steer and loped at an angle to cut it back into the herd.

The longhorn had been named appropriately. Its ponderous horns swung in their direction, the head turned back for the thicket, and the steer picked up speed. "Come on, boy," Jack yelled, urging the horse forward. The pinto was big and fairly quick for its size. Its long legs stretched out to cut the stubborn longhorn off. They had a good angle on the wide-horned steer. Jack, still far enough out of the mesquites to allow him to swing a loop, had shaken out his rope. The steer, no more than twenty yards from the treeline, cut straight back toward Jack as the pinto stepped into a gopher hole. It collapsed around the horse's right front hoof. The pinto's head went down, and he dove forward, dropping out from under Jack, but not before the saddle acted like a slingshot. The horse's back snapped up and followed its head, throwing Jack directly in the path of the falling animal and the confused steer.

The steer cut inside the horse, swinging his head and scraping the point of its left horn along the pinto's front left shoulder, leaving a gash. While this was happening, Jack rotated through the air, seeing steer, then open ground, then horse falling right at him. Jack hit the ground on his right shoulder, rolling like a tumble bug. All he could see was the horse's back and saddle driving down at him. The weight of the animal jerked past, slamming into the ground, and the wooden saddle stirrup whacked him in his nose and mouth. Then it was over. He jumped to his feet and leaned his head out, well clear of his body, because blood was flowing from both his nose and mouth.

Checking his position to make sure there were no other stragglers, he turned back toward the end of the herd and saw Bronco break away and ride toward him.

Pulling up and turning his horse alongside Jack's, he said, "Mighty pretty fall. Looked like you've figured out a new way to turn a steer. Just throw yourself at him."

Jack grinned wryly, hurting his lips. "I wouldn't recommend it as a normal operation. You mind riding flank while I change out my horse? He's gonna need a little doctoring."

"Don't mind at all. Thought you might be a goner there for a second. It's a wonder you didn't break your neck and your horse a leg. That looked like a nasty fall." Bronco gave Jack's mouth and nose a once-over. "Did you get kicked?"

"Naw. When the horse went over, the stirrup flopped around and hit me in the mouth."

Bronco shook his head. "You are one lucky feller. You was inches away from getting yourself squashed like a bug."

Jack grinned painfully again. "I'm just naturally a lucky guy. I'll be right back."

Bronco was shaking his head as Jack rode toward the remuda.

Buster saw Jack coming and untied his rope, shook a loop in it, checked the herd, and dabbed his loop over a strawberry roan with a white blaze. He led him from the remuda and waited as Jack pulled up.

Jack stepped down. "Needs some doctoring, Buster."

"You or him?" the boy said, grinning.

"How about you take care of the horse, and I'll take care of myself."

Buster nodded. "What happened?"

"Chasing a steer. Found a gopher hole."

Buster was examining the scratch on the pinto's shoulder. "I'll get this taken care of. He'll be good as new in a couple of days."

Jack switched tack and swung up on the roan. The horse stood steady. Jack patted him on the neck. "You're a good horse, Red." He turned to Buster. "You ready for the Brazos?"

Buster looked ahead. "I reckon. I sure hope Mr. Huff finds us a good crossing where we can walk across."

Jack shook his head. "I don't think those exist right now, Buster. Not with all the rain we've had. It's liable to be deep and running fast."

Buster frowned, his young face wrinkling. "That ain't good, Mr. Sage. Several of these boys ain't very good swimmers. Someone's liable to get hurt."

"I hope not." Jack lifted his right hand in a salute. "See you at the crossing."

See you at the crossing, Jack thought. Who knew Texas had so many creeks and rivers? They'd already pushed the cattle across the Llano, San Saba, and Colorado Rivers, not counting so many creeks it was hard to remember all the names. It seemed like he hadn't hardly gotten dry before they were crossing another. Now they had the Brazos coming up. All the rivers had been above normal, and Monty, who had ridden ahead, said the Brazos was the same. The banks were acceptable for the approach and exit, but worn and beaten, making them slick, from Jorgensen's and another herd that was ahead of them.

Monty had talked to the trail boss of the herd directly in front of them. Their crossing had been tough, but they'd managed to make it with no loss of life. The trail drive, even at this early stage, had been eye-opening for Jack. The men and boys who pushed these herds north earned every thin dime of their forty dollars a month.

He looked across the herd stretched ahead of him. The animals' horns clanked as they bumped each other, but they didn't seem to mind. They moved slowly, occasionally pulling at the already beaten-down bunchgrasses, little bluestem, side oats grama, and cup grass, among others he hadn't learned yet.

He was amazed at the myriad of colors of the longhorns. They ranged from almost solid black to white, reds and browns, tans and yellows, pinto, no two colored alike. With the exception of the random steer, like the one he had just faced, the majority of the animals moved placidly north. They would eat their way to Kansas. Monty had planned a nice, slow, ground-covering pace, which would fatten them on the trail and move them north at an average of ten or twelve miles a day.

Even as he watched, in the distance he saw the cattle slowing, beginning to bunch and mill. *Must have reached the river,* Jack thought, slowing Red while the horse moved around a large green prickly pear patch.

Bronco rode up. "Come on, Jack. Those boys can watch 'em back here. Let's head up front. Monty's reached the Brazos, and I'm guessin' he could use a hand."

The two riders urged their horses into a gallop.

The longhorns had strung out nearly two miles and were slowly closing in behind the leaders as Jack and Bronco galloped past. Nearing, Jack got his first glimpse of the Brazos, muddy, deep, and wide. The best thing he could say about it was the banks on both sides. They were sloped and hard. The approach was fairly open, but above and below the crossing, the river was lined with scattered pecan, elm, oak, and mesquite. The plan was to keep the cattle out of the tree-lined portion of the river, a great place for them to disappear into the forest. The Brazos River was a long one, originating several hundred miles north of the crossing and extending all the way to the coast, over a thousand miles.

Jack watched the first group of fifty head, led by Vern Kitchen and Bo Dawson. Both men had stripped down to their birthday suits, their wet white bodies shining in the sun. The big brindle steer that had been leading the herd was making good headway across the expanse of the moving river. Though they had drifted a little south of the crossing, they would still be clear of the trees and have a gradually sloping bank where they would exit the water.

Monty rode up. "Jack, you and Bronco take this next bunch across. You know the drill. Get over to the chuckwagon and strip down. Leave your clothes, valuables, and guns with Hamm. Make it quick. These longhorns are ready to go."

Jack and Bronco rode to the chuckwagon, swung off their horses, stripped their clothes and guns off, and tossed everything into the back of the wagon. Jack removed his saddlebags and rifle from his horse and also transferred them into the wagon, laying them next to his bedroll.

Bronco swung into his saddle, dressed only in his hat, his white and wrinkled body shining in the midday sun. He saw Jack grinning at him. "You ain't so pretty yoreself, boy. I wouldn't recommend lookin' in the mirror about now."

Jack laughed and turned Red, his chestnut. "Come on, Bronco. Let's go for a swim."

By the time they were back, Vern was walking his horse up the bank. He looked up at Jack. "Water's cold. Usually it's a lot warmer, but I guess all the rain cooled it off."

Monty trotted over. "Vern, go back and get the rest of the boys stripped down and ready. Leave Stinky back there to watch the drag. I don't suspect there'll be any quitters, what with all the water up here." Vern disappeared through the dust, and Monty turned back to Jack and Bronco. "Take 'em in a little above where the last bunch entered, and keep 'em headed above the landing. That should put those hardheads coming out just about right. Watch out, and stay clear of them horns."

With the help of Vern Kitchen and Jasper Gibson, they drove the reluctant cattle toward the moving water.

"Move out up front!" Monty yelled to them. Jack and Bronco worked their way to the front of the herd and led the first of their group into the water. It was hard to hear anything with the incessant bellowing of the cattle, the clanking of the horns, and the calls of the riders.

By now, Jack was comfortable with river crossings. He had done many in his lifetime, though until recently, never driving or leading cattle. The water pushed on his upriver leg and pulled on the downriver one. *Vern was right,* Jack thought. *This water is cold.* He felt it swirl around his knees, and moments later Red was swimming. A big longhorn followed just behind him. Something spooked the animal, and it leaped forward into deeper water, where it had to immediately begin swimming. Jack urged Red to speed up, but it was unnecessary. The horse was an experienced cow horse. He didn't want any longhorn pushing up behind him. His hooves dug into the water.

Jack glanced at Bronco, who was still seated in his saddle, his horse swimming. Bronco yelled over the din, "Current's not too bad. We should hit the bank just right."

Jack waved, and he felt Red sink farther. He looked around, still well in the lead of the cattle and safe enough, for now. He pushed himself up and over the cantle, then slid along Red's back, slipping off the animal and grasping its tail. He could immediately see, with the loss of his weight, the big horse rise in the water. The animal's laboring became less. Jack looked behind him, and the big steer, looking black from the water, was about to overtake them. He drew his legs up, and when the longhorn was close, he kicked him in the nose with the bottom of his bare feet. The steer jerked back, let out a bellow, but slowed. Jack glanced toward Bronco, who was still sitting his horse. Bronco waved. With his free hand, Jack waved back and then concentrated on hanging onto Red's tail.

The rest of his crossing went smoothly. Red reached the bank, and moments later Jack felt the bottom with his feet. He waded up to the chestnut and swung back into the saddle. The big steer was right behind him. Red trotted up the bank, followed by the longhorn. They moved to the side and pushed the cattle exiting the Brazos up and away from the landing area so they wouldn't block the next bunch that was on the way behind them.

The crossing went smoothly. Lester Pugh, everyone called him Stinky because of his last name, had a little problem with the crossing since he had never learned to swim, but he was the only one. The remuda also made it across safely. Jack watched Buster. *That boy was born for this,* he thought. Buster handled the horses smoothly, along with Dale. Neither had any difficulty with the water.

The chuckwagon came last. Jack waited and watched as Bronco, Monty, Vern, and Bo tossed a loop around each corner of the wagon. Roger swore the chuckwagon was sealed so tight it could sail on the Texas sea.

The only way water could get to the equipment stored in the wagon was if it turned over. The four riders with their ropes helped stabilize the wagon as it made its way across the river. The harnessed horses waded in, followed by the wagon, and just as Jack had seen it on the Colorado, the wagon floated like a boat, a little wobbly, but afloat. The horses swam valiantly, and within a few minutes, it was rolling up the opposite bank.

The cattle had continued grazing and were stretched to the northeast. The lead steer was already half a mile ahead. "Get dressed and get to work," Monty called to all of them. "If you boys want a night in Fort Worth, this ain't no time to be lollygagging."

At the mention of Fort Worth, a cheer rose from the cowhands, and they all galloped to the chuckwagon to get their things and get dressed. They were back in their positions quickly, whistling and calling, moving forward.

After getting dressed and picking up his gear from the chuckwagon, Jack rode up to Monty. "We're stopping in Fort Worth? I thought we were running behind time."

"We are, but not bad, and we need to stock up the chuckwagon. This next haul is going to be the long one. I want to give the boys a couple of nights in town. It won't hurt the cattle either. Any chance we get to put some weight on 'em will help."

Bronco rode up in time to hear Monty mention the time in town. "You're gonna have trouble. Happens every time."

"I know, but it won't be anything to worry about. There may be a scuffle or two, a few scratches, but it'll do 'em good to blow off some steam."

Jack had been in charge of men for most of his life, after leaving his home in Virginia. "I agree. It'll give them something to remember and look forward to on the trail."

Bronco eyed him. "I'm guessin' you've seen a lot more than what you're a-lettin' on. How old are you, Jack?"

Jack's eyes twinkled. "Thirty-six whole years, and after that crossing, I'm feeling every one of them."

Bronco nodded. "You fought in the war, didn't you?"

"Yep."

"How'd you keep from gettin' that big frame of your'n punched full of holes."

"I told you I was lucky."

Bronco eyed Jack's beat-up face. "You ain't lookin' too lucky."

Jack tossed right back at him, "I'm alive, aren't I?"

Bronco turned and released a long stream of tobacco juice. "You got me there."

Monty turned to his friend. "Leave it alone, Bronco. We've still got a lot of work ahead of us, and we need to keep these boys and the cattle moving."

"Yep, and I need to get back to riding drag. By the way, Mr. Trail Boss, sir, Francis is gettin' mighty good at it. I figure he could do it by hisself."

"Good," Monty said, "wait until we get to Fort Worth. Then you can move back to point."

Bronco shook his head, muttering as he rode away.

Jack turned Red to fall back to his right-flank position, when Monty called, "Jack."

He stopped the horse, turned, and braced his right hand on the cantle of the saddle. "What's up, Monty?"

"Bronco don't mean anything with the questions."

"No problem. I can answer anything any man asks. At least any man I consider a friend."

Monty gave a single emphatic nod. "Good." He raised his hand in salute and headed for the chuckwagon. Jack bumped the chestnut into a lope, surveying his cattle as the horse loped back toward the flank position. Movement along a far ridge caught Jack's attention. It was brief, but he knew he had seen something.

Something that looked like a man. A man on horseback and wearing a red shirt, but the instant he saw him, the man disappeared over the ridge.

I wonder who that was. Just a traveler, but if he had been only a traveler, he wouldn't have been so shy. He kept his eyes peeled.

10

Jack and Monty sat side by side, gazing at the herd. Over a thousand head of tired longhorns drank their fill of water and settled down for their last few snatches of grass before calling it a day. A couple of miles to the east lay the city of Fort Worth, Texas.

"Look at that," Monty said. "Made it all this way with more wet crossings than I've ever done, and we ain't lost a cow. I'd say that's a miracle."

Jack grinned at the cattleman. "I'll take luck any day. How far along you figure we are?"

"All in all, we're a couple of days behind schedule, but that ain't all bad. We've had some green hands who had to learn, and now they're straightened out mighty fine. Our first two hundred miles are behind us, and we did it in twenty-one days." Monty pointed, swinging his arm across the gathering cattle. "The best thing is those longhorns are fat and sassy. They've put on quite a bit of weight so far. They'll lose some of it in the Oklahoma hills, but not much."

"Music to my ears." Jack pointed down at the chuckwagon and the cowhands beneath the hill where they sat. "I'm thinkin' if you don't turn some of those boys loose soon, you'll have a mutiny on your hands."

"Let's go." Monty pushed out ahead with Jack following. They rode down the grassy slope to the camp below.

"About time," Bronco said as they rode up. "I've got some young fellers here who are hankerin' to get themselves into town."

Monty swung down, opened his saddlebags, and pulled out a leather sack and a ledger. He laid both on the dropped tailgate of the chuckwagon. "Alright, boys. I'm givin' you each a ten-dollar advance. You worked out who's going into town tonight and who's going tomorrow? No more than four drovers, and I need at least one wrangler here all the time."

The men were standing around. Some with gloomy faces and others bright and raring to go. They all nodded their heads. Jack was watching Buster. The boy grinned with several others.

"Buster," Jack said, "you're not planning on going in tonight, are you?"

The boy frowned. "Why, yes, sir, I sure am. Porter said I could go with him and Bo. I'll be just fine."

Jack couldn't help the frown that settled on his face. He had promised the boy's mother he'd look after him, but Jack wouldn't be going into town until the next day. "Why don't you wait until tomorrow. We can go in together."

Buster's spine stiffened, and he stood taller, his young chin jutting out. "No, sir. I'll be fourteen in a couple of months. I'm big for my age, and I can take care of myself."

Jack gazed at the boy, and Buster returned his gaze, a defiant gleam in his eyes. Jack had made a promise, but he couldn't embarrass the lad in front of his peers, men he looked up to. Though he felt a twinge of misgiving, he nodded his head. "Have fun, but stick with Bo and Porter. Fort Worth is a wild town."

Buster capitulated, the defiance vanishing from his face as he broke into a grin. "I sure will, Jack. I'll be real careful."

Jack waited until Buster had received his pay and was signing Monty's register. He walked quickly to Bo's and Porter's side, grabbing an arm of each. He spoke in a low and threatening voice. "You two had better protect that boy with your life. If he comes back harmed in any way, you'll be answering to me. Do you understand?"

Porter said, "Sure, Jack, we'll take care of him."

Bo leaned in to Jack, his voice also low. "You don't need to threaten me for me to do my duty," and yanked his arm from Jack's grip.

Stinky and Jasper joined the group. All five of them had washed up in the creek, put on clean clothes, and dusted off their hat, boots, and saddle. Slicked up, paid, and ready for a night on the town, they mounted their horses and, yelling, raced toward town.

Roger shook his head. "Chow's on. Those boys were too anxious to wait and eat. With that money in their pocket, they'll eat big tonight."

"And drink," Bronco said. "They won't be worth a plugged nickel tomorrow."

Monty nodded. "Makes no difference. Drunk, hungover, or sober, they'll be sittin' a saddle tomorrow." He turned to Francis Dilton. "You're up first tonight, with Jack. Then it'll be Vern and me. Bronco, you'll have it till sunup by yourself. If you need any help or see anything, sound out. Dale, keep an eye on the remuda."

Everyone nodded and stepped up to the fire, where Roger was dishing out venison stew with hot biscuits. The peach pies sitting on the lowered gate of the chuckwagon hadn't gone unnoticed.

Jack took a bite, savoring the venison. He had killed the young doe this afternoon, well away from the herd. The food was excellent, but he couldn't get his mind off Buster. If anything happened to that boy, he'd never forgive himself. He remembered Amelia's big eyes and worried face when she finally gave in. He understood. The woman couldn't bear losing her son this close to the loss of her husband. It would be devastating to her.

He started to put his plate down, mount Smokey, and follow the boys into town, but he couldn't do it. He had to let them go, but they had best protect Buster. He continued to eat, filling his body with nourishment, but barely noticed the taste.

∼

THE SOUND of riders returning woke him. It was still dark, way too soon for their return. He pulled his watch from his vest pocket, opened the cover, and held the timepiece so the reflection from the fire's coals would illuminate the face—two thirty. He could hear moaning as the riders pulled up at the camp. He closed the watch, dropped it back into his vest, yanked his boots on, and stood, swinging his gun belt around him as he rose.

"Help us," came the plaintive, young voice of Buster. "It's Bo and Jasper. They're hurt bad."

Jack stepped up to the horses, grasping the first rider.

It was Bo. "I tried to do what you said, but there were too many. They came out of the alley. Hillbilly types. Quick and mean. I think they broke my roping arm."

Jack eased the man from the saddle. Monty and Bronco were helping Jasper. Ralph tossed wood on the fire, and in moments they had a blaze going. By the light of the fire, the damage to Jasper's face was stark and obvious. His nose had been broken, and he had a slash down the left side of his cheek. Both eyes were almost closed from swelling. The boy's face was a bloody mess.

Jack lowered Bo to the ground and felt his arm. The forearm was swollen to almost twice its size. Jack gently ran his hands from wrist to elbow. "Rotate your hand."

Bo slowly rotated his hand through ninety degrees.

"Nope, I don't think it's broken. I'm guessing the blow bruised either one or both of the bones, and your arm is gonna be useless for a few days, but you're lucky. All the heavy work in the past strengthened those bones so they could take the blow. You'll be good as new in a few days." He looked up at Ralph, who was bending over, watching, with both hands on his knees. "We need to keep this thing stationary for the next few days. I need something to make a splint, about a foot long."

"I've got just the thing." Roger turned and hurried to the chuckwagon. There were the sounds of drawers opening and closing, then he was standing close with two flat boards the correct length. In his other hand he held several lengths of cloth, like strips from a torn sheet.

"Hold on a second." Jack laid the boards on opposite sides of the man's arm, and Roger wrapped the cloth over the splints and arm until they were secured tight and steady.

Jack reached up and checked Bo's bandanna. It was tied close to his neck. He yanked the bandanna loose, tied the ends together, took the man's hat off, and slid the bandanna in place. Once he had it positioned with the wide part at the bottom forming a rest, he slid Bo's forearm into it. "Keep it there for a couple of days. When it starts feeling better, you can take the whole contraption off."

Ralph leaned over again and looked at Jack's handiwork. "Not bad. You've done this before."

Jack nodded.

Ralph glanced at Bo. "When you're done with them boards, give 'em back to me. Someone else might have a need before we get to Ellsworth."

"Sure enough," Bo said, "and thanks." The last was directed to both Jack and Ralph.

"You hurt anywhere else?" Jack asked.

Bo shook his head. "Not bad, maybe a couple of broken ribs, but Jasper took the worst of it. They jumped us out of an alley. One of 'em grabbed Buster."

"It was Cletus," Buster said. "I'd recognize his ugly face

anywhere. Bo yanked me loose and knocked Cletus clean across the alley. He wasn't moving. But then Harley, right then, when Bo's arm was sticking out and Cletus was falling, slammed his rifle barrel across Bo's forearm. He hit him something fierce. You could hear the forearm of that rifle hit Bo. Whop! Then Harley drove the butt of his rifle into Bo's side, but Bo wouldn't turn loose of me, so Harley hit him again." Buster couldn't take his eyes from Bo's face. "He *never* turned me loose."

Jack looked at Buster. "Are you alright, boy? Did they hurt you?"

"I'm fine, Jack, no thanks to the Moulds. They were trying hard to get me. But Bo slowed 'em down, and then Jasper and Porter came dashing in just as it looked like they had us."

Jack looked around. "Where are Porter and Stinky?"

Jasper spoke up, his speech muffled through smashed lips. "We left Stinky at the roulette table. He was winning and didn't want to leave. The folks who helped us took Porter to the doctor. He was pretty banged up and out cold."

"Why didn't they take you two with Porter to the doctor?" Jack asked.

Bo jumped in. "We wouldn't let 'em. By the time folks started gathering around, the Moulds had disappeared. We figured it was best to get Buster back here."

"Good thinking," Jack said. He looked at Monty, who was working on Jasper. "How's he doing?"

Monty shook his head. "He'll carry a mark from that knife for life. I'm gonna have to straighten this here nose, or he'll never be able to breathe. You hurt anywhere else, boy?"

Jasper shook his head. "No, sir, just my face and nose hurt like the dickens."

Monty nodded. "It's gonna hurt worse afore it feels better. Bronco, hold the boy's head still."

Bronco, who had silently been watching Monty work on Jasper, grasped the young man's head in his hands.

In the firelight, Monty looked directly into Jasper's nearly closed eyes. "You're gonna need to hold still while I straighten this nose of yours. I'm gonna have to squeeze it, 'cause there's some bones in there that need to line up, and I'll have to move and pull it. You feel free to yelp if you've a mind. You understand?"

Jasper gave an almost imperceptible nod.

Monty looked at Bronco and nodded. Bronco locked the boy's head in his strong hands while Monty grasped Jasper's nose, which was flattened and pushed to the right. A grunt came from the boy as Monty squeezed, pulling the spread sides of his broken nose together. The skin stretched as he then pulled Jasper's nose slightly away from his face and moved it back to where it was almost straight.

Bronco said, while holding Jasper's head steady, "You got anything else to do, do it now. The boy's passed out."

Monty looked at his work, grasped the nose again, and moved it a bit more to the left. He felt along the sides of the nose, slid his finger and thumb down near Jasper's cheeks, and nodded. "I think that'll do it. It may not be perfect, but I think it'll work."

Roger stepped up with a pot of hot water, a cloth, needle, and thread. "You want to clean that cut and sew it up?"

Monty pointed his chin toward the ground and took the cloth.

Roger set the pot next to Monty, and the trail boss commenced to clean the wound. It went quickly. First the cleaning, and then the sewing. Fortunately, Jasper was unconscious throughout the remainder of the ordeal.

Jack stood and glanced at Dale Slade. "Get Smokey." He strode to his bedroll, rolled, tied, and picked it up, along with his rifle and saddlebags, and stopped alongside Monty.

The trail boss washed his hands in the remainder of the water in the pot. He looked up at Jack. "Going after the Moulds?"

"Yep. I should have helped your sheriff friend when I was first asked. I don't like hunting men for money, and I knew you needed me here."

"We still do."

"I know, but the Moulds need to be stopped."

"You don't have to be the man to do it."

Jack looked across the dark backs of the cattle, most still and sleeping. He could make out the faint outline of the nightrider and hear his out-of-tune singing. The cattle didn't seem to mind. "I think I do. I've got more experience than most, and if I leave them alone, they'll end up killing or maiming more innocent people. I can't let that happen."

"Why did they try to grab Buster?"

Jack turned to the boy. "You have any idea why they were after you?"

Buster was still standing next to Bo. He turned a rock over with the toe of his boot. A scorpion dashed into the darkness. "I heard old man Mould yelling for Cletus to hang on to me. He said Ma would pay to get me back. That's all I heard."

Jack looked back to Monty. "They must have found out I bought her cattle and horses. Stay on the alert. I don't think they'd be crazy enough to try to hit a cattle drive, but I also don't think any of that bunch is operating with a full deck."

"Look, Jack," Monty said, wiping his still wet hands on his trousers, "now ain't the time for you to leave. That bunch could be riding out here to hit us and grab Buster. Your leaving puts us one more down, plus I've got all these hurt men."

"Two down."

Monty's head jerked back to stare up at Jack. "What do you mean, two?"

"I'm taking the boy with me. He'll be safer with me than herding along those horses."

"Jack, you leave me in a heck of a bind. I'll have to find a wrangler as well as a drover, and when you get back, there might not be a place for you or for Buster."

"There'll be a place. You're not paying for me, and I'll personally take care of whatever extra expenses are incurred from having an extra drover and wrangler. You're making out, Monty, getting two free men instead of one."

Bronco spoke up. "He's right, old hoss. Plus, the pressure will be off us. We won't be havin' to watch out for Buster."

"I can take care of myself!" Buster stood, small fists clinched and pressed against his hips, his jaw jutting out.

Jack stepped over, put down his saddlebags, and placed his hand on the boy's shoulder. "Listen to me, Buster. One day, you'll be able to take care of yourself just fine, but that day isn't here yet. You come with me, and you can start your learning. Trust me."

The boy looked up at the big man's wide, honest face. "You mean it? You'll teach me?"

"I'll teach you, boy. Now, get your gear on your horse, and we'll be on our way."

Buster turned away and started packing his gear.

Jack turned back to Monty. "Like I said, hire another drover and wrangler. It's Fort Worth. I'm sure you can find plenty of out-of-work cowhands hanging around looking for a job." He stopped, leaned his saddlebags toward the fire so he could see inside, and opened them. Once opened, he fished out a leather bag, opened it, and counted out ten twenty-dollar gold pieces. After closing the bag and dropping it back into the saddlebags, he stepped to Monty's side. "Hold out your hand."

Monty did as he was told. Jack dropped the double eagles into the man's palm. "That should cover another drover, wrangler, and extra expenses while I'm gone. I'll be back as soon as I can. Take care of my cattle."

Dale had brought Smokey and Stonewall, Jack's mule, both saddled and ready to go. Jack nodded to the wrangler, slid the Spencer into its boot, tied the saddlebags and bedroll behind the saddle, and swung up. "Mount up, Buster."

The boy swung into the saddle.

"You hankerin' for company?" Bronco asked.

Jack shook his head. "No, thanks. The most important thing for you, Monty, and me is to get these cows to Ellsworth and get a good price for them. I'll be along before you get there." He raised a hand in salute and rode into the dark, Buster at his side.

He was on the hunt and felt little, other than being sorry the cowhands had been beaten so badly. He regretted he hadn't been there. He could have ended the Mould problem once and for all.

Bo, Jasper, and Porter were all good men, but they were cowhands. They would fight when necessary, and they would fight hard, but they didn't have the killer instinct he did. Sometimes it bothered him, the exhilaration he felt when he fought. But it had been a part of him for all these many years. They hadn't been fighting near as long or faced as many different enemies as he had. However, it wasn't just experience. Even with, or maybe especially with, the Foreign Legion, where he had spent so many of his younger years, only a small fraction of the men were then or ever would be true fighting men.

Most were young men, from all over Europe, looking for adventure. Many had never raised their hands in anger. Oh, there were a few. Some cruel, looking to hurt others, and some who had fought for survival since childhood.

Smokey stepped lightly toward Fort Worth. Jack leaned forward and patted the big grulla on his neck as he carried him toward the Moulds. "Good horse."

He straightened, glanced at Buster, and allowed his mind to drift back over the years, while his senses remained alert. He remembered being Buster's age, even younger. His first fight at four years old slipped into the forefront of his mind. It had been so long ago, but he saw it like it was yesterday.

11

A cousin, older and some bigger, not a great deal, for Jack was already large for his age, had shoved him to the ground. When his rear hit the ground, a realization blasted to the forefront of his four-year-old mind. It was as if he were out of his body and could see himself sprawled on the ground in front of his cousin.

The older kid stood grinning in triumph. In that instant, he knew he wanted to hit the boy who had shoved him, and he wanted to hit him hard. It didn't matter it was Sunday, or the two of them were at the bottom of the church steps with both boys' parents talking and laughing on the steps above, his mom lovely in her Sunday best.

All that mattered was his cousin grinning down at him, and he, lying in the dirt. The little boy, who would grow to be Jack Sage, surged to his feet, eyes locked on his cousin's big nose. He started the swing while his pudgy legs pushed off the ground. He heard his mother scream, "Jack!" but at that moment, he didn't care even a tiny bit. His arm and fist carried all the force his four-year-old body could muster.

He remembered the surprised look in his cousin's widespread brown eyes when he realized he was about to be hit. He remembered the feel of his little fist slamming into the bridge of the other boy's nose. The youthful cartilage giving way under his fast-moving fist. He also remembered the pain in his knuckles, but what had surprised him the most was the amount of blood a nose could yield. It first spirted all over his cousin's face and Jack's fist and white shirt. Then it poured from the screaming boy's nose. He also remembered the strong grip of his mother's white, lace-gloved hand, which closed around his upper arm, unfortunately on a part that had blood on it, but he couldn't take his eyes from his screaming, bleeding cousin. That is, until his father's wrinkled brow and jutting chin interrupted the view.

"What's funny?"

Jack looked at Buster. "What?"

"You were grinning. I was just wondering what was funny."

Jack shook his head. "Nothing much. I was just thinking about something that happened a long time ago."

"Must have been good. That was a mighty big grin."

"Actually, I was about to get into a mess of trouble."

In the breaking dawn, Jack could make out Buster's puzzled expression. Then the boy shrugged his shoulders. "You think the Moulds will still be in Fort Worth?"

"They might. It's a sizable town, but I suspect they've pulled up stakes. Tell you what. Why don't we stop at the doc's office and check on Porter. Who knows, Stinky may be there. After that, we'll grab us some breakfast. What do you think?"

Buster nodded enthusiastically. "Yes, sir, I could sure use breakfast. I'm mighty hungry."

"Yep, fighting'll do that to you."

They rode on in silence, day breaking around them. The three buildings just ahead had turned from darkened silhouettes to a store, a barbershop, and a livery barn in between. Buster pointed to the second story of the barbershop. "Doctor's office is up there."

The two pulled up to the hitching rail. Jack tossed Smokey's reins over the rail and followed suit with Stonewall's. Buster did the same. Dismounting, they crossed the boardwalk and climbed the outside stairs, their boots scraping on the weathered wooden steps and spurs jingling in the quiet of the early morning air.

Reaching the landing, Jack knocked lightly. After several minutes he heard feet shuffling on the other side of the oak door, and a young man appeared. He had obviously been sleeping, and his thick, uncontrolled blond hair tumbled in disheveled curls over his wide forehead. Deep blue eyes blinked at Jack like an owl with a burning-bright pine knot thrust in front of him.

"Is the doctor in?"

The man stifled a yawn, covering his mouth with the back of his slim wrist. "Yes, unfortunately, you're talking to him. I'm Dr. Franklin Jensen. Everyone calls me Dr. Frank or just Doc, and you'd be?"

"I'm Jack Sage, and this here is—"

"Buster Massey." The doc nodded to Buster. "Come on in. Coffee's brewing. You're welcome to a cup. I suspect you're here to check on Porter Odell." Dr. Jensen pulled the door wide, allowing Buster and Jack to enter.

Stepping through the door, Jack removed his hat and ducked low.

Doc Jensen grinned at the move. "I imagine that head of yours has found the top frame of many a door."

Jack gave the doctor a crooked grin. "Doc, you have no idea. You mentioned coffee?"

"I did. Follow me." He started toward an open door and glanced at Buster. "Are you doing alright?"

"Yes, sir. I'm fine. They didn't hurt me like they did the others."

"Good. How are they?"

Stepping through the doorway into the examination room, Jack saw Porter sitting up, leaning on a forearm. Above his eyebrows, his head was completely wrapped in bandages. Blood had seeped through in one spot, and the eye beneath the bloody bandage was almost swollen shut.

He looks spry enough, Jack thought. "They're beat up pretty good, Doc."

"How're you feelin', Porter?"

"I'm fine. Doc said I had a concussion, but I feel fine, ready to get back to work."

"You heard anything more about the Moulds?"

"I guess they cleared out, Jack. I been laid up here, so I ain't heard a thing. One of 'em slapped me with his pistol barrel, and I went out like a light. Ain't heard a word."

Dr. Jensen poured Jack a cup of coffee and handed it to him.

"You heard anything, Doc?"

The doctor poured cups for the rest of the men, including himself, and said, "Last night, I heard one of 'em say he wasn't leavin' town without a drink. I think they were headed to the Gilded Palace."

Jack's wide forehead creased. "The marshal didn't arrest them?"

Dr. Jensen carefully took a sip of his steaming coffee. "He's out of town."

"What about the deputy or deputies? Aren't they in town?"

Dr. Jensen shook his head as he stared into his cup. "That is some nasty coffee."

"I've tasted a lot worse, Doc. What about the deputy?"

"Mr. Sage, you've got to understand about the marshal's deputy. He's more of a jail custodian than an armed lawman. In fact, he doesn't even carry a gun."

Jack's wide gray eyes stared at the doctor. "You're telling me they were allowed to go free?"

"Unfortunately, yes."

"Did they leave town?"

The medical man shook his head again. "I don't think so. One of them said something about going to the Gilded Palace to wet his whistle. The old man wasn't happy about it, but the older boys wanted a drink. They didn't have to do much persuasion. It didn't appear he was too averse to the thought."

"Where's the Gilded Palace?"

"Couple of doors up the street on this side, just past the marshal's office. They never close, so if the Moulds went there, the bartender should be able to tell you about them."

Jack set his cup down and glanced at Buster. "You stay here. I'll be back in a minute."

"But Jack—"

"Don't argue with me, or you'll be going back to the herd. Remember what I said. I'll be back in a minute." He pulled his extra Remington Police from behind his belt, did a quick check, shoved it back, and let his vest front fall over it. Next, he slid the other revolver from the holster. Once checked, he dropped it back in place and made sure it was loose and ready. He started for the door, stopped, and turned. "Doc, you'd best get ready for business. You may have some shortly."

The doctor nodded, set his cup on the table, and headed for a back room. Jack left the office and started down the stairs.

Early risers were on the boardwalks. Fort Worth was coming to life. There would be plenty of witnesses, which was good. He stopped at the marshal's office, opened the door, and stepped in. An elderly man stood near the potbellied stove, his arm out, reaching for the coffeepot sitting on the flat top.

"Howdy, stranger. How can I help you?"

"This is a courtesy call. I'm stopping by to let you know your jail will be needed shortly if the Moulds are still in the Gilded Palace. They're wanted for killing a congressman in Austin."

"Well, I'll be," the old man said, pouring himself a cup of coffee with a shaking hand. He got it poured and unsteadily made his way back to the marshal's desk. He carefully placed the full cup on the desk, moved so he could grasp both arms of the marshal's chair, and slowly lowered himself into the chair. Once there, he let out a sigh, as if he was thrilled with the successful completion of his long-distance travel. "That's the first I've heard of that." He pointed to a peg near the open door with a palsied hand. "There's the keys if you need 'em. Cells are right through the door." He took a long sip of the coffee and relaxed deeper into the well-worn chair.

"Thanks, I'll see you in a minute," Jack said, and turned from the old man. With the marshal gone, he understood why there had been no repercussions from the Moulds' attempt to kidnap Buster. He pulled the door closed behind him and turned right. One of the wide front windows of the Gilded Palace was less than three steps from where he stood.

He could feel the blackness rising in him. It would be there until he could close the chapter on the Moulds. They had stolen Amelia Massey's cows, and now they had also tried to kidnap her son. He hoped they were here. They had escaped him once before, but wouldn't the second time. He strode past the window and pushed through the batwing doors. Early like it was, the saloon was brighter than normal, the lamps still lit.

He could make out everyone in the saloon clearly enough to see the features of their faces. He saw no Moulds. Three steps to the right took him to the bar. The bartender stood, both hands against the bar, watching him. "Morning, whatcha drinking?"

"Looking for information."

"Drink first, information later."

He had a wide, dark face, several scars from knuckles finding his cheekbones were present, and his nose had been broken, more than once. The big hands gripping the bar also showed scars of past battles. With all of the signs of mayhem, the man's eyes danced with humor while Jack looked him over.

"Would coffee do?"

"Same price as a drink. Fine with me."

"Coffee."

"Two bits."

Jack fished a quarter from his vest and dropped it on the bar.

The bartender scooped the quarter from the bar, turned, grabbed a coffee mug from the shelf behind him and a coffeepot. The pot had been sitting on a metal stand. He turned back, slid the mug across the bar, and poured. "Cream and sugar?"

"Black."

The man filled the cup to the brim, half-turned, set the pot back on the stand, and faced Jack. "Now what's your question?"

"More than one."

At this the bartender gave a one-sided grin. "That cup'll get you more than one answer."

Jack took a sip. It was better than the doc's coffee, but a lot more expensive. "What's your name?"

"Kevin's the name, Kevin O'Donnell. You can call me Kevin, Kev, or O'Donnell."

Jack took a long sip. "Good coffee. You seen any of the Moulds, Kevin?"

"I have. All of them rode out but one, and he's back to the outhouse. That fella sitting at the table in the corner is with him. Says his name is Curley Blaine Simpson. Said it like it's supposed to mean something, but I've never heard of him."

Jack looked at the mirror. The fella Kevin had pointed out wasn't much different from many of the folks he'd seen in saloons, other than being dirtier and more unkempt. His face was covered with stubble. He looked to be in his early thirties, and from where he was sitting, Jack could just make out the gun belt but not the gun. Curley must be left-handed.

The man's eyes found his in the mirror and held them for a long moment, then looked away. Jack took another sip of his coffee. "Where's the outhouse?"

"Can't miss it. Straight out the back door, and follow the path."

Jacked scanned the almost empty saloon in the mirror's

reflection. Besides the man at the bar and Curley Blaine, the only other occupants besides himself and the bartender were two men at a table. "Much obliged, Kevin. You don't have many folks here this early."

"Just those who don't have any other place to hang their hat." He nodded his head toward the man at the bar. "Toby's here all the time, and those two stagger between bars. If any of them want to sleep at a table or stretch out on the floor when it's slow, I let 'em. Doesn't hurt anything or anyone."

Jack's eyes had been on the mirror, but they moved back to Kevin, reassessing him. "A bartender with a heart. What does your boss say?"

Kevin rolled his eyes at Jack's first comment. "I'm the boss. I own the place."

"Really? Well, let me tell you this, since you own what might get broken or shot. I'm taking Mould to the marshal, and if Curley back there steps in, I'll be taking him too." Jack held his hand up as Kevin began to protest. "Don't worry. Anything gets broken, either I'll reimburse you, or those two will if they have enough money on 'em. How long's he been gone?"

Before the bartender could answer, the back door opened, and Axel Mould stepped into the saloon. He was readjusting his gun belt as he walked past the gambling tables to where his companion was sitting. Jack waited until Mould drew close to his table. He wanted the two of them close together. It would be more efficient, and there would be less chance of an innocent person getting hurt.

Jack straightened and, before turning to face the man he was after, said, "You might want to move from behind me, and take Toby with you."

Kevin nodded and walked slowly down the bar. Reaching Toby, he pulled a bottle from the shelf, bumped Toby with it, and nodded to the side door off the bar. Toby looked up, saw the bottle, and staggered after Kevin. He held tightly to the brass rail around the bar's edge, his eyes glued on the bottle.

When they were clear, Jack turned to face Axel Mould and Curley Blaine. He had watched Curley notice Kevin moving down the bar and leading Toby to the back. His eyes were now on Jack. Axel had missed it all. Jack could see the man had only one goal in mind, and that was to get back to the table and another drink.

Jack watched him approach the table. Mould reached for his chair. "Long time no see, Axel." Jack's voice echoed through the empty saloon. Mould's head jerked toward Jack. His eyes squinted as he tried to remember who the big man was. Finally, Jack saw a touch of recognition.

"I know you."

"You should."

"Where from?"

"Think about it. A dark night. A campfire. Cattle you had rustled from a defenseless woman. Does any of that ring a bell for you?" Jack could feel the coldness throughout his body. Every fiber relaxing, waiting for its command to strike pain or do harm to this killer who stood in front of him.

Mould glanced at his partner and licked his lips. "I know you. You're that big fella who bought Amelia Massey's cattle. What do you want with me?"

"You tried to grab Buster Massey tonight, and your bunch injured several of my cowhands, men I need to work those cattle. I aim to take you in to the marshal."

Mould gave a laugh, more like a grunt. "There's two of us and only one of you, and I'm fast. I'm not near as fast as Curley here, but I bet I can get a bullet in you before you hit the floor."

At his words Curley Blaine stood and grinned at Jack. "I ain't never killed me a man as big as you. You make an easy target."

"That's good."

Curley, his brow wrinkled and his head inclined slightly to the side, stared at Jack. "What's good?"

"What you just said. That'll look good over your grave. He thought he had an easy target."

Curley stiffened. "Ain't no man alive makes fun of me."

Jack grinned back at him while keeping a wary eye on Mould. "There you go again, another one. You keep it up, and we'll have to get you a downright giant marker to write down all your sayings."

Curley opened his mouth to say something else and abruptly closed it.

Jack, relaxed and ready, looked the two over. "Here's your one chance. Drop your gun belts and stick those hands high, and we'll march down to the marshal's office. He has a couple of rooms just built for you two."

Mould's face pulled into a grimace. His drooping mustache seemed to drip off the sides of his chin. "I ain't goin' to no jail."

The grin left Jack's face, replaced by a firm set to his jaw and a hard steely glare. "Good. I hoped you wouldn't. Now draw!"

12

At his command, Mould and Curley went for their guns. Jack's hand flashed to his Remington, and while bringing it up, he watched them, as detached as he had been at four years old with his cousin. They were so slow. He had faced men in Laredo much faster.

Mould's gun hadn't even cleared the holster before Jack's Remington leveled. Curley was the fastest, though not by much. He gave Jack time to place his shot. Usually Jack took no chances and fired for a heart shot, but not this time.

When Curley's revolver cleared his holster, Jack fired. The .36-caliber ball slammed into the man's Colt, taking the top of the hammer off and blasting it into the gunman's wrist. Curley let out a scream, dropped the weapon, and grabbed for his left arm. The ball, which was doing so much damage, was no longer round but a jagged piece of lead. It skittered between the two bones in the man's forearm, bouncing off of and breaking both before blasting through his elbow. If he lived, he'd never draw a gun with his left hand again.

While all of this was going on, Mould was working to bring his weapon into play. Hearing the screams of his companion, fear overpowered all other senses, and he opened his gun hand, allowing the big revolver to fly through the air toward Jack. For Jack, time had slowed. Seeing Mould release his weapon, he halted his trigger squeeze, for he had centered this shot directly on Mould's heart. He watched the now free and rotating revolver turning muzzle over grip, rising as it flew. He waited for a moment and, with his left hand, plucked the Colt from the air by the grip, appearing as if it had been drawn to his hand with a string.

"Well, I'll be danged if I've ever seen that happen before," Jack heard to his right. Still holding his Remington steady on Mould, he glanced in the direction of the voice. It was Kevin, and standing next to him was Toby shaking his head in disbelief.

"Why," Toby said, "it looked like that feller just threw you his gun."

Jack laughed. "I'll have to admit, I've never drawn on a man and had him toss me his weapon before. This is definitely a first."

Curley was holding what was left of his bloody hand and arm, wailing. "I need a doctor. Somebody get me a doctor. I'm bleeding to death."

As if on command, Dr. Franklin pushed through the swinging doors, assessed the room, and dashed to Curley's side.

"Doc, you gotta help me. My arm and hand, they're both killin' me. I can't move my hand."

The doctor shook his head. "Son, there isn't much left of that hand to move."

Jack watched Mould. It didn't look like he could get another inch of stretch out of his arms. When he'd turned loose the revolver, his hands had shot straight up as if he were trying to touch the high ceiling of the saloon. Now he stood frozen, staring at the muzzle of Jack's Remington.

Jack motioned. "Come over here, Mould."

"Don't shoot."

Mould was one of the men who had beaten his cowhands.

Surrounded with a gang, he was brave and fearless, but now he was almost peeing his pants. He watched the frightened gunman walk carefully toward him.

Kevin moved back to Jack's coffee cup. "Want a freshener? It's on the house."

"How can I turn down such an offer?"

Kevin emptied the cup into a barrel at the end of the bar and refilled it with fresh coffee. "What you gonna do with that feller's revolver?"

By now Mould had made it to the bar and was staring at Jack, eyes wide.

Jack looked across the bar at Kevin. "What'd you have in mind?"

"Well, I'll tell you, Mister...?"

"Sage, Jack Sage. Call me Jack."

"Well, I'll tell you, Jack. What just happened here is gonna be a story that travels all over this country. Folks'll come from miles around to see that Colt. It could sell a lot of drinks for me."

"What'll you give me for it?"

Mould had gradually let his arms lower and relax. His hands had lowered to even with his head. "Now, wait just a minute. You cain't sell my pistol. That there is mine. If anyone—"

Jack reached out and shoved his Remington in Mould's belly. "First off, get your hands up! I didn't tell you to lower them."

Mould's hands shot straight up over his head.

"Second, you're going to hang or go to prison. You won't have any need for a weapon." Jack turned to Kevin and motioned to the back. "You have a cook back there?"

Kevin gave a firm nod. "One of the best."

"Then how about this. These brave souls tried to kidnap a thirteen-year-old boy tonight. That boy's with me. His name's Buster Massey. How about you let Buster and me eat here, on the house, when we're passing through. How's that sound to you?"

"How long?"

"As long as you say."

"Fair enough."

Jack handed the .44 Colt over to Kevin. "Then we've got a deal. I need to get these boys to the jail and have a little small talk with them. When I'm done, Buster and I'll be back, and I'm feelin' mighty hungry."

Kevin held the Colt in both hands, examining it like it was a priceless jewel. "You come on. You won't regret this."

Jack looked over at Doc Franklin. "Doc, are you about finished?"

"I still have quite a bit of work left to do on this arm, Mr. Sage."

"Then you'll have to do it in the jail. Get up, Curley. You're headed for the jail." He waved the Remington toward Mould. "Get moving."

"Yes, sir," Mould said, and stepped past Jack for the door. Jack was about to warn him not to run into his partner when his hip struck Curley's broken and torn left arm.

"Look out, you idgit!" Curley gave Mould a hard shove with his good arm, causing Mould to stumble into the saloon door frame. Mould swung around, striking Curley's bloody arm again. The man screamed and doubled over with pain.

Jack, watching Mould, saw the smile of satisfaction on his face. "Knock it off, you two. The jail's a left turn out of here. Please try to escape. There's nothing I'd like better." Jack watched Mould's arms go higher.

It took a few minutes of grumbling for the deputy to get the cells open. After seeing how much Mould had enjoyed hurting Curley, Jack told the deputy to put them in separate cells. At first the deputy argued, but quickly gave in. The doc went into Curley's cell with him, and Jack followed Mould into the other cell, leaving the third empty and available for business. The deputy had departed back to the marshal's desk, tossing the keys to Jack.

Once he was gone, Jack turned Mould around to face him, and dropped his Remington into his holster. "Drop your hands."

Mould lowered them, and Jack watched the man's eyes flit from his face to his gun, his fists, and back to his face. "Where's the rest of your gang?"

The man shook his head, and Jack hit him. He drove a short, quick punch into the man's solar plexus. It didn't need to be hard. He had learned the move from a sergeant in the Foreign Legion, where he had served in his youth. The sergeant had been much smaller than Jack but had skills that he demonstrated to recruits, many whose lives those skills would save in the future. The sergeant had doubled Jack over with his single blow. Jack had labored for what seemed like eternity to get his breath. He knew what Mould was going through as the man collapsed to the floor, gasping.

"I can do this all day long, Mould, but you won't enjoy it much." He watched as the man writhed in pain and strained to draw breath into his paralyzed diaphragm. When the man succeeded in getting his first breath, Jack reached to the floor, grasped Mould's arm in a viselike grip and, almost gently, raised him to his feet.

Mould, gasping, eyes wide, and body trembling, stared at Jack.

"Where's your gang?"

Mould held up a hand. "Let ... me ... get ... my ... breath."

Jack waited until Mould was breathing almost normally, and lifted his eyebrows.

Silence.

He was about to release another blow when Mould held up his hands. "All right. Just don't hit me again."

Jack said nothing.

Mould took a long breath. "They're waiting for us up north. We've got a camp 'bout where Sweetwater and Catlett Creek join up. That'd be two miles west of where Catlett Creek runs into

Denton Creek, and that's about sixteen miles west of Denton. There's a hill just on the other side of Catlett. You cain't miss it."

Jack stepped closer, grasped the frightened man by the front of his shirt and twisted, making it nearly impossible for Mould to breathe. "You telling me the truth?"

The prisoner's hands flew to Jack's thick wrist, attempting unsuccessfully to dislodge the tightening grip. His voice was a croak. "I swear. It's all true. That's where they'll be."

Jack, in disgust, thrust the man hard against the rock wall. "They'd better be. If I find you've lied to me, I'll be back."

Doc Franklin was working on Curley Blaine Simpson's arm in the next cell. Between moans, Curley raised his face to Mould. One side of his mouth was drawn back in a contemptuous sneer. "They're your kin. You can't keep your mouth shut for a little beating? You ain't worth spit." A moan choked off his next comment. He just shook his head.

Jack ignored Curley. "How many?"

Words fell rapidly from Mould's quivering lips. "We've had a bunch more join us. We was gonna grab the kid and ride back down to Massey's place, take her money, and then head out to California. That's been all messed up. Pa was talkin' about robbing a bank, but he ain't said where afore I left."

"How many?" Jack asked again, his eyes narrowing. He moved impatiently toward Mould.

The man took a step back, the rock wall of the jail cell again stopping him. "I'm tellin' you truth, Mr. Sage. Don't hit me again. It's Pa and the other three boys plus four more who's tied up with us. That's eight. Would be ten, but you done caught Curley and me."

Jack looked at Curley. "When did you join up with them?"

Curley bent his sweat-stained face toward him. The doc had wrapped his arm from elbow to mangled hand. "Worst day of my life. I should've never let them talk me into it. It ain't even been a day, and now I'll never use my hand again."

Jack's cold eyes showed Curley no sympathy. "You got lucky, fella. If you had been with them when they were in Austin, you'd be hanging by their sides for killing that congressman." He wheeled and let himself out of Mould's cell and locked the door. "You ready, Doc?"

Doc Franklin stood. "Yes, that's about all I can do for him."

Jack let the doctor from the cell. The steel-barred door let out a piercing shriek when he pushed it closed. Once inserted, it was necessary to partially rotate the key several times in the lock to make it fit. Using a little finesse mixed with brute strength, he was finally able to turn the key. He locked the door, and the two of them stepped into the front office. The deputy, bent over a stack of wanted posters with one gripped in his gnarled hand, looked up as Jack walked in.

"Well, mister, you got yourself a real fast gun with that young feller Curley Simpson. That boy's wanted over in Shreveport for killin' a constable. Got him a five-hundred-dollar ree-ward on his hide." His lips pulled back in a grin, showing a wide gap where his front teeth should have been. "I found the circular on them Mould boys, too. They got a big price on their heads." His mouth snapped closed, the grin disappearing. "You ain't a bounty hunter, are ya? The marshal don't take kindly to folks who hunt men."

Jack shook his head. "No, but I won't turn down the money."

"Hee-hee. I reckon not. Marshal should be in this morning. You'll need to talk to him about your money."

Jack nodded and followed the doctor out the door. "Buster still in your office?"

"As far as I know. I asked him to watch Porter." The doctor stepped quickly to keep up with Jack's long strides.

"I'll get him. We need to eat, get supplies, and be on our way."

Buster was standing on the landing at the top of the stairs. "What was all the shooting?"

Jack let the doctor lead the way up the stairs. "Caught one of the Moulds and a partner of his. They're in jail."

The boy's eyes widened. "Really? Did you have to shoot one of them?"

"I'll tell you later. You hungry?"

Buster's face lit like the rising sun on a clear day. "I'm starved."

Stepping into the office, they met Porter. He was dressed and ready to go. "Thanks, Doc. What do I owe you?"

"Fifty cents will do it. You take it easy for a couple of days. If you start feeling groggy, get yourself off your horse and sit a spell. Barring a little dizziness, you should be fine."

Porter settled up, and the three men left the doctor's office. Reaching the bottom of the steps, Jack scanned the street and turned back to Porter. "Monty'll be looking for you. Why don't you head on back."

The cowhand nodded. "Adios." He headed for the livery while Jack, with Buster at his side, stepped out for the Gilded Palace. Their walk was in silence, Jack thinking about his next move.

Passing the marshal's office, the sound of the piano in the Gilded Palace began, and as Jack pushed through the swinging doors, "Camptown Races" attacked their ears. But it wasn't only their ears, smoke from cigars, pipes, and cigarettes combined with dust and the smell of unwashed men to assail their nostrils. Though the day was still new, the saloon's business had picked up.

Jack moved to a table, grabbed a chair where he'd have his back to the wall, and sat facing the door and bar. Buster dropped into the chair to his left. Kevin O'Donnell spotted them, stepped to the side door by the bar, said something to someone inside, turned, and waved. Jack waved back. Moments later, a beautiful young woman, dressed conservatively for a saloon, headed directly for them. The blue-bowed collar around her long neck exposed nothing, while her blue skirt labored unsuccessfully to hide an attractive figure. He watched her as she approached and noticed Buster was also watching her, closely.

Her hair, the color of a golden palomino, was parted in the middle, with several long, soft plaits circled and fastened behind her ears. Well-defined cheekbones, beneath rosy cheeks, gave her face a regal and healthy air. Dark blue eyes, matching the color of her dress, accepted the appreciative glances of admirers with friendliness but without familiarity. Her full lips, wide smile, and glistening white teeth unintentionally captured the hearts of any admirers who might be in range.

Reaching the table, she warmed both Jack and Buster in her radiant smile. "I understand you are Mr. Jack Sage." Before Jack could speak, she turned to Buster. "My brother tells me you are Buster and that you have a big appetite."

Buster's grin seemed to go from ear to ear. "Yes, ma'am, uh . . . I surely do. I'm mighty hungry."

"Well, I do believe that I can take care of your hunger. Would eggs, flapjacks, ham steak, and biscuits work for you?"

At the mention of the food, Buster's eyes grew even bigger. "Yes, ma'am! That'd be just fine."

She gave Buster a heart-tripping smile, "Then that's what I'll bring you," and turned to Jack.

"Mr. Sage?"

Jack looked into what had to be the most honest blue eyes he had ever seen. The last pair of eyes to capture him so had been in North Africa. A time of much joy and much pain. "Yes, ma'am. That sounds good for me, but you know our names. You have us at a loss. We don't know yours."

"You met my brother. He owns the saloon, so that makes me an O'Donnell, Kathryn Grace O'Donnell." She laughed, a tinkling, confident laugh. The laugh brought smiles to all the men at the surrounding tables, and to Jack.

Her cheeks flushed a shade darker. "I have no idea why I gave you my full name. I never do that. I think you must fluster me, Mr. Sage."

His smile, the first of its type since the passing of many years and miles, warm and friendly, shared her faint embarrassment, though if asked, he would not be able to explain why. "The feeling's mutual, ma'am. I'd be much obliged if you'd call me Jack."

"I shall, Jack, and you may call me Kat." Gathering herself, she said, "If you'll excuse me, I'll be back with your food in a few minutes."

She whirled, her skirt swishing against the chairs and table legs. Jack couldn't take his eyes from her trim body as she hurried through the side door, to the kitchen. Noticing the conversation from the other tables had died, he looked around. All of the men were gazing at the empty side door. Watching the others, he laughed to himself. *Don't be a fool, Jack. That girl probably has more suitors than she knows what to do with. Anyway, you've got a job and a long trail ahead of you. This is no time or place to get involved with someone. It's been so long, you probably wouldn't even know how.*

The batwing doors swung open, and Monty stepped in.

13

Monty glanced at the bar, waved to Kevin, spotted Jack and Buster, and headed to their table. Bronco was in trail.

"Pull up a chair. We're about to put on the feedbag."

Bronco nodded. "Sounds good to me. I'm almighty tired of eatin' Hamm's cookin'."

"Would eggs, flapjacks, ham steak, and biscuits work for you? That's what we've ordered."

Monty nodded, and Bronco said, "That'd tickle my gullet like a turkey feather, boy."

Jack frowned. "Does that mean yes?"

Bronco frowned back. "'Course it does. Don't you understand English?"

Jack shrugged, waved, and got Kevin's attention. He pointed to Monty and Bronco and, holding up two fingers, mouthed, "Two more of the same."

Kevin acknowledged the order and headed for the kitchen. Jack turned back to Monty and met his eyes.

"Hear you've been busy, Jack."

"Happened pretty fast." He explained all that had taken place since his and Buster's earlier arrival. At the mention of the Moulds' hiding place, Bronco looked at Monty, but didn't interrupt. "That's about it. I need to pick up some supplies and be on my way. Figure I might even meet up with the herd by the time you reach the Red River."

Monty leaned forward, placing his forearms on the table. "Jack, Bronco and I heard some sorry news this morning as we were coming into town."

Jack said nothing. After a moment his eyebrows rose, waiting, his eyes taking in the sadness on both Monty's and Bronco's faces.

Monty took a deep breath and let out a long sigh. "You remember the sheriff we met back down the trail, Bill Stanton?"

Jack nodded.

"He was found dead a couple of miles from his home. Feller said he was shot up so bad he could hardly be recognized. Said they must have shot him at least fifty times. Had a wanted poster nailed to his forehead."

Jack's face hardened, his jaw muscles standing taut like ropes on a longhorn. "The Moulds."

"The Moulds."

Jack Sage was not a swearing man. He had learned control from a man he respected, his father, but moments like these challenged his resolve.

Kat brought out the four meals, but seeing the serious faces she said nothing, placing steaming plates in front of each man.

Time clicked by while Jack stared out the window, picturing the burly, demanding sheriff. He hadn't liked the man, but Monty and Bronco had, which said a lot for his character. *A bad decision,* he thought. *If I had gone with him, Bill Stanton would still be alive. I let my own pride get in the way, and now he's dead.* "They get up a posse?"

Bronco leaned forward, swore, and slammed the table with his fist. "They didn't find a thing. You'd think, out of all those sodbusters and ranchers around there, they could've found one decent tracker. The Moulds got away with nary a scratch."

Monty just looked at Jack with those sad eyes. "Ain't your fault, boy. I hate to say it, but Bill was getting old. In his younger days he'd never ride into an ambush like that. Guess he was calculating what he was gonna do with all that reward money. Reckon he won't be finding out."

He raised a hand and pointed his finger at Jack. "It ain't yore job to be chasing after that bunch. You've already done more'n enough. You scratched their numbers by two. That'll help. Let the law get after 'em. They done killed a congressman and a sheriff. The rangers'll be on their tails before they know it. You've got a job waitin' for you, gettin' them cattle to Ellsworth." Monty leaned back, lifted his left hand, and pushed his hat to the back of his head, showing the accumulated wrinkles of experience across his forehead. "Hamm's in town with the chuckwagon. Soon as he gets his supplies, we'll be on our way. Join us."

Jack sat silent, thinking about the dead man. Tasting nothing, Jack ate knowing he would need the nourishment. His mind was filled with thoughts about his bad decision. He'd made plenty in his life. While in the wars, he'd been involved in a couple that had cost lives, but this one couldn't be laid at anyone's doorstep but his. It was up to him to fix it. His gray eyes focused on Monty. "No. I'm going after the Moulds."

Bronco yanked his hat off and slapped it against his leg, dust flying up in a cloud. "Danged, you are one hard-headed man."

Jack laid a frigid grin on his friend. "I've heard that before, but I do want to make a change in plans." He turned to Buster, who was just finishing the last bite of his ham steak. When the boy looked up, Jack said, "As much as I'd like for you to ride with me, I think Monty and Bronco need your skill and understanding with the horses."

Buster gazed up at the big man who had saved his family and

given him his first real job. Absently he placed his knife and fork on the plate. "But I could help you."

Jack laid a big hand on the boy's shoulder and squeezed gently. "I know you could. You'd be a big help, but the drive needs you more. What with the new men Monty's hiring, we need someone who knows and understands horses, and you're the man for the job."

Jack saw the tears spring to the boy's eyes and felt a pang of regret, but told himself, *Ignore your feelings. This is for his own good. The Moulds are no longer interested in Buster. They're going after a bank. He'll be safest back with the herd.*

Buster looked down, jammed his hat on his head, and pulled the brim low, hiding his eyes. "I'll do what you want. I don't like it, but I'll do it."

Bronco, sitting next to Buster, slapped him on the back. "I'm glad to hear it. We was wonderin' what we were gonna do, 'cause we knew we couldn't replace you."

The men stood. Monty said, "We'll be going to the general store, and I still need to hire a couple of hands. Buster, why don't you meet us there."

Buster nodded.

The swish of a skirt caught Jack's attention, and he turned to see Kat approaching. He greeted her smile with his, while the rest of the crew stood watching. "Kat, how much do we owe you?"

"Fifty cents for your two friends." She tossed a smile to Monty and Bronco. They reached for their vest.

Jack shook his head. "I've got it."

Bronco winked at her. "Mighty fine food. If I was ten years younger, missy..."

She laughed. "I just bet."

Monty nodded to her, and said to Jack, "Thanks."

She turned back to Jack. "I think Kevin is rethinking his deal with you, especially after he saw all that Buster ate. He might throw a fit over all the food I gave him."

Buster's face, which had brightened with her approach, went somber until he saw she was joking. He flashed a big grin and stuck his chest out. "If he does, you tell him to come see me."

All the men broke into laughter, relieved to be able to vent the tension. Kat reached past Jack, her face serious. "Thank you, Buster. If he does, I will." She gave his cheek an affectionate pat and turned to Jack. "You, big fella, owe me nothing for you and Buster, just the fifty cents for your friends. Can you handle that?"

"Yes, ma'am, I think I can." From his vest, he pulled a shiny gold half eagle, and lifting her hand, he cupped it in his and dropped the five dollar gold piece into her palm. He felt the soft strength of the back of her hand, and the long fingers touching his wrist. It brought about a tingling that reminded him of how his hair felt in an intense lightning storm.

Kat broke the spell first. "Yes, I guess you can. Thank you, kind sir." She hesitated, slowly sliding her hand from his. "I know what you're about to do. Be careful."

The feel of her smooth skin sliding across his lingered in his hand. "Don't you worry, Kat. I'll not only be careful, but I'll see *you* again."

"See that you do." She spun and marched back to the kitchen.

Jack watched her disappear through the kitchen door, then moved his gaze up the bar to Kevin. The big man was watching him. He cleared his throat. "Best get moving. We all have a lot to do. Buster, stick with me for now."

Monty and Bronco shook hands with Jack.

"Luck," Bronco said.

Monty gripped his hand hard. "I ain't agreein', but I'll be lookin' forward to seein' you on the Red."

"See you there, and take care of yourselves." He put his hand on Buster's shoulder. "And take good care of my friend, here."

The two men nodded and disappeared out the saloon door. Jack looked back to Kevin, raised a hand in salute, and relieved, saw it returned. He followed Buster through the batwings.

Earlier, he had spotted the gunsmith's shop across the street. Dodging between freight wagons, horses, carriages, cow and horse droppings, the two made their way across the busy Fort Worth main street. Jack stepped onto the boardwalk, and Buster jumped up beside him. They stopped to look through the window at the numerous weapons upon the counters. In the reflection of the glass, Jack could see Buster's eyes shining.

Opening the door, Jack saw an older man, with thick salt-and-pepper hair, watching them from behind the counter. The man motioned. "Come on in. Glad to see you. It's been a slow morning."

Jack nodded, examined the gentleman, who he assumed was the gunsmith and proprietor. He was a tall man with wide shoulders, a little under six feet. "We're looking for a Winchester '66, a Yellow Boy."

The man waved an arm toward a long-gun shelf behind him. "I've got several, just a matter of you deciding on what you like. Prices range from fifteen dollars to fifty-five."

"So how about you explain the difference in prices and show us some rifles."

"The one at fifty-five is new and hand engraved. A special from the factory. Some gents like that. The three at thirty-five are also new, just out of the box. I've only shot them to make sure the sights are dead-on at a hundred yards. The other five are used, some more used than others. A couple downright beat up, but let me assure you, sir, they are all good shooters. If I can't bring a weapon up to snuff, it doesn't go up there."

Jack eyed the used rifles. Past the Winchesters were several nice-looking Spencers. He only glanced at them and pointed to three of the Winchesters. "I'd like to see that one, that one, and that one." He had chosen three, one rifle and two saddle-ring carbines.

"Good choices depending on your needs," the gunsmith said. He pulled each from the shelf, opened and checked the breech to make sure it was unloaded, and laid each weapon on the counter. "Name's Chester Wyatt."

Jack picked up the first of the carbines, closed and opened the lever rapidly several times, and threw it to his shoulder. He was surprised the way it fit. He tried the next one, and finally the rifle, which was longer. He liked the carbine. He'd give up a couple of rounds for the carbine's quick pointing characteristics. He gave the rifle back to Chester. "Jack Sage. You can put it up." His big hand closed around the other carbine, and he handed it to Buster. "Try it."

Jack had already seen how Buster handled a rifle when the Moulds rustled the cattle. Now he watched as the boy almost exactly duplicated his and Chester's movements by checking the rifle to make sure it was empty, and exercising caution with the muzzle, even knowing the weapon was empty. "How do you like it?"

Buster lowered the rifle and laid a longing gaze across the Yellow Boy. "It's mighty nice, Jack. You replacing your Spencer?"

Jack nodded. "I might need a little more and faster firepower, and I'm willing to give up some range for it."

"Yes," Chester said, "the Spencer is a fine weapon, much better at the longer ranges, but it can't push out the number of rounds the Winchester can."

"How much?"

"This is a fine rifle. I took it on trade for a new one. I know the man who owned it. As you can see by the weapon, he took excellent care of it. I can let you have it for an even thirty dollars."

"What if I bought two? Include the other carbine."

The man's eyes widened slightly. "In that case, I could let you have both of them for fifty-eight dollars."

Buster, eyes wide, was staring at the rifle in his hand with amazement. His head moved back and forth, from the new rifle to Jack, unable to believe what his friend had said.

Jack picked up the other carbine. "I'll pay your price if you'll throw in a hundred rounds of ammunition. Plus, I'll buy another hundred."

Chester didn't hesitate. He thrust his hand across the counter. "Deal." The two men shook, after which Chester bent over and reached under the counter. He pulled out and stacked four boxes of .44 rimfire ammunition next to the two rifles.

Once stacked, Chester straightened, and Jack paid.

When the transaction was completed, Chester asked, "You have a Spencer?"

Jack nodded.

"Interested in selling it?"

"Not right now. Maybe when I come back through. I'll need another scabbard for this Winchester." The thought hit him, *Buster will, too.* "I forgot, the boy will also need one."

"I've got a couple of used ones. They're in good shape. I'll let you have them both for three dollars."

"We'll take 'em."

"Be right back." Chester disappeared through a back door.

Jack nodded to the ammunition on the counter. "One of those is yours. Load up. Weapon's no good to you empty." Buster nodded, and the two of them slipped rounds into the side loading gate on the rifles. Jack worked the lever, throwing one into the barrel, and added the additional round. "Go ahead. You know to never point that muzzle at anything you aren't aiming to blast. Shove one up the chute."

Buster followed Jack's example as the gunsmith returned with the two scabbards. Jack looked them over. They were worn, broken in for the carbine, but in good shape. He paid Chester the three dollars, chose a scabbard, handed it to Buster, and watched him slide the Winchester into the leather. It fit snugly and slid in nicely. Jack followed suit. "We'd best be getting out of here while I still have a couple of dollars left."

Everyone laughed, with Buster laughing the loudest while he admired his new rifle.

"Don't forget to stop by with that Spencer when you come back through," Chester said.

"Adios," Jack said, and they walked out into the hot Texas sun.

On the boardwalk, Jack turned to the boy. "Buster, you'd better get on over to the store. You don't want to keep Hamm waiting."

Buster turned a serious face toward Jack. "This is the first rifle I've ever owned. I'm obliged, Jack. I'll pay you back when we get paid."

"Forget it, boy. I wanted you armed so you could protect my string and my cattle. Speaking of string. I need to ask a favor of you."

"Yes, sir, anything."

"You mind taking Stonewall back with you and watching out after him? I'm thinking he'll be more hindrance than help for what I'm planning."

"Sure, Jack. I'll be glad to. I'll take real good care of him and all your horses."

"Good." Jack shoved his hand out to the boy, who slid the box of shells under his left arm and grasped the big hand. "You take good care of yourself, Buster. I don't want to have any explaining to do to your mother when we get back. You hear?"

Jack could see Buster was having a tough time keeping the tears back, but he succeeded, giving him a firm grip.

"Yes, sir. I sure will, and you do the same. You watch out for those Moulds. They're sneaky and conniving, and don't believe a word that comes out of their mouths. Like my pa used to say, 'If their lips are movin', they're lying.'"

Jack grinned down at the boy. "Good advice. Now git."

Buster turned and walked down the boardwalk to the general store. Jack watched him until he had entered the store. *I like that boy*, he thought. He turned and crossed the street for the marshal's office.

A different man sat in the chair behind the desk when Jack

walked in. This man was bigger than average, older than Jack. His brown hair was sprinkled with a little gray, as was his thin mustache. His gray eyes showed no emotion. "Yeah?"

"I'm Jack Sage, Marshal. I—"

"I don't have your money yet." The marshal's voice was frustrated. "You just brought 'em in."

Jack told himself to be patient. "What's your name, Marshal?"

"Marshal Parrish, and as I was trying to tell ya, it'll take a week or so for it to be authorized. As a bounty hunter, you should know that."

The last was said with a touch of disdain, and Jack could feel his hackles rising. "Look, Marshal, I didn't come here to ask you about the money. I came here to find out if you're interested in catching the Mould gang."

"What, a bounty hunter willing to split his bounty? You are new."

Jack took a deep breath. "Marshal Parrish, I'm not a bounty hunter. I'm here to see if you want to help catch the Moulds. I also want to talk to Axel again. I've still got a couple of questions for him."

"Ezra's already told me how you questioned him in my jail. You won't get a second chance to beat a prisoner while I'm here."

"Alright, Marshal. I've got some more news for you. The gang your prisoners belong to shot and killed Sheriff Bill Stanton. He was shot over fifty times, and then their wanted poster was nailed to his forehead." Jack leaned toward the marshal. "You still want me to leave him alone?"

The marshal broke eye contact with Jack and stared at his desk. "Bill's dead?"

Jack said nothing, for he knew it wasn't a question for him. It was a question of disbelief. He waited.

Marshal Parrish looked up. "Coffee?"

He shook his head.

The man nodded toward a chair. "Sit."

He walked to the chair, spun it around, sat, and leaned forward, resting his arms on the back, and waited.

The marshal stared out the window. Dust hung over the main street from the wagon and horse traffic. Kids chased and yelled at dogs barking at the wagons and horses, while teamsters yelled at the kids to get out of their way. People moved along the boardwalk, speaking about the heat of the day, or the lack of rain, or the price of cattle, or the marriage of someone's daughter. Life went on outside while they sat inside the marshal's office and thought about a life that had ended violently.

"When'd it happen?"

"I don't know for sure. I'm with a herd passing through. The trail boss is Montana Huff. He brought me word this morning that Sheriff Stanton had been killed nine days, maybe two weeks ago."

The marshal swore. "He was getting older. Last time I saw him, he talked about retiring, just wanted to save a little more." He lifted the Mould wanted poster from the top of the stack. "Guess he figured five thousand dollars would be enough. It would for me."

He looked up at Jack. "He say anything about Barbara, Bill's wife?"

Jack shook his head.

"She's a fine lady. Martha and I have known them for over twenty years. Once, out around Weatherford, we fought off Comanches together." He shook his head. "Good friends." He cleared his throat and squared his shoulders. "So, Mr. Jack Sage, you'd like to have a discussion with the prisoner?"

Jack gave a single nod. "I would. It won't take long. I just have a couple of questions for him. You may not even need to let me in the cell. He's gotten familiar with my methods."

The marshal stood. "Come on back."

14

Axel was sitting on the edge of his bunk, eyes wide with fear. It was obvious he had heard much of what had been said, and recognized the voices. As soon as the jail entry door opened, he said, "Marshal, don't let him near me. I've got my rights, and Curley here is a witness. He'll tell if Sage lays a hand on me."

Parrish looked at Curley, who was sitting on his bunk, holding his injured arm. "I'm not seeing Curley caring much as to what happens to you. Looks to me like he's got enough on his plate to hold his attention." He motioned to Jack. "Ask him your questions."

Jack stepped to the bars. "How're you doing, Axel? I enjoyed our little talk earlier. You want to pick up where we left off?"

"Stay away from me, Sage. The marshal's here, not that old geezer. He'll stop you. He don't allow folks to abuse his prisoners."

Parrish handed the keys to Jack. "Told my wife I'd be home early. Hang the keys up when you're through." He walked out the jail entrance, and moments later the front door banged as it closed. The marshal's footfalls could be heard disappearing down the boardwalk.

Jack kept his eyes on Mould. A cold, mirthless smile parted his lips. "You're all mine, Axel. We're going to have some fun."

He started shuffling through the keys.

"Wait, Sage."

Jack found the key and inserted it into the lock.

"Just wait!" Mould yelled, his voice shaking.

Jack paused with the key and waited, eyes still on Mould.

Sweat rolled down the man's face. His shirt was dark with the stain.

"Where are they hitting the bank?"

His voice still raised, Mould said, "I told you, they hadn't decided. I don't know."

Jack shook his head and turned the key. The bolt released with a clank.

"Alright, alright, it's Denton. They're robbing the bank in Denton."

Jack caught movement in the other cell. Curley was shaking his head.

"Which bank?"

"Which bank? There's only one. It's the Cattlemen's Bank."

"When are they hitting it?"

Mould swung his head back and forth. "I don't know, Sage. I just know they're going to rob it. Pa didn't tell me the time."

Jack slowly pulled the cell door open. The hinge let out a long raucous squeal. He waited for a second, then moved to step in.

Mould jumped to his feet, both hands extended in front of him as if he might keep the big man away. "Alright, alright, I'll tell you. They plan on hittin' it day after tomorrow. Pa said it'd be late, just when most folks are sittin' down to supper. That old banker stays late. He'll be able to open the safe. They plan on driftin' into town a couple at a time, earlier in the day. Make it all a surprise. That's it—all of it. Now, just leave me alone."

"Not yet."

Mould's body seemed to shrink. "I told you everything. There ain't no more. I swear."

"Tell me about Sheriff Stanton."

"Who?" The word came out small, shaking.

"Now's not the time to play games with me, Axel. I found out what you and your kin did to the sheriff, and I want to know how it happened."

"I got to sit." Mould dropped to his bunk.

"Tell me, Axel. I'll leave, and you won't ever see me again. Tell me now."

Jack watched the killer's shoulders slump. His head dropped. He stared at his feet. He had seen men like this before. It could happen to most men, weak or strong. There was a point, when pushed by pain or fear, whether for themselves or loved ones, they would break, give in, spill their guts. For Axel it was shallow, near the surface.

It poured out. "Pa had sent Jethro to town. He's my youngest brother. He don't really fit. Too soft, but he'd gone and got a few supplies, not a lot. We didn't want anyone to be gettin' curious, just enough to keep us going for a while." He stopped for a moment, took a breath, and scuffed his boot sole on the rock floor.

Jack waited, saying nothing.

Now Axel was calm as he spoke, almost in a trance, the words pouring out. "When he come back, he told Pa all the town was talking about them, and the sheriff had paper on us and was looking to catch us. Pa just laughed like he does when he starts thinkin' bloody. He said something like, 'I reckon we oughta let him catch us, boys,' and everybody laughed. Pa was startin' to plan like he does." He stopped again.

Jack said nothing.

A mockingbird sang its song in the cedar tree behind the jail, and pigs could be heard fussing and rooting at a trough.

"We was riding along that trail, mindin' our own business, when lo and behold if the sheriff, his badge shining bright on his vest, just don't come around that bend right in front of us." Axel turned his face up to Jack. "I swear it was like it was supposed to happen, like a gift. Cletus, he's a tad older'n me." Mould nodded, agreeing with himself. "He's bloody, like Pa. But he's fast, too. He can slick that iron out faster than a rattlesnake. He whipped that big ole .44 out and shot that sheriff right through the belly. I'm tellin' you, Mr. Sage, he was about the most surprised sheriff I think I've ever seen. I don't even know if he recognized us, but it ain't made any difference. All them other boys pulled out their guns and went to blasting.

"The sheriff fell on the ground, and they kept on shooting. Why, it sounded like a young war there for a bit. Both Pa and Cletus emptied their guns and pulled out their other ones and emptied them, too. Then Cletus must not have been satisfied. 'Cause he took out his Winchester, he's mighty good with that rifle, and shot until Pa made him stop." Axel shook his head. "I don't know when that sheriff died, but he sure had a lot of bullet holes in him. Pa got down and went through his pockets. He found the circular." He looked up at Jack. "You know they got a five-thousand-dollar ree-ward out on us? I ain't never seen that much money, and they want to give it to whoever catches us. You gettin' some of it, Mr. Sage?"

"Go on. What happened next?"

Axel must have seen the deep disgust and anger reflected on Jack's face. His voice started quivering again, and he looked at the floor.

"I ain't pulled a trigger nary a time, Mr. Sage. It was all them other boys. They're a bloody bunch. I woulda stopped 'em if I could."

Jack's voice came out low and threatening. "Axel, don't make me ask you again."

Axel's voice was equally low but cautious. "It were Pa's idea.

He thought of it all hisself. He told Jethro to bring him a nail. Pa likes nails. Anytime we travel, he carries nails with him. So Jethro climbed down off his horse and found the nails in the pack and brought one to him. I swear I didn't know what he was about to do. If'n I had, I woulda stopped him for sure. Pa, he lays that wanted circular on the sheriff's forehead, sticks that nail over it, picks up this big rock, and pounds that nail straight into the sheriff's head, right there in front of everybody."

Mould cut his eyes up in a sideways glance at Jack. "I swear it made me sick. I almost puked. I surely did."

"Is that it?"

Mould nodded his head vigorously. "Yes, sir, Mr. Sage. That's every bit of it, I swear."

Jack looked up at the barred window. "Did you get all that, Marshal?"

An intense voice, low and heavy with anger, said, "I got it, and so did our town clerk, who was kind enough to join me and write down every word. I'll be right in."

Jack turned, exited the cell, and threw the bolt. He looked down at Axel Mould, a man not even thirty years old. "I'll be gone, Axel, but even though I won't be here to see it, it's gratifying to know you'll be swinging with the rest of your worthless kin."

Mould, shocked, sat staring at Jack, his jaw slack and his mouth hanging open.

Curley Simpson began laughing from the adjoining cell. "They got you good, you rat. I ain't knowed in my whole life a man who would sell out his family. I hope they don't hang you near 'em. I wouldn't want those folks to be tainted with the likes of you."

Jack let himself out of the jail and into the office, thinking, *Tainted. That's how I feel just from being around Mould. Any human being would be tainted by the likes of the entire family.* He stopped and thought, *Except maybe the youngest. I think his name is Jethro, and their ma, I don't know anything about her.*

The marshal walked back in, his face red, brows pulled tight together. He went straight to his desk, waved at the chair in front, and dropped into his. "Sometimes I hate this job. I'd like to be fishing, not listening to a spineless killer like Mould spill his guts."

He shook his head. "They saw a man with a badge, so they just shot him." He jerked his hand up and pointed toward the jail. "I'm going to enjoy seeing the likes of Mould stretch a rope. Him saying he never shot. You know he was right in there with the rest of the bunch."

Jack said nothing.

Marshal Parrish sighed and looked across his desk at Jack. His mouth drooped at the corners, showing wrinkles running to the sides of his chin. "Thanks for letting me blow off a little steam. I guess you're headed for Denton?"

"As quick as I can. If you could give me a name and a letter of introduction, that might smooth the way. Since Axel and his partner haven't shown up at their camp, I'm not too sure the old man might push up the robbery. It could be today."

The marshal pulled out a piece of paper and a pencil. Laboriously he began to write. When he finished, he handed it to Jack. "That'll introduce you. As you can see, the man you want is Sheriff Arthur Colson. He's a steady man. With this letter, he'll listen. There's plenty of good men up there, so if you can get there before the Moulds, he'll have a fine party waiting for them.

"As far as the town marshal is concerned, he's nothing more than a political appointee who's way in over his head. He was appointed by the mayor. The problem is, the mayor is the marshal's brother. Marshal Dylan Rush is young, inexperienced, and headstrong. I'm surprised he hasn't been shot before now. So do your best to get to the sheriff."

Jack stood, folded the letter, and shoved it into an inside pocket of his vest. "Much obliged, Marshal."

"Good luck. Hope you get 'em all. That kind of vermin don't need to be loose in this country."

"Thanks. How far to Denton?"

"About thirty-five miles. Head north. Where the road splits, take the one to the northeast. It's not that far, but it's hotter than the hinges of hell out there and gettin' hotter."

"I have a good horse," Jack said, striding to the door. He stepped out onto the boardwalk and turned left to head for the livery. *I hope Smokey is rested,* he thought. *We've got a fast trip to make.* He pulled out his silver pocket watch. His thumb ran softly over the emerald set in the engraving of an exploding grenade. It had been a gift from a girl in another time, another place. Every time he opened it, the emerald reminded him of her—so long ago. He shook his head and checked the time. How had it gone by so fast? It was past one o'clock.

He felt the heat of the sun beating down on him. Traffic had died in the street. Most folks were having dinner or taking naps, anything to get out of the sun. This would be a hard trip for Smokey, but he knew his horse could do it. They had to get there before the gang hit the bank.

A boy greeted him as he walked into the livery. "Hidee-do, mister. Want to rent a horse?"

Jack nodded. "Hi, boy. Nope, I'm after my grulla. Did he get some corn and water?"

"Yes, sir. He ate mighty well."

"Good," Jack said, continuing to Smokey. At his voice, the big head turned to watch him. He brushed off the horse's back, making sure it was clear with nothing to irritate under the blanket and saddle. Laying and smoothing the blanket, he glanced at the boy. "How about getting his bridle."

The boy reached to where the bridle was hanging and pulled it down.

Jack threw the saddle across Smokey's back. "You go ahead and put it on. He won't bite."

"I ain't afraid. Most horses like me." The kid stepped up and slipped the bridle on while Jack finished fastening the cinch.

"How much I owe you?"

"It's twenty-five for the stay and twenty-five for the corn."

Jack pulled out a half-dollar and a nickel. He flipped the two coins to the boy, watched him deftly catch both in one hand, swung into the saddle, and turned Smokey toward the stable door.

"Thanks, mister."

"My pleasure." He pulled his gray Stetson down tight and bumped his horse with the spurs. "Let's go, Smokey."

The horse launched from the stable. A fat man near the entrance jumped back and yelled, "Watch out."

Jack knew he continued yelling, but the sound was lost in the hoofbeats and rushing air. The grulla accelerated and was running at full tilt by the time he passed a wagon tied at the north end of the stable. Jack leaned low over the horse's neck and let him cut around the traffic ahead. A bunch of chickens had moved dangerously close to the street and flew up cackling in complaint at the racing horse. Several pigs squealed as their short legs churned to get them out of the way of the flying hooves. Jack grinned. Sometimes it was just plain fun.

They left the town and turned right on the road to the northeast. A wooden arrow-shaped sign with Denton burned into it confirmed they were headed in the right direction.

Jack let Smokey run for what he figured was about a mile and slowed him to a walk. The horse was good for three miles before he even started breathing hard, but he wasn't going to press him in this heat. He let him walk for another mile, then bumped him up into a ground-covering lope. *This should put us in Denton in about three hours,* Jack thought. *If old man Mould moved the robbery up a day, it's going to be tight.*

∽

TIME HAD PASSED QUICKLY. It had taken almost four hours. Because of the heat, they had stopped twice to water Smokey. The horse had picked up a rock only minutes after their last stop. Luckily, Jack managed to pop it out from beneath the edge of the shoe. He examined the hoof and shoe carefully, no damage. After he'd walked Smokey a short distance, the animal was ready and anxious to get moving.

He entered Denton at four fifty. The first man he saw, he guided Smokey near him. "Can you tell me where to find the sheriff's office?"

The man stopped and pointed in the direction he was going. "Can't miss it. Keep going up the street. It'll be on the left, next to Mason's Mercantile."

"Thanks." Jack started to move Smokey along.

"Won't do you any good."

He turned to look at the well-dressed man. "Why's that?"

"He and his deputy are out of town, escorting a prisoner. Don't reckon they'll be back for several days."

Dang, Jack thought. *I hate it, but I'll have to depend on the marshal.* "How about the town marshal?"

The man rolled his eyes. "Same direction, but you won't find him there."

"Where will I find him?"

"At the Cattlemen's Club. Still straight up the street. It'll be on the right. Can't miss it. Best saloon in North Texas. He'll probably be in a game of cards about now. He does like the gambling. He . . ."

Jack heard nothing of the man's remaining sentence, for he had Smokey galloping up the street. The Cattlemen's Club was only a short distance. Jack pulled Smokey to a sliding halt in front of a hitching rail with a watering trough. He leaped from the horse, but before his feet hit the ground, Smokey's nose hit the water. Jack tossed the reins over the rail and strode into the saloon.

The name changed nothing. It was a typical saloon. Maybe a little nicer, but still a saloon, packed with cowhands, ranchers, city folks, and dance-hall girls. The noise and smell of tobacco smoke, liquor, and unwashed bodies rolled past the batwing doors onto the boardwalk. The saloon was doing a booming business. It looked like all of Denton had chosen to congregate here.

He ignored the bar and looked to his left, where the tables sat. They were filled with men drinking, talking, and playing cards. Jack had no idea what this marshal looked like. His only description was young and headstrong. That would describe most of the occupants.

His eyes went from table to table. He passed over one, then jerked back to it. There were five men sitting around the table, all looking toward the sixth, whose back was toward the door. He was holding a deck of cards and regaling the other players. He wore a derby hat, and his frock coat was draped over the back of his chair. His vest, a portion visible over his shoulders, was maroon brocade with heavy gold trim.

Jack leaned to a man standing next to him. "Where's the marshal?"

The man pointed to the brocade vest. Jack started across the room. Nearing the table, a large man stepped in front of him and held his hand up to stop him. Jack grabbed his wrist, twisted and shoved. The marshal's protector piled in a heap on the floor at the foot of a big man at the next table.

The big man stood. He was older, a full head of gray hair showing under his wide Stetson. "Now see here, sir. We'll have none of that in this establishment."

"Look, mister. I need to see the marshal on an urgent matter. It can't wait, so move out of my way."

The brocade vest stood and turned.

15

He looked Jack over from boots to hat.

Jack was aware his stature was impressive, but he also knew his appearance was dusty, unshaven, and unkempt. He reached inside his vest and pulled out the letter. "If you're the marshal, you need to read this."

The man Jack saw was young, no more than twenty-five at the most. Taller than average, around six feet, he was slim, and Jack figured the women might call him handsome in a pretty, sly sort of way. There were few wrinkles on the man's face. His hair and clothing were immaculate. He was the perfect picture of a riverboat gambler, yet he wore a nicely polished, silver marshal's badge. He gave a slow nod, and Jack extended the letter to the marshal.

With large but almost delicate hands, the marshal took the letter, which was now soaked with sweat. "My name is Marshal Dylan Rush." He held it carefully by one corner and flipped it open. His gaze drifted slowly over the letter and looked up. "You are Jack Sage?"

"Yes, Marshal, and you need to get some good men to the bank right now."

"But this says your witness indicated it would be tomorrow, and *you* suspect it will be today." The marshal looked up at Jack, reached with both hands to the bottom of his vest, and pulled it tight, then straightened his tie. "If the witness told you it would be tomorrow, why do you suspect it will be today?"

The marshal pulled out a gold pocket watch, flipped the cover open, and stared at the time. "It's almost five thirty right now, and it seems nothing is happening."

Jack reached out and yanked the letter from the man. He folded it and shoved it back in his pocket. "Those men who plan on robbing your bank are not only thieves, but killers. They killed Sheriff Bill Stanton. Anyone they find in your bank stands to get shot. You need to get armed men to that bank right now."

The big man who had stepped up to Jack turned to the marshal. "Dylan, he's talking about a bank robbery."

The sounds in the saloon had fallen quiet. Jack figured there were a lot of men who had money in the only bank in Denton.

"Jeremy," the marshal said, "the letter is from Marshal Parrish in Fort Worth. He says the witness believes the robbery will be tomorrow. This man Sage only suspects it will be today. It sounds like he's overreacting to me."

The man called Jeremy turned back to Jack. "Why do you think it will be today?"

Jack, almost exploding with frustration, leaned toward Jeremy. "Does it really matter? If I'm wrong, what have you lost? Deputizing a few men for an hour or two? But what if I'm right? You lose what's in your bank and very probably the people also."

Jeremy turned back to the marshal. "He's right, Dylan. Why don't you deputize a few men. I will authorize the funds. The council won't vote against me. It can't—"

Gunfire erupted from up the street.

Jack spun and dashed for the door. He heard a yell behind him, "The bank, get to the bank!"

Up the street, he could see men charging out from a large,

brick building. He recognized Mould in the group. He ran to Smokey's side, yanked out his new Winchester, and leveled on the old man. The bank robbers were in various phases of mounting and dashing north out of town. Jack filled his sights with the old man and squeezed the trigger, but just as he fired, one of the other thieves yanked his horse around to get past Mould. The bullet took him in the back of the head, blowing brain, blood, and bone in a red spray in front of him and over his horse. Lifeless, he toppled to the ground.

Mould didn't glance back. He slammed in the spurs and, in the middle of the gang of bank robbers, dashed to freedom.

Jack racked the .44 Winchester's lever, throwing a fresh round into the chamber, and sighted on the back of another escaping thief. He fired and watched the man jerk, almost falling from the saddle, but catch himself and hold on.

By now multiple weapons were barking, but all were handguns, until a Spencer roared next to Jack. At the blast of the Spencer, another robber toppled from his horse. Then the gang of robbers disappeared behind a treeline on the outskirts of town.

There was yelling and confusion. Rush was trying to pull a posse together. Jack turned and saw the man behind him holding a Spencer and staring down the street. It was hard to tell where dirt stopped and human began. Jack figured he must look similar after all the riding he'd done today. "Good shooting, though I don't know if I'll be able to hear anything for the next day or two."

"Sorry about that. Figured I didn't have time to stroll out into the middle of the street to take a shot." He made a point of looking Jack over. "Anyway, you cover a lot of territory."

"Reckon I do." Jack extended his hand. "Name's Jack Sage."

Marshal Rush pulled his horse toward Jack with a group of excited men he had deputized into a posse. "You coming with us?"

"No."

Rush jerked back in the saddle, surprised at Jack's answer. "No? Aren't you the man who wanted to catch them?"

"You're going to catch nothing. It'll be dark soon, and they'll be long gone. You oughta stay and see who's hurt in the bank and what was taken. You can get on their trail early in the morning."

Rush shook his head and yelled, "There's no time to waste!" He turned to his posse. "Come on, boys." With Rush in the lead, his derby pulled tight, they roared out of town.

The other man waited until the noise died down. "Theodore Dewitt. Folks call me Ted." He nodded toward the disappearing posse. "Mighty excited bunch of folks. Think they'll catch anything?"

"Maybe a little lead, but that'll be about all. I suspect they'll have themselves a brisk little ride and be done. That's about all a posse's good for."

"Ain't that the truth."

Ted turned back to a buckskin tied next to Smokey. He slid the Spencer into the empty scabbard. "I'm tuckered and famished myself. You interested in some beef and beans?"

Jack moved around to Smokey, picked up the reins, and swung into the saddle. "Sounds attractive to me. First, I'm going to mosey up to the bank and take a look. I like to know who I shoot, plus it'd be nice to find out if anyone else was hurt, and how much that bunch made off with." He pulled a couple of rounds out of a bag hanging from the pommel and shoved them into the loading gate of the Winchester, then dropped it back into the boot.

Ted had mounted and was watching.

"What?"

"Cautious man."

"I've been around too long. Never know when you might wish you had the last one fired."

Ted nodded. "A fact."

The two men rode the fifty yards to the bank. From his saddle, Jack looked down on the man he had shot. Falling from his horse, the bank robber had ended up on his back. Part of his forehead hung over his eyes, held only by skin.

Jack rested his elbow on the saddle and looked down at the dead man. "Don't know him. I can tell he's no Mould, but that's all."

Ted had been examining the man he had shot. "Don't know this one, either. Reckon thieves would rather keep it that way."

Jack eased Smokey through the press of people staring at the dead men in the street, and pulled him up to the bank's hitching post. After dismounting and looping the reins, he headed for the bank, Ted behind him. The mass of people separated. He saw the big fella called Jeremy, who he assumed was the mayor from his conversation in the saloon, and stepped to his side. The mayor was looking down on a white-haired gentleman, who lay dead on the floor with a big .44-caliber bullet hole between his eyes. He was lying next to another man, whose green visor still rested on his head, and blood seeped from a nasty hole in his shirt just above his navel. He lay moaning while an elderly gentleman knelt over him.

"Doc," Jeremy said, "is Peter going to make it?"

The doctor ripped Peter's shirt open. He examined the wound for a moment and shook his head. The wounded man opened his eyes in time to see the doctor's response.

He grimaced and grabbed the sawbone's arm. From tight lips, his strained voice asked, "I'm dying, Doc?" When the doctor didn't answer, the man spoke again. "Tell me the gospel, Dr. Jenkins. Have they killed me?"

The doctor straightened, removed his glasses, and wiped the sweat from his forehead with his shirtsleeve. He patted the hand that was gripping his arm. "I'm afraid so, Peter. There isn't any way to fix this wound."

Tears filled Peter's wide-open eyes. "What's Molly going to do?"

From the bank entrance, Jack heard small, rapid footsteps

and a female voice calling, "Peter! Oh, someone please tell me Peter's alright. He was supposed to be off early today. He was going to take me to the doctor. Let me through. Please, let me through."

The crowd parted. Jack moved to allow the young woman access to her husband. She was attractive, healthy, and very pregnant. Stepping even with Jack, she saw the shoulders of Dr. Jenkins and then the bank owner's body. The back of her hand flew to her mouth.

Her voice was small, soft. "Mr. Richards?" As she moved forward, his head came in sight. "Oh, poor Mr. Richards. They killed him." Then she saw her husband. "Peter? You've been shot?" She fell to her knees alongside the doctor. "Oh, my poor Peter." She placed her hand gently on his exposed belly. He winced. She gasped and jerked her hand away. "Did I hurt you?" Her cheeks were wet with streaming tears, which flowed past her full lips and dripped from her soft chin.

Jack watched, his heart going out to the poor girl who was seeing the future, which only moments ago seemed so stable and safe, disappear in gun smoke. It had been shattered by the bank robbers.

Peter rubbed his wife's arm. "Honey, be strong. For the baby."

Molly turned wet, innocent blue eyes on the doctor. "Dr. Jenkins, please tell me Peter will be alright." She leaned toward him as if to persuade him to say what she wanted to hear. "He will, won't he?"

The doctor took a deep breath. "Molly, like Peter said, you've got to be strong for your baby."

Her face stiffened, and her voice became sharper. "Doc, tell me."

The old man shook his head. "No, Molly, he won't be alright. Your husband is dying." He put his arm around her shoulder, but she shrugged it away, completely unaware of the tears pouring from her eyes, and turned back to her Peter. Her hand caressed his cheek, words coming out between sobs. "I love you. Oh, Peter, what am I going to do without you?"

Jack had had enough. He grasped the mayor's arm and, with his head, motioned outside. Jeremy Rush nodded and led the way. They moved off a distance from the crowd. "Was the teller able to tell you how much money they got?"

The mayor nodded. "Not much. The cash at the teller's station and what Frank, he's the dead man, bank owner and president, had at his desk. Frank's the reason they shot them. He refused to open the safe. Peter said that one of the robbers was supposed to know how to get into the safe, but he couldn't. The robbers had a big argument over it. He said one of the younger fellas threatened to shoot the safe man. He—"

"Sorry, Mayor, but how much did they take?"

"Oh, yes, a total of three hundred dollars. He said there was over twenty thousand in the safe. But that hard-headed old man wouldn't open it. Told those thieves the money belonged to honest hardworking people, and they could go straight to hell. That's when the younger one shot him, then turned the gun on Peter, who was doing absolutely nothing but standing there with his hands up."

The feeling was coming over Jack again, or the lack of feeling. He knew the Moulds would be caught, and they'd be caught by him. He believed in the law, and a part of him preferred they stand trial before they were hanged. But it was the other part that scared him. The part that hoped they resisted, for if they did, he'd kill every one of them. They'd brought pain and suffering to a number of people now, and who knew how many they had killed or injured before he had ever heard their name. His right hand drifted lightly over the butt of the revolver behind his waistband. The cold metal felt comforting, promising. The time would come and soon.

"Thanks, Mayor. Wish I'd made it here sooner."

The mayor shook his head. "Mr. Sage, thank you for bringing

us the information. If we had acted immediately, we might have prevented these killings."

Jack's granite-hard gray eyes locked on the mayor's. "Wishes and ifs don't count for much."

The mayor shook his head. "No, they don't."

"Now, me and my horse need to eat and rest. Where would you recommend?"

"Zane's stable is the place for your horse." He pointed across the street, where a large stable door stood open. "Mable Nestor's Boarding House, north, just before you ride out of town, is the place for food and rest. Food's good, and you don't have to worry about bugs."

Jack nodded his thanks. "I'll be pulling out in the morning."

"You going after the robbers?"

"Oh, yeah. I'll be going after them, and I'll be catching them."

"If you do, we'd love to have the trials here."

"I'll keep that in mind. Adios." Jack turned to find Ted leaning against the building. He had broken a thin splinter from the hitching rail and was picking his teeth.

"Wondered if you were gonna talk all day. I'm hungry."

"Time for talking is way past, but Smokey and I'll be resting up for the night. I'm stopping first at the stable." He nodded across the street.

The people just naturally moved out of the way of the big man as he walked to his horse. Swinging up into the saddle, a forlorn scream ripped from inside the bank. Several of the ladies who were gathered in the crowd began to weep. Jack eased his horse out, turned him, and rode across the street. A man with straw caught in his shirt stood watching the tragic scene and brushing the loose straw from his clothing.

Jack nodded and stepped from the saddle. "This your place?"

"It is, though sometimes I wonder why. I seem to never catch up."

Ted pulled up next to Jack and dismounted.

Jack looked through the wide, opened door. "I need to leave my horse for the night. He needs a good rubdown, a bait of corn, plenty of feed, and water. He's come a fast pace from Fort Worth."

"I can handle it. Fifty cents up front. That way you can pull out anytime you like without havin' to look me up. He'll be fed and well taken care of." He looked at Ted. "You?"

"I'll have the same."

Jack paid the man, pulled his Winchester from the scabbard, and untied his saddlebags. Ted did the same with his Spencer. The two men, chaps flapping and spurs jingling, walked side by side toward Mable Nestor's Boarding House.

"You heading after 'em in the morning?"

Jack nodded. "Yep. Daylight."

"You want company?"

"Wouldn't mind, but I call the shots, all the way."

Ted looked up at Jack. "You know what you're doing?"

"Yep. If you ever feel uncomfortable, you can ride out. Won't hurt my feelings."

Jack had already assessed the younger man. He wasn't a big man, about average, except for the wide shoulders and thick arms. It was obvious he had worked hard since he was a boy. He had a confident air about him and a steady gaze. Not cocky like so many of the younger folks were, just confident in his ability. He had already shown his willingness to step up. His curly brown hair was hardly contained by his hat, which seemed to habitually ride back on the crown of his head, and his pale green eyes constantly surveyed his surroundings. Jack guessed him on the shy side of thirty by three or four years. He got a good feeling from him. It'd been a long time since he'd had a sidekick, but having a pardner could make life easier.

"Good," Ted said. "Let's get to Mable's. I'm starving."

16

It was still dark when they left Mable's. She was already up, filled them with coffee, eggs, bacon, and biscuits, and sent them on their way, each with a lunch. Jack felt like a new man. He had managed to get a bath, which he needed badly, and a good night's sleep. He had been so tired he almost fell asleep in the tub.

Neither he nor Ted had spoken much, but now the younger man asked, "How are you planning on picking up their trail?"

Walking along in the dark, Jack shook his head. "I'm not. I know where they're camped, or at least where they were camped. I figure they were planning on going back after the robbery. Whether they stayed or not makes no difference. We should have a trail to follow. One that hasn't been cut up by a posse. Speaking of posse, did you hear them come back last night?"

"Yeah, they were pretty quiet. There was no celebrating going on."

"All they accomplished was blotting out tracks. That's the way with posses if you don't control them." Reaching the stable, Jack opened the side door and stepped through. The horses were ready and saddled. Zane rose from mucking out the stalls. He stopped, straightened, and walked to the wide door. After unlatching it, he pushed it open while Jack and Ted secured their gear. The two men swung into their saddles, and Jack led the way out.

Zane nodded when they rode past. "Luck."

Jack touched his hat and turned Smokey north, out of town, the same direction the robbers and posse had taken. Ted, following Jack, ignored the man.

From their right, daylight slipped over the green trees and grassland. Out of sight of town, Jack turned left and walked Smokey into the high grass. He pulled him to a stop, waiting for Ted to pull up alongside.

He stopped and looked at Jack questioningly.

Jack pushed his hat back. "Something you need to know."

Ted remained silent.

"There's a reward out on the Moulds, five thousand dollars."

Ted let out a long, low whistle.

"I don't chase men for rewards. I'm not a bounty hunter. It just happened, so there it is. When it's over, we'll split it, but like I mentioned before, if possible, we bring them in alive. All bets are off if they start shooting."

"Fine with me," Ted said. "I wouldn't mind having twenty-five hundred bucks in my pocket."

"Questions?"

"Nope."

Jack bumped Smokey in the flanks, and the gray horse broke into a lope through the high grass.

The two men alternately walked and loped their horses. After an hour, Jack began to move from one spread of timber to the next. He had slipped the field glasses from his saddlebags, and they now hung by their strap, wrapped around the saddle horn. Before riding into patches of open land, he would stop and glass the area. He had become familiar with the importance of binoculars in Africa, and he always had his with him.

They had said little since leaving town. Jack motioned Ted near. "They aren't far." He nodded toward a hill less than a mile to their front. "There's a creek right behind the hill. They should be located across this creek. It's in a fork formed by two creeks. We can slip into this next patch of timber just below the hill. If you'll stay with the horses, I want to climb up and around to the south side to get a look. I might be able to spot them from there."

Ted crossed one leg over his saddle and stretched his back. "How many you reckon?"

"Can't be more than six, probably five's more accurate. We each killed one, and I wounded another. They only had eight to start with." Jack gave Ted a close look. "Ready?"

His pardner swung his leg back into the stirrup. "Let's go."

They rode out into the open grassland, made it across, and worked their way through the timber until it started thinning. The hill lay in front. Jack tossed his reins to Ted, pulled his rifle from the scabbard, swung his right leg over the saddle, and slid down. "I'll be back shortly."

Bending low, he began working his way up the back side of the hill. It was covered with grass and scattered scrub oak, with a taller elm here and there. Fortunately the sun was behind him and would be in the eyes of the robbers. He slipped from brush to brush and eased around the side of the hill. Nearing the edge where he might be seen, he removed his hat and laid it on the ground, then slowly lifted his head above the scrub. He saw nothing. The two creeks were heavily wooded with elm, pecan, and willow. The canopy of the trees provided an almost solid covering.

He waited. Jack Sage had stalked men, singly and in groups, many times before and knew the key was always patience. Raising his glasses, he studied a section of timber just back from where the two creeks joined. The foliage was thick. He moved the glasses slowly, taking in and identifying everything visible until moving on. A flash of red momentarily filled his glass.

He froze.

There it was again, a shirt. He made out an arm. A hand came into view, gripping a coffee pot. Then he saw the faint drift of smoke from below the trees. The canopy of leaves did an excellent job of screening and dissipating the smoke, but it wasn't one hundred percent effective. The arm stretched out again, came back without the pot, and disappeared.

Jack continued his slow visual search of the two creeks. A short distance west of where he saw the arm, he caught additional movement, a horse, and then he made out several more. He heard the faint sound of a man's curse, then unintelligible words, followed by the word money and another curse. He figured the gang was upset over the small amount of cash they'd come up with in their bank robbery. *Too bad,* he thought. *The old banker threw a hitch in your get-along, and now you're upset.*

Through another opening, he caught movement. A man, stretched out on the ground. No healthy man would be down like that during the middle of the day. It must be one of the wounded. He'd seen enough. They needed to probe the camp to learn more. He eased back to his hat and far enough around the hill to ensure he was well out of sight of his quarry. Standing, he made his way down the rocky hillside to Ted. His partner was watching his approach, thick black eyebrows raised in a question.

Jack, speaking softly, said, "They're just across the creek. I can't see them all because of the leaves. We'll have to get up closer to make out how many there are and what kind of shape they're in. We'll leave the horses here. Grab your rifle. You might want to take some extra ammunition."

Ted nodded and turned to his horse, while Jack switched extra .44 cartridges from the bag on his saddle to the lower front pockets of his vest. He took his additional Remington New Model Police out of his saddlebags and slipped it behind his waistband. He glanced to his pardner. "You ready?"

Ted was turning from his horse with his Spencer in one hand

and his Blakeslee reloading box in the other. He strung the strap over his head, hanging the box under his left arm.

"How many reloading tubes does yours hold?" Jack asked.

"Ten. It can get heavy over a long haul, but I like having those tubes filled with ammunition. They make mighty quick reloading."

"I know," Jack said, thinking about his Spencer and Blakeslee box. Ted was right, the box could get heavy, holding up to thirteen tubes. Each tube in the box held seven rounds, and if all the tubes were full, could weigh over nine pounds, heavier than the rifle. To reload the Spencer, the release on the butt of the stock was turned, the spring extracted, and a tube poured into the magazine. It was as simple as that. Put the spring back in and a man was ready to fire, but it wasn't a Winchester with up to fifteen rounds, and it couldn't be fired as fast. That was why he'd given it up for this newer rifle, more rounds and faster fire. He motioned with his head, and they moved forward in silence.

The advance was quiet enough. Jack was finding out Ted wasn't the woodsman he had expected, which made him think, *I don't really know very much about this young fella*, and immediately put the thought aside, concentrating on their approach.

Moving closer to Catlett Creek, and to prevent the Mould gang from hearing them, he used hand signals to communicate with Ted. Nearing the creek, Ted spooked an armadillo, which was hard to do. They were nearly blind, but when spooked, they made a loud grunting sound, and their claws scraped on the gravel, rocks, and brush. Fortunately, the boys at the camp were feeling safe, for their loud voices could be heard across Catlett. Jack motioned Ted down, and they crawled through thick brush and brambles beneath the tall trees to the edge of the creek. There, Jack motioned his companion to stay put and carefully parted the underbrush.

They were almost on top of the camp, except for being on the opposite side of the creek. He could see the men around the small fire. His count had been right. Five men looked to be in good health, while one was stretched out, being mostly ignored, and obviously in pain. Even from here, the large stain of blood on his right side, covering his shirt, was obvious. Most of the blood had turned a dull brown, but one area showed shiny red, still bleeding.

Jack could see clearly into the camp. He and Ted were on the high side of the creek at the base of the hill from where he had spotted them. Their position gave him a clear view. That was the good part. Unfortunately there was also a bad element. If they tried to approach the camp from this angle, they'd be spotted. To make matters worse, it looked like the gang was preparing to break camp and move out.

Jack looked over the approach. From where he lay, there was no way they could move forward without being seen. It was possible to crawl back from their current position and slip farther down the creek, but it might take up to an hour, maybe more. The Moulds would be long gone before they could reach the camp. He'd seldom seen such lucky thieves. With all the shooting that had taken place in town, not a one of the Moulds appeared to be injured. Of course, the other fella had taken his shot for old man Mould, but the family continued in good health.

He crawled back until he was next to Ted, whose view of the camp was blocked by brush, and spoke in a low whisper. "We can't cross here, and they're getting ready to move out. It looks like five of them are in good shape, and one's wounded. We'll have to back out of here and move down the creek. Let's go. We need to make it quick."

Jack started to push his large body back through the brush. Ted touched his shoulder. "Wait. Being on this hill should give us a good line of fire. Why don't we just drop 'em and cross leisurely. With the two of us, they won't stand a chance. We know they're killers, and you said the reward was dead or alive. I'm for finishing it right now."

Jack's jaw tensed, and he stared at Ted. This was why he operated by himself. His voice was low and hard. "They're the murderers, not us. I'm not going to be responsible for killing out a whole family." He gave a small motion with his head. "Back out of here quietly. If you don't want to do it my way, then head back to your horse and wait."

Jack saw something flash across Ted's face, anger? Then it was gone. The younger man held up a palm and almost obsequiously said, "I didn't mean to buck you. It was just an idea. You're right. I'll be right behind you."

They backed out to the edge of the treeline and, with the trees and brush between them and the camp, ran down the creek.

Jack figured they had gone far enough, reached a long arm and touched Ted on the shoulder. When he had his attention, he motioned toward the creek. They had thick brush protecting them from view. Bent over, they ran toward the edge. Catlett Creek was like most other Texas creeks. For most of the year, water flowed in a narrow stream in the middle of a wide, deep-cut creek bed. Tall pecan trees, occasionally mixed with elm, and willow close to the water inhabited the tall banks above the creek. The banks were so high a man of six feet could stand in the creek bed and not be seen by a person a short distance back from the bed's edge. Also, the creek, if it was running, was usually flowing over a shallow rocky bottom, except for in the deeper holes.

But it had been raining more than usual, and now the creeks across North Texas were flowing steady, wide, and in many places deep. Jack started along a deer trail through the brush. He signaled for Ted to follow. They eased, as best they could, through the thick brush in the shade of the tall trees. Once again as they neared the edge, Jack motioned for Ted to get down. They started crawling. The greenbrier caught and pulled at their clothing and skin. Jack could hear Ted cursing under his breath.

The briars were tough, with short, sharp thorns that could scratch and tear. They were thick and infested the creek.

Reaching the edge, Jack peered down the trail. It dropped at a steep angle into the creek bottom, which was flowing bank to bank, but looked to be no more than knee deep at the deepest part. He raised his eyes to the activity in camp just in time to see Eli, the old man, walk over to the wounded man on the ground. He leaned over, said something, and straightened. The man stretched up and grasped Eli's arm. Eli said something to one of his boys. *I think the one he's talking to is Cletus,* Jack thought.

Cletus had been loading the horses. He shook his head, as if it was a bother, and walked to his pa and the man on the ground, pulled his revolver, and as cool as if he were shooting a snake, shot the man in the head. He said something to Eli, shoved his revolver deep into the holster, and marched back to the horse he was loading.

Eli went to the fire and poured himself a cup of coffee.

Ted had jerked at the weapon's discharge, but Jack laid a hand on his shoulder, leaned close to his ear, and said, "They just killed the wounded man."

Ted nodded.

"Come on," Jack said, his voice cold with fury. They slipped down the steep trail into the creek. Here was where they were at their most vulnerable. If someone happened to be near the opposite edge of the creek and spotted them, they'd quickly be two dead bodies floating in the current, and the Moulds would be free to go on robbing and killing.

Jack maintained a steady, but careful pace across the bottom. The water was cold as it rushed in, pouring over the tops of his boots and filling them. He could hear Ted muttering and thought, *After this is over, we need to have a talk about the need for silence.* He kept moving forward, and the water rose. Reaching his knees, he could feel the unrelenting force of the water pushing, trying to knock his feet out from under him. He kept moving forward. It began to shallow.

The deer trail continued up the opposite bank. It looked steep, but not so steep they couldn't make their way. Reaching the bank, he glanced back to make sure Ted was still there. He was right behind him. Jack slowly ascended the trail, removed his hat before his head broke the plane of the high bank and eased his eyes above it. It was just as he expected. More brush, more briars. They were completely hidden from the killers. He eased farther up the trail. As it climbed, he bent over to remain beneath the level of the brush and greenbrier.

He could hear them now. They were loading the animals and cursing Mr. Richards, the banker, for not giving them the combination to the safe. They were no more than twenty yards distance. Jack looked at Ted and nodded. He bent over and slipped his hat on. Together they straightened, Jack rising high above the waist-level brush. Nobody noticed them.

Eli had his back to them. He was by the fire, drinking his coffee, watching the others load the animals. Occasionally he would glance at the dead man, shake his head in disgust, and turn back to watch the loading. The boys, plus the remaining outlaw who had joined them, were all working with the horses. Jack pulled the hammer of the Winchester to full cock, and Ted joined him with the Spencer. The multiple metallic clicks cut through the conversations and movement of the outlaws. They froze in position.

Jack felt good. He was in his element. "You boys have a choice to make. Drop your guns and live, or draw and die. Your choice."

Eli's cup of coffee had been headed to his mouth when Jack spoke. He continued with it, took a sip, lowered it, and slowly turned. Seeing Jack, his eyes filled with hate. "You. We shoulda killed you when we had the chance."

"But you didn't. Now drop that weapon, or die right here."

Eli slowly moved his cup to his left hand. "You got you a pardner, I see. How's his shooting?"

Ted grinned. "You're so close, old man, it don't have to be good to blow you away."

"Make up your minds, boys," Jack said.

"They ain't but two of 'em," the new man said. "They's five of us, and if they take us in, we'll all be headin' for a hanging."

"Shut up, Krank," Eli said.

Jack looked at the youngest Mould and remembered Amelia Massey had said he wasn't like the rest of the Moulds. *Give him a chance,* he thought. *Any wild bullet could catch him if the shooting starts.* "Jethro, drop your gun. You haven't started living, boy. You don't want to end it before your life begins."

Jethro looked at the old man. "Pa?"

"Go ahead, boy, drop your gun. Yore ma'll skin me alive if anything happens to you."

"Well, I ain't goin' to a hangin'!" Krank shouted, and went for his six-shooter.

Before his gun had cleared leather, both .56-caliber Spencer and .44-caliber Winchester slugs smashed into the outlaw's chest. His revolver dropped back into the holster, and Krank dropped straight to the ground. He twitched twice and was gone, but before the last twitch, Eli yelled, "Git 'em, boys!"

Jack figured Eli must've thought because both men had fired, there would be a split second of opportunity. He was right, as far as the Spencer was concerned. He didn't know who was the fastest, but he supposed it must be Cletus, because Axel had spoken of him almost reverently. But it didn't really matter, for Eli was the closest, and he was fast enough.

The old man's revolver lifted from its holster. The muzzle began to rotate upward, and Jack shot him. Jack felt a tug at his left shoulder. If he hadn't been in so many battles, it might have turned him off his target, but his experience kept him focused on the front sight of the rifle. It settled on the old man's left eye, and

Jack squeezed the trigger. He heard the blast of the Spencer in his right ear and thought, *That fella's gonna deafen me yet.* While he was thinking, he was leveling on Harley. Cletus was already down.

Harley's third shirt button below his chin rested on Jack's front sight, and he pulled the trigger. He saw the momentary slap of the bullet and spray of blood. Harley was backstepping, but he was leveling his revolver to fire again. Jack saw the blossom of flame, felt a jab at his right leg, and began tilting to the right, the leg no longer supporting him. The Spencer roared again, and Harley jerked backward, arms flying wide, his revolver sailing through the air. Jack continued to fall. *Not the briars,* he thought, falling straight into a thick bed of the vicious thorns. Falling, he caught sight of Jethro, his gun belt on the ground, looking at death all around him, tears flowing down his cheeks. Jack's last thought was, *At least the boy made it. Amelia will be happy.* He felt a crushing blow to the back of his head, and his world went black.

17

Jack slowly drifted upward through the blackness toward a tiny spot of light. It grew larger and brighter until it made his head hurt. It made it hurt something terrible. He kept his eyes closed and pressed his hand against the back of his head—something soft but pressing on it made his head hurt worse. He took a deep breath. His chest hurt, too. He opened his eyes.

A young boy, no more than nine or ten, stood close to his bed, leaning over. Staring at him. His freckled nose only inches away. Then the boy's mouth gaped open, and he yelled, "Ma, he's awake!" The boy's breath smelled of milk and cornbread.

Jack's eyes slammed shut with the pain. He managed to grit out, "Shh, boy, not so loud." The yell had crashed through his head like a thousand church bells. Moments passed until he felt strong enough to face the light again. Cautiously he opened his eyes.

The freckled nose and blue eyes were still inches from his. "You alright, mister?"

Jack moved his lips into what he hoped was a grin. "I'll be alright if you step back a bit and don't yell again, okay?"

The head nodded solemnly as he took two steps back and continued to stare at Jack. "Sure, mister. How'd you get so shot up?"

A handsome woman in her mid thirties stepped into the room, wiping her hands on a flowery blue and white calico apron looped over her head and tied around her waist. "Nathaniel Hackett, get out of the face of our guest. Don't you have chores to do? Have you fed the chickens? What about the eggs? Have you picked up the eggs? That egg-sucking dog of yours better not get any of my eggs, or it'll be the last he eats. Now get out of here."

"No, ma'am. I mean, yes, ma'am. He don't eat eggs!" The last statement was shouted as Nathaniel dashed from the bedroom. Jack winced, his head almost exploding with the boy's shout. He could hear him rummaging in the other room, then bare feet were slapping across the floor. The door slammed, and there was the happy barking of a dog.

Blue eyes, the same color as her son's, flashed at Jack. "I am so sorry about him. It doesn't matter how many times I've told that boy to stay out of this room and not bother you, he keeps slipping back in here. For some reason, I think you fascinate him."

His headache was starting to let up a little, still there, but now only a low beat with his heart. From a dry throat, he croaked, "Where am I?"

She immediately poured a glass of water, sat in the chair next to the bed, held his head, and helped him drink.

The water was wonderful, wet, and cooling. His throat felt like it had been ripped from his body and staked on the Sahara for a week. He emptied the glass and looked up at the woman. Her son was a spitting image of her, down to the freckles across the bridge of her nose and on her cheeks. Her dry, blonde hair was pulled back in a loose bun, tied sufficiently to keep it out of her way when she worked. He saw an open, kind, no-nonsense face. "More?"

She filled the glass only half-full. This time he was able to take it in his right hand. The hand quivered as he moved it to his mouth. What was wrong with him? Hand quivering? Head hurting? Shoulder hurting? Now he felt his right leg. It was also hurting. The water had an alkaline taste, but it was the very best liquid he had ever put to his lips. His voice became a little less croaky, and he smiled at her. "Thank you."

She returned a concerned smile. "I am Dorothea Hackett. Call me Dot, everyone does. You've met my persistent son, Nathan. May I ask your name, sir?"

After drinking the glass of water, Jack collapsed back on the bed, his head propped up on two pillows, and handed the empty glass back to Dot. "Certainly. My name is Jack Sage, but what am I doing here? How did I get here? How long have I been here?"

The mouth, shaped by smiles, was now pulled down at the corners with concern. "Mr. Sage, you have been with us for a month."

Jack felt the shock surge through him. A month? His mind raced. *The herd. They must be far past the Red River, maybe already into Kansas. What about the Mould gang, Ted, Jethro? Where is everyone? How did I get left behind?*

The blonde was talking again, a pleasant voice. "Mr. Sage, my husband, Robert, found you and brought you to our home. We fully expected you to die. You were shot up so badly, and the back of your head was bashed in something terrible. It looked like someone hit you with a fencepost. Why, with the head wound, the blood loss, and the infection, you should have been dead weeks ago."

Jack, mystified, slowly shook his head against the pillows. "I don't understand. Your husband found me? I was alone? My head . . .?" He stared up at the ceiling, trying to remember, to put the pieces together. The last thing he remembered was seeing Jethro, tears on the boy's cheeks, and falling toward the brambles. He felt his face lightly.

Dot said, "I didn't mention the scratches. You fell into a greenbrier patch face-first. You were scratched up worse than if a mess of cats got after you. You've pretty much healed by now, at least the cuts and scratches, though you'll carry a few of their marks for a while."

He could feel several of the channels left by the thorns, which had cut across his face.

The door opened, and steps sounded in the other room.

"Bob," Dot called, "come in here. Our guest is awake."

Jack turned his head to see a tall man bend low, stepping through the doorway. He looked older than Dot, but not by much. He was a well-built man, like a cowhand, slim waist, wide shoulders. His face was broad, with wide-set green eyes, honest but inquisitive eyes, protected by thick, bushy eyebrows. Straight brown hair fell carelessly over his forehead. A big smile lit his face upon seeing Jack awake. "Welcome back. We thought you was a goner for sure."

Jack grinned at his rescuer. "Too ornery to die. Reckon I owe you my life, you and your wife, here."

They both shook their heads, Bob responding, "Shoot, no. You'd done the same thing. We're just almighty happy to see you awake. How're you feeling?"

Jack grinned. "I'll have to admit, I've felt better, but it's good to be awake."

Dot jumped up. "What am I thinking? I'll get you some soup. I just made some fresh chicken soup. I'll be right back." She was gone.

Bob smiled after his wife. "That's Dot. She don't stop. She's always doin' for something or someone." He turned back to Jack. "How's your head?"

"It still hurts like the dickens. The funny thing is I don't remember getting shot in the head by any of those fellas."

Bob shook his head. "No, sir. It weren't a gunshot. Somebody hit you a bad blow with what I would guess was the butt of a rifle. The doc said it would kill you. He said you'd never recover from it. He was talking about what happens to the brain when it gets a blow like that, but I didn't follow what he was saying. Everything he said just meant you was going to die. I guess smart folks don't know everything."

"I'm glad he was wrong. By the way, my name's Jack Sage. Your wife told me your name is Bob. Alright if I call you that?" Without waiting for his answer, Jack continued, "How did you find me?"

Bob leaned back in his chair. "Mighty interesting how it happened. I was looking for strays and ridin' down Sweetwater Creek. A lot of times they'll corner up where Sweetwater runs into Catlett. So I'm getting close to the end, and I see where there's blood on the ground. Then I see blood all over the clearing, no men, no horses. The ground was cut up. There'd been a camp and horses, but that was at least a day before. While looking around, I hear a groan from the briars. That kinda gets my attention. So I ease over to 'em, and there you lay, facedown in them nasty things."

Unconsciously, Jack reached up and ran a hand over his face.

Bob nodded. "Yes-siree, you was some scratched up, besides having the life darned near shot out of you. And my goodness, man, you're big. I had to ride my horse into that mess, and he didn't want to go, so's I could hoist you up into the saddle. I hated to do it like that, but I swear I figured you was dying anyway."

Jack waved his hand. "Don't worry about it. You did what you had to do to get me out of there, and I'm grateful to you. So, you didn't see anyone around?"

"Nary a soul. I didn't look much, right then, since I was hankerin' to get you back here and go get the doc."

Jack's disappointment must have shown in his face. Bob went on quickly. "But the next day, I went back to check it out. I covered those creeks. Jack, I used to do some scouting for the army. What I mean is that I can read sign pretty well."

Jack pushed himself higher on the pillows. His headache was letting up.

"I seen where another fellow was standing close to you. His casings lay on the ground. He was shooting a Spencer." Bob pulled a .56-56 case from his pocket and tossed it to Jack.

He caught it and looked at the rimfire. After studying it, he looked back up at Bob.

"Well, sir, it looked to me like the two of you took down all of those fellers exceptin' the one who was already dead. Somebody shot him in the head while he was lying on the ground."

Jack nodded. "I saw it happen. The gang was the Moulds. One of the gang members was shot when they tried to rob the Denton bank the day before. He was the man lying on the ground. Cletus, one of the Mould boys, shot him."

Bob shook his head. "That's a cold man who'll do that kind of thing, but like I was saying, there was a feller standing close to you."

"That was my pardner, Ted DeWitt."

Disgusted, Bob shook his head. "With a pardner like that, you ain't in need of any enemies."

Jack's head jerked back in surprise, and his eyes tightened from the pain of the sudden movement. "What do you mean by that?"

Bob was sitting close to the bed. He leaned forward, gazing at Jack. "You got hit in the back of the head. Who do you think did it?"

Jack thought. His head began to shake, and his jaw locked, the muscles standing out like cords. He stopped and stared at Bob. "Tell me what you found."

"I found where you had been standing when you were shot, and I found where this Ted was standing. He took a step forward, and you could see where his weight transferred, like he was swinging a rifle. He's the one who slammed you in the back of your head. I'd be willing to bet, if he hasn't cleaned it, your scalp can be found in the butt of that Spencer."

Just the thought almost made Jack sick. *I trusted that man. I was willing to split the reward with him. I read him as honest.* Doubt filled Jack's mind. To have made a mistake of this magnitude. What did that say about his judgment? "Did you find my horse?"

Bob continued, "Like I said, after getting the doc, I went back. I thoroughly checked the area, then following the trail of the horses, I came to where two horses had been tied. They were gone. I'm guessing your pardner made off with both of them."

Jack's eyes closed. *Smokey, gone. His saddlebags with his remaining stake, gone.* "What'd I have on me when you found me?"

Bob shook his head. "Though they scratched you up, those briars helped you, too. They were so thick, I think this Ted hombre couldn't get to you, or wouldn't brave their scratches to get to you. Everything you had on you is here in the house. Your rifle, pistols, and money are all here and safe."

A sardonic grin settled on Jack's face. "I never thought those briars would be a good thing, and I thought Ted was as honest as a loaded gun. Guess I need to keep a bridle on my judgments."

Bob shook his head. "You can't be too hard on yourself. Some people live to fool others." He paused. Light footsteps approached the room.

Dot came in carrying a tray. "Mr. Sage, you need to eat. This will do you good, so sit yourself up and try this chicken soup."

Jack could smell the soup and the fresh-baked bread. Suddenly hunger hit him like a blow to the belly. His stomach growled. "That smells mighty fine, Dot." He smoothed out the sheet, and she placed the tray on his lap. "Now, you eat up. There's plenty more where that came from."

He picked up the spoon and noticed his hand was no longer shaking. Just the aroma of the food seemed to strengthen him. A big chunk of chicken floated in the first spoonful, surrounded by soup and vegetables. The taste almost overwhelmed him. It was better than the best steak he had ever tasted.

"Don't eat too fast." Dot watched her patient closely.

"Leave him alone, honey. The man's hungry."

She punched her husband on the shoulder. "Alright, mister, you can clean up the mess when it comes right back up."

Bob held up both hands, feigning fear. "Yes, ma'am, just don't hurt me."

Jack smiled inwardly as he devoured his soup and bread, thankful this good man had found him in the briars. His countenance changed when the vision of Ted slipped in front of his mind's eye. *How could I have so easily been duped? A greenhorn, yes, but not me, not with my experience. I've seen liars and charlatans in all sorts of dress and a variety of nationalities, but he completely fooled me.*

"Would you like some more, Jack?"

He held out his bowl. "That soup beats a high-priced steak, and the bread, I was afraid it was going to float right off my plate."

Bob grinned. Dot laughed and said, "You are full of it, *Mr. Sage,* and I don't mean soup."

She took the bowl and disappeared into the kitchen.

~

ANOTHER WEEK PASSED before Jack had the use of his right leg. The bullet had bruised the bone. Thankfully it wasn't broken. It was mending well, his limp almost gone.

Two more weeks slipped by before he began to feel like himself again. His strength returned, and he moved from the Hacketts' bed to the barn. They argued with him, insisting he could sleep in the house, but he preferred to give them the privacy they had missed for so many weeks.

Nathan was his constant shadow. He at first helped the boy with his chores and then started lending Bob a hand with such things as barn repairs, fencing, and even a little plowing. He admitted to himself, he would never make a farmer. He quickly grew tired of his constant view of the mule when plowing.

But he mended. His body healed and grew stronger. Nathan watched with awe when he split firewood with a single blow, driving the axe blade deep into the fiber of the logs. Though he was anxious to get moving, to find Ted, and exact a little justice, his soul enjoyed his part in this little family. He enjoyed having Nathan around, though the boy was full of questions, and he felt the love the family shared.

Then it was time. Almost two full months had passed since he had collapsed into the briars, and he had healed, at least physically.

He stood in the dusty clearing that passed for a yard in front of the house. Bob sat in the buckboard, holding the reins, waiting. He stooped and swooped Nathan up high in the air. There was a little catch in his shoulder, but it wasn't bad. The doc had said it would bother him when he was older, but older was a long way off. Nathan's laughter was like music he knew he would miss.

As he lowered the boy, Nathan threw his arms around Jack's neck. "Do you have to go, Uncle Jack? You could stay here. Pa says, as big as you are, you'd make a good hand."

Jack laughed and then grew serious. "I do have to go, Nathan. There are folks depending on me. In fact, I imagine some of them might think I'm dead."

Nathan pushed back in Jack's arms until he could look into his face with those bright blue eyes. "Uncle Jack, you sure wouldn't want folks thinkin' you was dead. It just wouldn't be right."

Jack set the boy down and roughed his hair. "You're right, but you never know when I might stop back by to see you and get more of your ma's cooking." At that he looked at Dot. The woman actually had tears in her eyes.

"We'll miss you, Jack. You've been good for our boy and for us." She glanced up at her husband, who watched from the wagon, smiling. "You take good care of yourself, and if you ever find yourself in this country again, you had better stop in."

"Yes, ma'am." He placed his hands on her upper arms and held her at arm's length. "Dorothea, you saved my life, you and your fine man, Bob. I'll never forget that, or you. Thank you. If you folks ever need anything, get word to me. I'll come a-running."

He turned and walked to the wagon. Bob popped the reins, and they were off. Jack turned and waved. Nathan's little arm, his hand held high, swung back and forth.

"He'll wear you out," Bob said.

Jack continued to wave until Nathan, then Dot, then the house disappeared from view behind a patch of oaks. He turned forward, a feeling of emptiness falling over him.

18

Jack towered above the man. He was exercising every last smidgen of his self-control to keep from reaching across the clean and polished desk, grabbing the dandy of a marshal, and yanking him out of his overstuffed chair.

"I am sorry, Mr. Sage, but your partner"—he paused to pick up a paper and examine it—"Mr. DeWitt, Mr. Theodore DeWitt, to be exact, was paid the full amount of the reward, minus the part covering Axel Mould. Including the two hundred dollars each for Dallas Krank and Mason Duncan, it came to a total of four thousand six hundred and fifty dollars."

Jack was speechless.

Marshal Dylan Rush continued in his smug and condescending tone. "We of the town are extremely grateful for Mr. DeWitt's brave sacrifice. He was wounded. Fortunately for him, it turned out to be only a flesh wound, but his willingness to accompany you and, when you fell, to face the desperadoes alone was gratifying beyond measure. Though he proclaimed, and I do believe he was completely sincere, his interest was justice and justice alone, I was happy to expedite his payment of the reward."

Jack dropped into the chair in front of the marshal's desk, his long legs stretched out in front of him.

In a low, resigned voice, he asked, "Where's my horse?"

"Why, it was awarded to Mr. DeWitt, since we, and he, believed you were dead."

"So it's gone?"

"Yes. In fact, I believe Mr. DeWitt liked it so much, he switched from his to yours. I am truly sorry there was a mix-up, but you have to see it was an honest mistake."

Jack had never been a bounty hunter, though he had collected several bounties from taking outlaws who had paper on them. He had to admit, though, he had been counting on the extra money from the return of the Moulds. It would have gone a long way to financing his planned ranch, but it was gone, along with the remaining portion of his stake he'd had in his saddlebags.

The thought of the saddlebags brought Smokey to his mind. *I'd give up everything in those saddlebags to keep my horse. Hopefully, one day I'll find him.*

He nodded toward the wooden door behind which were the jail cells. "When's Jethro's trial?"

Marshal Rush stared at Jack, his face blank. Finally he said, "Jethro? Is he one of the Moulds?"

Jack sat up in his chair, a cold feeling of foreboding washing over him. "Jethro, Marshal, was the youngest of the Mould boys, only nineteen. What happened to him? Where is he?"

The marshal leaned forward, placing his forearms on the desk. "Oh yes, the youngest. Mr. Sage, he was shot dead. In fact, I remember Mr. DeWitt saying how surprised he was when you shot the young man. In his recalling of the incident, he said the boy was just standing there, and you shot him. He mentioned you said it was easier to carry a dead man than a live one." The marshal raised a hand from the desk and pointed a finger at Jack. "I personally find that sort of comment reprehensible, sir. If I could, I would arrest you for murder, but you are protected by the law."

Jack's mind was racing. After bashing him in the head, DeWitt had killed the unarmed boy? *How could I have misjudged the man so seriously? Ted DeWitt is the picture of evil on two feet, and I missed it.*

"If you have all of your questions answered, Mr. Sage, I am asking you to leave my office, and I'm telling you to leave this town. We don't need your kind around here."

Jack had been staring at his boots. His head slowly came up, and the cold gray eyes turned on Marshal Rush. "You listen to me. I never killed that boy." He removed his hat and pointed to the back of his head. "See this scar? This is where DeWitt slammed me in the head with the butt of his Spencer. Jethro was standing, with his gun belt on the ground, when I went down. He was the last thing I saw. DeWitt killed him and attempted to kill me to get the reward money. He's a lying horse thief. My saddlebags had a substantial amount of money in them, and he's taken my horse."

Rush leaned back in his padded leather chair and looked up at Jack. "I would expect some such story from a man who'd shoot an unarmed boy."

Jack slowly rose, stepped to the front of the desk, and rested his knuckles on the polished wood. "You're lucky I'm a patient man, but if you call me a liar again, I'll kill you. Has DeWitt left town?"

Rush stared back at Jack. "Don't threaten me, Mr. Sage. I don't buffalo."

"Mister, that's no threat. It's a dyed-in-the-wool promise. Where's DeWitt?"

Rush waited a moment and then said, "He headed north."

"How long ago?"

The marshal continued to glare at Jack. "Weeks. I managed to get him paid quickly. He was only here for a few days."

"Did he say anything about why he was going north, or where?"

Jack watched the marshal. He was good at reading men, at least he had been before DeWitt. The marshal was thinking.

His glare softened. "I thought it was funny he was in such a hurry to get his money and get out of town. It was like he felt guilty for the killings. In fact, we were in the saloon, and everyone was anxious to buy him a drink. I noticed he didn't appear to be feeling so good about his actions, and I said something to him. I told him he had done the town a great service in bringing the criminals to justice. For a moment, I could see a touch of remorse, and then this facade seemed to drop over him. He gave me a big grin, thanked me, and asked if there was anything I could do to speed up the money. Of course I said I could. I got my brother the mayor involved, and we had authorization to pay him in no time. Let me see your head again."

Jack turned where the marshal could clearly see the wide scar.

After looking it over for what seemed like minutes, he said, "I want to check something." He stood, reached back, and lifted a Spencer from the gun cabinet. Stepping forward, he laid the butt carefully in the indentation in Jack's head. Except for the hair growing out, it fit perfectly.

Marshal Rush returned the Spencer to the gun cabinet, sat, and shook his head. "He fooled us completely. I believed every word that man said, and felt sorry for him." The last was said with disgust.

Jack took a deep breath. "You weren't the only one he fooled. I let him get behind me, the most greenhorn act there is. Marshal, did he say why he was headed north?"

He nodded. "He said he felt like it was his responsibility to catch up with your friends and let them know what happened to you. At the time, I thought that was an admirable goal. Why do you think he would do such a thing?"

Jack sat back down, thinking. *Why would DeWitt take the chance of contacting Monty or Bronco? There's no good reason. It doesn't make sense. Anything he does, he would have his fortune first and foremost. How could he benefit by telling them I'm dead?* Jack continued to chew on the problem.

"Marshal, I hate to ask, but he stole my stake, and I'm running low. Would it be possible for you to send someone to Marshal Parish in Fort Worth to collect the reward they're holding for me? I'm sure the authorization is in by now."

The marshal thought for a moment, then leaned forward, grabbed a piece of paper, a pencil, and started writing. When he was finished, he shoved it in an envelope and jumped to his feet. "There's a stage leaving right about now. If we can catch it, Parish will have this in a few hours. He can send the response back on the next stage, which is in the morning." He rushed out.

Jack followed and watched the marshal trot up the street to the freight office, where the stage was loading. He spoke to the stage driver, handed him the letter, and jogged back.

"Done. You'll have it in the morning, and I'll personally take you to the bank. It's not the amount you would have gotten for all of the gang members, but at least it'll help. Do you need a loan to tide you over until morning?"

Jack shook his head. "No, thanks, but I appreciate the offer. I've got enough to manage."

"Good. I'll spread the word about what happened. Thanks to DeWitt, there's a lot of folks around here who don't think too highly of you right now. I'll do my best to correct DeWitt's lies."

"Thanks again." Jack started to turn away and stopped. "Maybe you can help. My grulla was a fine horse. He could haul my weight far and fast. In all my years, I've never had a horse like him. Do you know of anyone around who might have something that could come close?"

"I saw that grulla when you were on it. It fit you, but that big horse made DeWitt look kinda small. There is a rancher, east of town, who raises some fine horses. I don't know if you will find what you're looking for, but he's the only one I can think of who might have what you're looking for. His name is Truman Shelby."

"Thanks, Marshal. I've got to head out. I'll check with you in the morning." He headed for Zane's stable.

Zane was sitting under the shade produced by the front of the building. He slowly stood when he saw Jack. "I thought you were dead."

"Not yet."

"Dead or alive, you ain't welcome here."

"Zane, I don't have time to explain. What you've heard are all lies. You'll be hearing the straight of it from Marshal Rush, but for now, I need to rent a buckboard for the afternoon."

Zane was confused. He moved his tobacco cud around to the opposite side of his mouth and let loose with a long and nasty spit. After wiping his mouth with his sleeve, he looked Jack over. "I wish folks would get their stories straight. Nowadays, a man don't know what to believe. Come on and give me a hand."

Jack helped the man hitch a bay gelding to the buckboard.

"Fifty cents for the afternoon."

Jack pulled out a half-dollar and dropped it into the man's hand. "How far is Shelby's ranch?"

"Ain't far, maybe five miles. Ranch sits a couple of miles off the main road. Called the Rafter 3. Big sign and entrance. You cain't miss it." He leaned close to Jack, bringing a strong smell of body odor and chewing tobacco. "Be ready. He's got some fine horses, but he's mighty proud of 'em. You offer him two-thirds of what he starts with and he'll take it. He's proud, but he likes to make a sale." He stepped away and walked back to his chair.

Jack took a deep breath of the fresh Texas air. It smelled sweet without Zane's blend. "Thanks for the information." He popped the reins, and the bay trotted out. The afternoon was hot, and he wasn't in such a hurry he needed to push the bay. He let him trot for a ways and pulled him back into a walk. He needed time to think. Why would DeWitt intentionally approach Monty or Bronco? Jack had seen he was a confident man, but he had no idea he had this kind of confidence, but what was he after?

He mulled the question over and over, looking at it from one direction and then the other, but he couldn't come up with the answer. Turning it loose, his eyes drifted across the grass and the rolling hills. This was pretty country with plenty of water. He crossed three running creeks before he came to the entrance of the Rafter 3. He turned down the road, passing under the arch that not only proclaimed the ranch's brand, but displayed an engraving of a running horse.

Rounding a patch of oak, the main house and barn burst into view. Jack was surprised at the large size. it looked to have at least five or six bedrooms. The house was plank with cedar shingles. The same material was used for the barn and the bunkhouse. The barn was high-roofed, with an abundance of room for hay storage and stalls. The bunkhouse was low and long. Jack guessed it could hold twenty men, but doubted there were anywhere near that number living there.

Cowhands were coming and going, with one working in the barn. Jack swung the buckboard toward the trough at the barn and pulled the bay to a stop. "Howdy."

"Howdy, yoreself. What can I do for you?" The speaker was on the long side of forty. Jack guessed he could be pushing close to fifty, but it was always hard to tell with a cowhand. These hard-working ranch hands lived their lives in the elements. If the sun wasn't burning them, the wind was, or the cold winter was freezing their skin. They all tended to look older than their time on earth.

Jack stepped from the buckboard and stretched. "I need a horse."

"A big one, I'd say."

"I'm looking for one that can carry my weight all day and then outrun a pack of mad Indians. Got any like that?"

"We got a lot of good horses, mister. Let me get Mr. Shelby. He does the horse trading around here. I'll be right back with him."

There was a hand pump by the water trough, and Jack walked over to it, pumped it a few times to get it flowing, and then cupped his hands under the spout. He splashed the cool water on his face and neck, removed his hat, and combed his wet hand through his hair.

"Nasty scar," a man said, approaching him from behind.

Jack turned. "Yeah, when I catch up with the man who gave it to me, I'm planning on a little discussion."

The slight man extended his hand. "I'm Truman Shelby."

Jack took the offered hand. "Jack Sage."

He felt Shelby's hand stiffen in his. The man's head pulled back, turned slightly, and his right eye partially closed.

Jack spoke up. "Mr. Shelby, the marshal is spreading the word right now. Everything Ted DeWitt said was a downright lie. He is a horse thief and a murderer. I intend to catch him. I want you to know I'd never shoot down an unarmed boy. I hope you believe me."

Shelby's black hair was going gray. Though he was of slight build, he stood erect. There was no stoop to his shoulders. He held the handshake for a moment longer while examining Jack. "I believe you, sir. How might I be of assistance?"

"Thank you." For some reason, Jack felt gratified this man believed him. "DeWitt stole my horse, a fine grulla, strong, with plenty of bottom, yet fast in a quick run. I am looking for an animal that might fill some of those requirements."

Shelby looked up at Jack. "So you don't want all of those requirements filled?"

Jack could see the twinkle in the man's brown eyes. A smile crossed his lips, and he dipped his head to the side. "It would be nice. However, I feel it might be very difficult."

"Let us see," Shelby said. "Shall we use your buckboard?"

"Sure." The bay had finished drinking, and Jack stepped in.

Shelby stepped to the barn, picked up a bucket and a large wooden spoon, and climbed into the buckboard. The rancher pointed to his right. "Start out south from the back of the barn. We have a few animals out there. I have one in mind that might suit you. If not, there are several more we can examine."

Riding slowly across the pasture, Jack felt envious. Shelby had exactly what he wanted, a ranch and a home. "You have children?"

Shelby nodded toward a rider on a large black stallion approaching at a lope. "My oldest. I couldn't ask for a better son, and he loves this ranch as much as I do."

The rider smoothly pulled the black alongside the buckboard on Shelby's side.

"Art, I'd like you to meet Mr. Sage."

Jack saw the look. He was growing tired of explaining, but Truman Shelby spoke up. "Son, I believe the gossip we heard about Mr. Sage is completely untrue. He seems to be a fine gentleman."

Art touched the brim of his black Stetson. "Pleased to meet you, sir."

Jack nodded. "And you."

"Son, bring the herd Pepper is in to the barn. I'd like Mr. Sage to see him. We're going after Dusty and Thunder."

The young man waved and raced away.

Jack watched Art race away. "That's a fine horse, a little small for me, but if you've got bigger stock like him, I'm sure I'll find what I'm looking for."

Shelby smiled. "I'd bet on it."

They spotted a small herd of nine horses ahead. Shelby reached back and picked up the bucket and spoon. "Stop here."

The horses had been grazing, but now all heads were up, watching them. When they had stopped, Shelby shoved the spoon in the bucket and ran it rapidly around the inside. The rough burring sound drifted across the pasture, and all nine of the horses broke into a trot toward them.

"Turn around, Mr. Sage. They'll follow us to the barn."

Jack turned the wagon toward the tall barn, visible in the distance, and started the horse back at a trot. He could hear the horses behind them break into a run until they passed them, racing into the corral, where several of the hands had opened the gates for the bunch following Art.

Jack laughed and nodded at the bucket and spoon. "That's a nice tool. It would sure come in handy on a roundup or cattle drive."

"It does. These horses are trained from colts to come to the bucket and spoon. We start them with treats until they develop the habit, then only occasionally do we reward them."

Jack pulled the buckboard to the corral and got out to tie the horse.

Truman Shelby stood in the buckboard and called, "Men!" He motioned for the cowhands around the barn, corral, and yard to move in where they could hear him. Once they stood around the wagon, he began. "This is Mr. Jack Sage."

Immediately the men started murmuring and giving Jack hard looks.

Again Shelby waved his arms for silence. "The scandalous fabrications you have heard about this man are all lies. I am as good a judge of men as I am of horseflesh, and Mr. Sage is a good man. I expect him to be treated as such." He stepped down from the buckboard and motioned Jack toward the corral.

The two of them climbed up and sat on the top rung. Shelby swept his arm across the milling horseflesh. "Do you see anything you like?"

19

Jack was no newcomer to horses. He had dealt with them for most of his thirty-five years. He knew he was looking at exceptional horseflesh. The animals were solid, well muscled, and calm. Even though the group of horses in the corral was large, there was little nipping or kicking. Unfortunately, most were too small for his weight. They could carry him for a short time, but not day after day, over hundreds of miles. However, he had seen four horses that were big enough and looked like they might match most, maybe all of his needs.

"Mr. Shelby, all of your horses look like exceptional animals, but I see four that might fit just what I'm looking for."

Shelby smiled in response to his words. "Thank you. Which are the ones you've picked?"

Jack motioned toward a big dun stallion. The horse, with his arched neck, strong shoulders, and thick body, looked powerful.

Shelby shook his head. "You choose well, but I'm afraid Sandy is not for sale. He is a valuable asset to this ranch. Several of the geldings in this corral are his sons. I cannot part with him."

Jack nodded understandably. He pointed at three other

horses. "Then how about the gray, the palomino, and the chestnut."

"You have chosen the three that were brought in for you to examine. I must tell you, my daughter named all three of them. She has an uncanny knack for coming up with good names." He shrugged. "Of course, she is my daughter. She's been naming them since she was six. The chestnut is Pepper, the palomino Dusty, and the gray Thunder."

He called to the hands, "Reward all of them. Keep Pepper, Dusty, and Thunder in the corral."

The hands gave each horse a treat and released all except the three Shelby had named. The animals raced out of the yard toward the pastures.

Jack watched. The horses genuinely liked the treats. The hands had been getting them from a bucket they had brought from the barn. He stepped over to the bucket and picked one up. He held it in his hand, broke off a piece, rolled it around, examining it, and then tasted it. It was pretty darn good.

Shelby picked one from the bucket and held it up. Each treat was about two inches long and an inch thick. "My father's recipe. It is made of oats, carrots, apples, and molasses to hold it together. Then I bake it for almost an hour. They endure the heat well, and the horses love them. I think the cowhands sneak one every once in a while, too."

"I can see why. Those things are tasty. I wouldn't mind having one out on the trail."

"True. I've been known to eat a couple myself. Now, would you like to try the horses?"

The cowhands had saddled the three horses, and the animals waited calmly, watching him.

"Thanks, I think I'll try the gray first."

"Thunder," Shelby reminded him.

He nodded and walked up to the big animal, softly talking to it. He scratched Thunder behind his ears, walked around him, patting and rubbing the horse. The big gray stood patiently, occasionally turning his head to watch the newcomer. Jack gathered the reins in his left hand, slipped his foot into the stirrup, and swung aboard.

"Take him around the corral and then out for a run. Spend some time with him."

Jack walked the gray around the corral. The horse had a rocking walk to his step. He would be comfortable to ride for long distances. He nodded to the cowhand at the gate. The man swung the gate open, and Jack clucked to Thunder. The horse trotted through the gate and turned south, answering Jack's neck rein. Clearing the buildings, he urged Thunder into a gallop. The horse was fast. He stopped, started, turned, and exploded from a standing start. This was a fine horse, willing to give Jack whatever he asked.

He took Pepper and Dusty through the same routines, and when he was finished, he knew which horse he wanted. All three had responded with willingness and effort, but for him it was Pepper. The red horse seemed anxious to give him whatever he wanted, almost anticipating his commands. He knew it was crazy, but he had a feeling, a rapport, with Smokey, and now he felt it with Pepper. There was a connection.

When he finished, he rubbed the big red horse's muzzle. He looked at the bucket and then at Shelby. "You mind?"

"No, go right ahead."

Jack pulled another treat from the bucket, placed it in the palm of his hand, and held it up to Pepper. The horse pulled its lips back and gently lifted the treat from Jack's hand, then crunched the baked oats, carrots, and apple greedily.

"Looks like you've made up your mind."

Jack nodded. "Only if we can agree on a price. I may end up buying a broken-down mule to get me to Kansas because I can't afford anything else."

Truman Shelby laughed. "I'd truly hate to see that happen,

for you and the mule." He motioned to the cowhand standing near. "Mr. Sage, let Tom take Pepper while we go inside and see if we can agree on a price."

Jack handed the horse over to Tom, and he and Shelby went inside the large home. Stepping through the door, Jack could hear children's laughter coming from upstairs and in the kitchen. The aroma of baking filled the home's interior.

Next to the wide fireplace, an oversized, well-used, cowhide-covered easy chair and ottoman clashed with a room filled with expensive Victorian furniture.

"Come this way, Mr. Sage." Truman Shelby turned right, behind the flowered Victorian divan, toward an open door through which Jack could see a large comfortable office. Family portraits hung on every wall, along with paintings of horses and cattle. Shelby motioned to one of a pair of easy chairs. They were similar to the one in the living room and located on either side of a low table. A rock fireplace was built into the wall opposite the table and desk. "Have a seat."

Jack lowered himself into the chair.

"Care for a drink or maybe coffee?"

"Coffee would be great."

"Good." He stood, walked to the door, and called, "Could we get coffee in the office, please?"

"Yes, dear," came floating back from the kitchen.

Shelby stood by the door until a lady entered the room carrying a tray, with a pitcher of coffee, cups, and cookies.

Jack rose. "Thank you, ma'am. I'm much obliged."

She was a handsome lady, with skin darkened from wind and sun. He noticed her strong hands as she placed the tray on the table and poured two cups of coffee.

"Darling," Sage said, "this is Mr. Sage. He's interested in buying Pepper."

She straightened and offered a strong hand. Jack took it in his. "Ma'am."

"A pleasure to meet you, Mr. Sage. I'm sure you will enjoy Pepper." Releasing his hand, she turned to her husband. "You have business, and I have an appointment in town." She kissed him on the cheek as she passed, pulling the door closed behind her.

The two men sat, and each lifted their coffee, appraising each other as they took their first sip.

The room was silent until Shelby said, "What do you think the red horse is worth, Mr. Sage?"

Jack grinned at the man's first gambit. Lead with a question. "I'm sure way more than I can afford to pay."

"Normally, I wouldn't think of letting that prime animal off my land for less than six hundred dollars."

Jack, shaking his head, set his cup down and began to rise.

Shelby's face showed a moment of humor and possibly just a tiny bit of appreciation at Jack's move. "Just wait, Mr. Sage. I said normally. Please sit back down."

Jack waited a second and eased himself back into the thickly padded chair. He picked up his cup again and watched his host.

Shelby waved his arm, describing the expanse of land outside the home. "As you saw, I have too many horses. The army has not made their usual trek to my door, so I find myself with an overabundance of horseflesh." The man set his cup down and raised both hands, palms up, toward Jack. "Don't get me wrong, I love my horses." He paused. "But I don't love what they're costing me."

Jack gave Shelby a wry grin. "We all have trials in our life, don't we?"

This time Shelby laughed. "Yes, we do, but I need to sell a horse. First, I do have a question. I hate to pry, but would you mind sharing what you have planned for Pepper?"

Should I trust this man? Jack thought. *I don't see how telling him would in any way compromise my goals, but* . . . "It's a long story, and I'd hate to bore you."

Shelby relaxed into the deep comfort of his chair, holding his cup in both hands. "Mr. Sage, I have nothing major planned for the rest of the day."

Jack launched into an abbreviated tale of the Moulds, DeWitt's betrayal, his portion of the herd, and his responsibility to keep his promise and return Buster safely home to his mother. When he was finished, he could see the anger of an honest man boiling beneath the surface of Shelby's calm veneer.

"So you see why it is important for me to get to Ellsworth. I have no idea what DeWitt is up to, but whatever it is, it isn't good."

Shelby was silent, chewing over what Jack had told him. Distracted by the tale, he took a sip of what had become cold coffee. Without comment, he set the cup on the table. "Jack, may I call you Jack?"

Jack nodded, and the man continued, "As good a horse as Pepper is, he will not survive such a ride to Ellsworth. He will give you everything he has until he dies under you. You will not have a choice. Even now, they will either be nearing Ellsworth or already there. You have days of hard riding ahead. You need more than one horse. In fact, you need more than two. What you need are Pepper, Thunder, and Dusty. With those three, your trip will be faster, and you won't kill any of the horses in the process."

Jack shook his head. "Mr. Shelby, assuming the money arrives tomorrow as I expect, and it is the amount I expect, I might barely be able to buy the horses. However, I wouldn't be able to purchase supplies and have enough remaining for necessary expenses along the way."

Shelby was still thinking. "If this DeWitt stole your horse, he must have your tack also. That will be another expense." His expression distant in thought, he muttered softly, "Call me Truman."

Jack nodded. "Which, Truman, is another reason I can't afford to buy more than one horse."

Shelby's face remained thoughtful, quiet, still thinking. Jack took a sip of his cold coffee.

Finally he spoke up. "You are coming back this way?"

"Sure, I've got to get Buster home."

"Then I have an idea. What if you took Thunder and Dusty and sold them in Ellsworth? I'm sure you can get a premium price for such animals, especially with all the cowhands getting paid off."

Jack shook his head. "I don't think that'll work. The cowhands usually sell their strings, with the exception of a horse or two they might keep to ride back to Texas. I don't think they'll be in a buying mood."

A faint smile touched the corners of Shelby's mouth. "You do not know cowhands very well. They live on horses. They know horses. If they see the likes of my animals, they'll sell whatever crowbait they're riding and buy mine. I can promise you that. I will sell you Pepper and give you an authorization to act as my agent for the sale of Thunder and Dusty, and I will include tack in the price. How does that sound to you, Mr. Sage."

Jack shook his head. "I can't let you do that. Those horses are your property. You said yourself you needed to make a sale. You stand to lose too much on this deal. What if one of the horses breaks a leg or both of them? What if they're snakebit or stolen by Indians? You stand to lose a lot of money. I'll not be responsible for that."

"Stop and think, Jack. This is a good deal for both of us. I will get more for my horses in Ellsworth than I will here at the ranch. Also, I will not have the cost of feeding, and you get there sooner. It is a win for both of us. Think, Jack."

Jack stared across the room and through the window. The day would soon be coming to a close, and he still had much to do. He applied his mind to Shelby's suggestion and looked at the man's idea from all sides. Would it help Shelby? Yes. Would it help him? Yes. *Then why am I being so danged stubborn?* The only problem was the loss of Truman Shelby's magnificent horses, and Jack knew in his heart he would do everything to prevent that from happening. If it did, though he prayed it wouldn't, after his cattle sold, he would repay Truman.

He rose from the chair and walked to the window he had been staring through. In the distance, he could see cowhands working a small portion of Shelby's large herd of cattle. One of these days, no matter how long it took, he hoped to have a place similar to this one. He smiled to himself as he pictured his home, without the Victorian furniture, he promised. Jack turned and stood with his back to the window, his size blocking much of the light. "I'll accept your generous offer, for which I thank you, but I will accept it on one condition. If anything should happen to either Thunder or Dusty, I will reimburse you for the horse or horses out of the proceeds of the cattle sale."

Truman Shelby rose and began to extend his hand, but Jack continued, "I think we do need to establish a price for Pepper and the tack."

At that, Truman turned to his desk, sat, and folded his hands. "Since you rented your rig from Zane, I assume he told you how to bargain with me?"

Jack felt a jolt of surprise. "He did have a couple of suggestions."

"Yes, that rascal has cost me a hefty profit on several good sales, but I still get a reasonable price. He normally tells folks to settle on two-thirds of what I initially ask. Does that sound familiar?"

Jack grinned and said, "Exactly."

"I knew it. No wonder I can never get an asking price." Truman waved his hand as if knocking a nuisance fly away. "Alright. How does this sound. A good saddle horse will set you back about two hundred dollars. Pepper is a lot more than just a saddle horse. He's worth more. I figure about three hundred, so I would have given you a price of four hundred and fifty dollars.

You would have countered around three hundred, and I would've accepted. Then you would've wondered if you shouldn't have offered less. Does that sound about right?"

Jack nodded.

"Good. In the process we would have bickered back and forth, but I would not have sold him for less than three hundred, which was the price I had in mind to begin with. So, if you are in agreement, that will be the price for Pepper, three hundred dollars."

Jack grinned. "That's about the easiest horse trading I think I've ever done."

"We're not over yet. I've some good used rigs in the barn. I'll give you a choice for, say, fifty?"

"More than fair, and I'd prefer a used saddle if it isn't smashed flat. Fewer squeaks and pops. Those little noises can sometimes get a man in a heap of trouble."

Businesslike now, Truman reached for paper and pen. He wrote a bill of sale for Pepper, and an agent contract for the sale of Thunder and Dusty. After he had allowed the ink on both documents to dry, he handed them to Jack. While Jack looked them over, Truman gave him a sly look. "To tell you the truth, I'll be surprised if you sell either one of those animals."

"What? Why do you say that?"

"Because those are not good horses, they are great horses. By the time you get to Ellsworth, you won't be able to part with any one of the three."

Jack's reply was thoughtful. "You might be right." Then he brightened. "In that case, when I get back, I'll buy them both."

The two men shook hands over their deal.

Jack pulled out a hundred dollars from his vest and handed it across to Truman. "Here's my guarantee. As soon as the authorization for the rest of my money arrives on the morning stage, I'll be out to pick up the horses and be on my way."

Truman shook his head. "Keep your money. As far as I'm concerned, your word is more than enough, and I'll meet you in town, with the horses. The stage usually arrives around eight thirty, and the bank opens at nine. I'll be there before the bank opens. Purchase all of your supplies at the Denton Mercantile and tell the owner, Jay Davies, I sent you."

Now the two men shook hands.

Truman looked up at the big man. "It's a pleasure to meet you and do business with a man who can appreciate my horses."

"Thanks, Truman. I can't tell you how much I appreciate what you're doing, but I've got to get going. I still have much to do in town. I'll see you in the morning."

The two walked swiftly to the front door. Jack's horse and buggy were waiting.

Tom was giving the horse one of the Shelby treats. He had been patting the animal's cheek. He stopped and glanced at the approaching men. "Thought you might be about ready."

"Thanks," Jack said and headed for the buckboard.

"Your tack?" Shelby asked.

"I trust you. If you don't mind picking it out. It's getting pretty late."

"I'll be glad to, but you'll have to put up with what I choose."

Jack grinned at the ranch owner. "I'll take my chances. Adios." He popped the reins and headed back toward town.

20

Jack pulled Pepper, the big chestnut, up after crossing the Red River. They had traveled fast. Having three big animals made traveling much easier. Catching up with and passing two herds of longhorns heading for Ellsworth had slowed him some. The trail bosses weren't happy at being so late, but they had to get the cattle off the home range. Even with grabbing some chuck from the second herd, he had covered the roughly forty miles from Denton to the Red in four hours. He didn't plan on keeping this pace, but the horses were fresh, and so was he. He had started on Dusty, the palomino, and changed once to Pepper. Now it was time to change to Thunder.

He threw one leg over the pommel and slid to the ground. He was near the outer edge of the strip of thick forest that followed the river. The dark green leaves of the oak contrasted with the lighter and larger leaves of the tall sycamores. A red-tailed hawk sat watching his movements from a long limb of an elm.

He patted Pepper. "You're a fine horse, but now's the time for you to get rid of this weight. That should feel good." He quickly changed the gear, switching to Thunder, the big gray. After pulling the cinch tight, he checked the saddle for movement, firm and solid, and pulled three treats from the big sack Truman had given him. He slipped one to each horse and swung into the saddle. "Let's go, Thunder."

The three animals were off at a lope. A wide cloud of dust was visible in the far distance ahead. Another herd. Bronco had explained how the drives lined out, one after another, all the way to Kansas. Who'd think that many cattle could be sold for the prices being paid. Of course these later herds would bring less, but still the drive, for all of them, unless enough animals were stampeded or lost on river crossings, or driven too fast and burned fat off, would be profitable.

He spent his first night with one of the drives. The one he had spotted from the Red. The horses rested, had a bait of corn each, something else Truman had insisted he take. Morning came, and he was on his way.

Both he and Truman had figured, with the three horses, he should be able to make it in a maximum of eight days, and possibly six, barring any trouble. That included stopping for six hours a night.

Time passed quickly, and the miles fell behind him. He was into his third day, and he was surprised there was no dust ahead. Tonight he would be camping alone for the first time since leaving Denton. His right leg ached where he had been shot and so did his left shoulder. Neither compared with his back. He tried leaning forward, to the side, and to the rear. He was on Pepper again, and the big chestnut didn't like the shifting weight, but he moved along. Jack had the horses in a lope. It was easier on his back. A trot sent streaks of pain down his legs. He thought, *I'm getting too old for this. I can remember the day when I would look forward to a forced march. Not now.*

The sun was drifting nearer to the hills in the west. He'd have to be pitching camp soon. The horses needed rest, and so did he, more than they did. They were holding up well. He could see the three days had eaten a little weight from their big bodies, but they were still in good shape and eager for more.

He had crossed the Canadian River a ways back and was eyeing a treeline in the distance. He thought, *Must be the North Fork of the Canadian. I'll camp there tonight.* He stopped on an oak-studded knoll and pulled his new field glasses, purchased at Denton Mercantile, from his new saddlebags. Jay Davies, the owner of the store, had extolled their virtues, and they were pretty good. Not as good as the Swiss glasses DeWitt had stolen, but functional. He studied the thick treeline of the river.

Most of the Indians were friendly through the Oklahoma territory with the exception of a few renegades. On the other hand, one man, with the type of horseflesh he had, would be a temptation for the best of them. When he had scanned and cleared the area ahead, he moved toward the river. Shadows were lengthening. He would find a spot, build a fire, eat, and get some sleep.

Jack found a perfect site for his camp under the tall cottonwood and elm trees lining the river. A grassy area at the edge of the trees provided a perfect place to stake the horses. First thing, he stripped the saddles. Truman had tossed in a light packsaddle, making it easy on the horses carrying his minimal gear. He gave each one a good rubdown, took them to water, and staked them with plenty of room to graze. Each received a couple of handfuls of corn before he moved a ways down the river to where he planned on having his fire. He collected dried wood so it would produce little smoke, and quickly got a pot of coffee going. Using his new bowie knife, he opened a can of beans, poured them into the pot, and cut up several lengths of jerky. Not restaurant fare, but it would stick to his ribs.

When the beans and jerky were ready, he leaned back against an elm's thick trunk and enjoyed his dinner with a hot cup of coffee. The horses looked good. They were tired from the miles behind them, but after a good night's rest, they'd be ready to hit the road in the morning. The juice in the beans helped soften the jerky somewhat, and the meal tasted pretty good.

For dessert, he reached for a can of peaches. He could never get enough of canned peaches. It was hard to beat a fresh peach picked from the tree, but out on the trail, a can of sweet peaches hit the spot. Again, using his bowie knife, he was soon pouring the peach halves, along with sweet juice, into his mouth. Finished, he had two more cups of coffee and poured the rest over the fire. Jack checked to make sure there were no remaining embers, picked up the pot, skillet, and cup, and headed to the river to wash them.

After cleaning the utensils, he made his way back to the pack, stowed the gear, and grabbed his bedroll. He had bought an extra blanket. He figured tonight it was best used for what he had planned, so he carried it back to the dead fire. Near the fire, he pulled up a bit of brush and covered it with the blanket. He stepped back and examined his handiwork. *Very good*, he thought. *If I saw that in the night, I'd swear it was a sleeping man.* He walked back to the horses. During his meal, the sun had disappeared, giving way to the light of the full moon rising in the east. From under the trees, he could see it topping the far horizon, and it looked like a huge yellow ball. He would prefer a dark night, but a fella took what he was dealt.

He had staked the horses a hundred yards from the campfire. If anything smelled the fire and approached, they would be expecting him to be curled up in his bedroll near the fire's remains. Not tonight. Tonight he'd sleep with the horses. All three of the big animals took turns coming over and nuzzling him for a treat, but he had to save them. Jack patted and scratched the ears of each horse, slapped them on the rump, and laid out his bed.

His saddle made a good pillow, and the saddlebags and packs were laid close. After slipping his moccasins on, he placed his Winchester across the pack and his gun belt next to him, both revolvers ready. Then he stretched his long legs. Moments after his head hit his saddle, the last thoughts passing through his mind were of a blonde, blue-eyed Irish girl back in Fort Worth, and he was asleep.

He awoke to the murmur of low conversation. Jack always had a good sense of time, and he figured it must be around two in the morning. He listened. The voices were soft whispers. At least three, maybe four men. He was lying on his side, and the voices sounded like they were coming from where he had built his fire. He slowly opened his eyes. Sure enough, the moon illuminated four men sitting not more than twenty feet from what they supposed was a sleeping man. He moved slowly so as to not alarm the intruders, and reached for his rifle. Once he had it in hand, he waited. The men hadn't noticed the horses back under the trees, which meant they hadn't noticed him, either. It sounded like they were arguing.

Finally, Jack could see all four of them draw their revolvers. *Not a good move, boys,* Jack thought. *Up to now you were just cowhands, but by pulling those guns, you've branded yourselves as murderers, and all bets are off.*

Jack heard the click of hammers being pulled back, and he closed his eyes. Almost immediately, the calm night was ripped apart with the roar of continuous discharges. It seemed like it was never-ending, but finally it did. Silence filled the night, magnified by the recent blasts of the six-guns. He immediately opened his eyes. The bright flashes had penetrated his closed eyelids, but not so severely his night vision had been hampered. He could still see the four men. In fact, he could see the eerie picture of smoke in the moonlight, rising from their six-guns' muzzles.

"You played the dickens, now," he called, and shot one from the saddle. The three, cursing, wheeled their mounts, but before they could race away, he fired again. Another of the marauders jerked and toppled from his saddle. The remaining two men raced away, followed by his bullets urging them onward. He lay still, listening.

The moans of a wounded man filled the evening. The man called, "You've got to help me. I've been shot, bad."

Jack remained quiet. The furthest thing on his mind was walking up on a wounded man in the dark. Only a crazy person would make that move, or a greenhorn. He lay quiet, listening.

More moaning came from the man. "Come on, man, have mercy. I'm hard hit. I'm dying."

Jack reached into his vest pocket and removed his pocket watch. His thumb slid back and forth over the emerald before he opened it, shielding it so that no reflection from the moonlight reached the wounded man or any of his friends. Jack checked the time, two fifteen. *Still plenty of time to get a little more sleep,* he thought. Quietly, he closed the watch and slipped it back into his vest. The man's moaning had stopped. He was either dead, slipping up on him, or dying. Jack knew where his bullet had struck, and he wasn't worried about the man crawling up on him. Plus he had the horses.

He turned his head to look behind him and check the animals. Truman had told him they were used to gunfire, and they proved it. With the initial blast of the revolvers, they had jerked and backed up, but there had been no more movement from the animals when the rifle fired. He placed his rifle within easy reach and laid his head back against his saddle. The horses would wake him if anyone came near. His eyes closed, and he was sound asleep.

Jack awoke three hours later. He'd had a good night's sleep. It was time he moved out. He lay still, looking out past the trees and across the prairie. There was a small herd of buffalo grazing along in the moonlight. An owl hooted from among the trees, and a fox barked, all indications of the absence of men. He needed to investigate the man he had shot. When he'd removed his boots, he had slipped on a pair of moccasins. He had learned that trick from an old mountain man who was a scout back east, during the war. This was another time he was thankful for all he had learned from so many men and women in his past. He half-rose and, bending low at the waist, slipped past the trees into the tall grass.

He worked his way through the grass, around and past where he believed the man to be fallen. Once there, he squatted and listened. Nothing. He felt sure this was where the man went down, but in the grass it was hard to tell.

Silently, he slipped a short distance farther, came out of his bent walk, and kneeled, softly placing the butt of the rifle on the ground. He listened, waited. Nothing. Then just as he was about to rise and move forward again, he heard something. It was low, barely discernible.

He heard it again, low, raspy breathing occasionally interrupted by a light cough. He continued to wait. Once pinpointing the man's position, Jack silently eased forward until he could see the man propped against a rotting log. In the moonlight, he could see the glint of a revolver gripped in the wounded man's hand. Slowly, he placed one foot after another on the ground, working to ensure even the grass didn't crinkle. An owl hooted nearby in the trees, and something small skittered through the grass. Near enough now, he slowly eased the cold muzzle of the Winchester toward the back of the man's neck until it contacted the flesh just above his collar.

With the touch of the muzzle, the man jerked, then sat as if frozen. Only his hand moved to allow the revolver to drop to the ground. His voice was soft, low, as if fearing to break the silence of the night. "You're mighty quiet, mister."

Jack, with the muzzle of his rifle remaining against the back of the man's neck, stood. "You've been waiting all this time."

The man's laugh deteriorated into a long bout of coughing. After he'd finished, he said, "You done kilt me. I ain't had anything else to do. I was hopin' you'd come over to check your handiwork."

"How'd you find me?"

"Smoke. We smelled it, just followed the smell. We eased up to the river, and there you be, all stretched out in the moonlight, sleepin' like a baby." He coughed again. "Only you wasn't."

"No, I reckon not."

"You got any whiskey? I could sure use a shot of whiskey about now."

"No."

The man sighed. "Leave it to us to jump a teetotaler. Drink of water would be good."

"Why should I give you anything? A few hours ago you tried to kill me."

"Would have, too, if you ain't been so he-coon smart."

Jack eased forward, squatted, and picked up the man's gun, slipping it behind his waistband. He patted the man down to make sure he didn't have any other weapons. When he'd finished with the man's boots, he stood and turned toward the horses.

"Don't leave me, mister. That ain't the Christian thing to do."

"How would you know?" Jack walked to his bedroll, sat, removed his moccasins, and put on his boots. He laid the man's gun on the bedroll. Standing, he picked up his gun belt, swung it around his waist, and fastened it. Then slid his extra Remington behind his belt. He picked up his canteen and walked back to the man.

The eastern horizon was beginning to break with the light of the coming day. Jack dropped the canteen in the man's lap.

The killer grunted, picked it up, pulled the stopper, and lifted it to his lips. Jack could hear the gurgle of the water as it was gulped from the canteen. He started to warn the killer about drinking too much, but then thought, *What difference does it make? He'll be dead soon.*

The man held up the canteen, and Jack took it, slipping the stopper back in. "What's your name?"

"Emmett Perkins." The man looked at Jack as if the name should mean something to him, then burst into a fit of coughing. Blood ran from the corner of the killer's mouth.

Jack nodded toward where the other body lay. "What about him?"

"You played hob when you shot that feller. He's Chester Haley. You ever heard of him?"

Jack shook his head.

"He's the onliest brother of Knox Haley." The man's face wrinkled in pain, followed by disbelief when he saw Jack's blank expression. "I know you've heard of Knox Haley. The Haley gang?"

"Nope. I don't keep up with two-bit local bushwhackers."

"Mister, you're dead and don't know it. Knox put a lot of store in his younger brother. All the rest of his kin was killed in the war. Chester was all he had left."

"He should have set him on an honest path and not that of a thief and killer."

Perkins clutched his abdomen and broke into another paroxysm of coughing. When he spoke again, it was in a whisper. "You gonna bury me, mister? I don't hanker to being eaten by them buzzards up there."

Jack tilted his head toward the sky. Above them, in the pale morning light, four buzzards, looking for an early morning breakfast, sailed in slow easy circles, knowing their meal was coming soon. They were patient.

"Were you planning on burying me?"

Jack looked at the dying man for a long moment. "Were you planning on burying me?"

Perkins motioned him closer. Jack bent over. In a weak voice, Perkins said, "You're a hard man, mister, but Knox'll find you and leave you for the buzzards." After his last word, his breath poured from his body in a long, slow current, never to be drawn in again.

Jack stood looking down on the dead man. He pulled the man's gun and went through his pockets. Nothing. No letters, no addresses, just a dirty plug of tobacco and a rusty pocketknife. He unfastened and stripped the gun belt from the dead man's body, tossed both the knife and the plug of tobacco into the grass, and looked across the prairie.

Nothing was to be seen except the herd of buffalo and the buzzards, now more visible in the brightening day, lazily circling the two dead men. He walked to the other man. He had a five-dollar gold piece, nothing else. The man looked to be near Jack's age, and all he had to show for his life was a five-dollar gold piece and a six-gun. Jack shook his head, stripped this man's gun belt, and walked back to the horses. Three strong heads stared at him.

"Alright, boys. We're about to be on our way." He saddled Dusty, the palomino, cinched the packsaddle on Thunder, and dropped the extra gun belts and six-guns into the pack. He swung up into the saddle and headed for the river. "You boys ready for a drink? We've still got a long way to go."

He found an easy spot to cross, and allowed them to drink their fill. Jack walked them to the treeline edge, gave the tall-grassed countryside ahead a close examination for anything possibly unfriendly, and walked them north. He was as anxious as the horses to leave this place. Jack bumped Dusty in the flanks, and they were off at a ground-covering lope.

21

The evening of the fifth day on the trail, he caught up with the last herd before Ellsworth. The drovers had pushed the cattle across the Arkansas River and were allowing them to graze on the remnants of nutritious big bluestem and Indiangrass. The grazing would add a few more pounds to the steers before reaching Ellsworth, which was only one day for Jack, but another four days for the drovers. Cowhands gathered around the chuckwagon, from which tantalizing aromas rose and traveled on the breeze, reaching Jack and causing his belly to growl in anticipation.

He was riding Thunder, the big gray, with Pepper and Dusty on leads. For some reason his back was feeling better, for which he was extremely thankful. The leg where he had been shot hurt occasionally, but except for it, he was fine other than being stiff as a corpse from the continuous riding over the past five days.

It was still daylight when he rode in.

A tall, slim, wide-shouldered man, whom Jack took to be the trail boss, stepped out from the chuckwagon. "Howdy."

Jack pulled the horses to a stop. "Evening. Name's Jack Sage, and that grub smells mighty good. I'd be willing to pay for a meal if that's allowed."

The tall man said, "Meals allowed. Payin' ain't. Name's Brad Ruff. I'm trail boss of this sorry lookin' lot. Shuck yourself outta that saddle and grab a plate." Before Jack could swing down, Ruff said, "Mighty fine-lookin' Shelby horses you got there. You seem to be in an awful hurry."

Several of the hands had also noticed the brands on the horses and were watching him closely.

Jack figured there needed to be an explanation and fast. "The chestnut I own. For the other two, Mr. Shelby has me acting as a sales agent once I get them to Ellsworth."

Ruff looked him over. "I've known Truman Shelby for quite a spell. He's mighty particular about who he sells his horses to. You have paper to show it?"

Jack nodded. "I do." He turned, pulled the bill of sale and agent copy from his saddlebags, and handed them down to Ruff. The man looked over both of the documents, folded them, and handed them back.

"Should have taken your word, but this far from home . . ." With his statement, the cowhands relaxed and went back to eating.

Jack swung down from the saddle. "Think nothing of it. I woulda done the same thing." He shoved the folded papers back into the saddlebag.

"Mind if I spend the night? Both me and the horses are a mite tuckered."

"Welcome to. Run your animals with the remuda if you like. Wranglers are about to take 'em down for water."

"I'm much obliged."

One of the wranglers had just finished eating. He walked over. "I'm Billy Mann. If you'll strip your gear, I'll take 'em on over."

"Thanks."

Billy pitched in helping Jack remove the tack from the horses. Jack nodded to the wrangler. "Much obliged. They're all yours."

Billy looked the three horses over before swinging into his saddle. "Mighty fine horses. You say they're gonna be for sale in Ellsworth?"

Jack looked at the three of them. "Maybe. The past few days I've grown attached to all three. It might be hard for me to part with any of them, but look me up. If you're interested, and they haven't sold by the time you get there, we can talk."

Billy swung into the saddle. "I'll do that." He herded the three horses toward the remuda.

The cook had been watching. "Come on over and git a bite, mister. You look like you could use it."

"Thanks." Jack walked with the trail boss to the end of the chuckwagon, where a big bowl of hot biscuits sat alongside several thick steaks.

He looked at the steaks and then at the cook. "Buffalo?"

"Heh-heh." The man chuckled and announced to anyone in earshot, "This big feller knows his meat."

Jack grinned. "Not so much. I just can't picture butchering one of those fine steers when you're so close to turning a good profit."

Brad Ruff laughed and slapped Jack on the back. "You got that right, Jack. Come on over and join us at the fire. Beans are bubbling in the pot. I imagine a man your size'll be glad to wrap himself around a few of 'em."

Jack grinned at Ruff. "You have no idea. We've been pushing hard since leaving Truman's place. This is my first opportunity to fill the pit."

A good-sized cowhand on the other side of the fire commented, "Looks like a pretty good-sized pit to fill."

The other drovers hooted at the statement while a smaller man, with thick black hair protruding from under his hat, and eyebrows to match, gave the commenter a long look. "Tiny, with all you eat, I'm surprised cookie doesn't run out of food danged near every meal."

Laughter erupted from around the fire, with others adding, "Yep, sure thing, ain't that the truth," to the conversation.

Tiny shot a mock frown at the group. "I need a lot of food 'cause I got to babysit all you saddle warmers." Turning toward the chuckwagon, he called, "What's for de-ssert?"

The cook stopped what he was doing and stepped out from behind his chuckwagon, pointing a long spoon at Tiny. "Nothing for you if you don't leave me be!" which brought more hooting and hollering.

Tiny grinned at the cowhands around the fire and went back to eating, and the men went back to low conversations, discussing what they would do in Ellsworth, only four tantalizing days away.

Bradley Ruff turned to Jack. "None of my business, but mind telling me what's got you so anxious to get to Ellsworth?"

Jack finished chewing a big piece of juicy buffalo steak, swallowed, and shook his head. "Don't mind at all. I own part of a herd up ahead that's probably already been sold. A fella I thought was a friend ambushed me, left me for dead, and for some reason I can't figure out, has gone north to meet my partners. Whatever he's got up his sleeve can't be good."

Ruff let out a low whistle. "Good reason to be riding hard. What's this fella's name?"

Jack had taken the opportunity to spoon in a couple more bites of beans while Ruff asked his questions. His appetite seemed to be growing as he ate. "When I knew him, it was Ted DeWitt, about six feet, brown hair, and real pale green eyes."

One of the cowhands who had been listening pointed his spoon at Ruff. "Boss, that feller came through our camp maybe a month or so ago. Those eyes got me. They were so pale, almost spooky, but a friendly guy."

Ruff nodded. "I remember him. Seemed a little too friendly to me, but we never turn a man down for a meal."

"He was real slick. He suckered me, and I've been over a trail or two." Jack took his last bite of steak. "Seconds allowed?"

Cookie called, "Come on, big fella, I'd rather you eat 'em than them complainers you're sittin' with."

Jack rose and disappeared behind the back of the chuckwagon.

He had been gone only moments when a call came from outside the light of the fire. "Bradley Ruff, mind if we ride in? This is Monty and Bronco with the remainder of our crew."

Ruff yelled back, "You two old codgers get in here. You got a surprise waitin' for you."

They've sold the herd, Jack thought, *and are headed home. I missed most of the drive.* Then with a thrill of excitement, another thought flashed. *Is DeWitt with them? Could I be so lucky?*

Ruff called to the cook, "Better whip up some more vittles. We got bellies to fill."

Cookie called out to Roger Hamm, the cook for Monty's crew, "Hamm, git yoreself over here, and give me a hand. You can fill me in on Ellsworth."

Roger swung down and handed the reins to Buster, who took them without a word. The boy's mouth hung open in shock. His eyes were glued on the man who stepped out from behind the chuckwagon.

"Howdy, boys," Jack said. "Good to see you."

There was silence, then muttered exclamations, followed by expletives.

Buster looked like he would burst into tears. Eyes wide and lips trembling, he muttered in disbelief, "You're alive."

Jack left his plate on the table stand of the chuckwagon and strode out, first to the mounted boy. He reached out and grabbed the boy's forearm. "I'm alright, Buster. I promised your ma I'd see you home, and I will. You go ahead and take care of the horses, and I'll talk to you later. It's mighty good to see you."

All Buster could do was nod and say, "Yes, sir."

Jack was surrounded by Monty and Bronco and the drovers. Statements and questions flew. "We thought you were dead." "What happened to you?" "Where have you been?" "Did you get shot?"

Finally, Jack held up his hands. "Easy, boys. I'll tell you everything. Just give me a minute." The crew quieted down. "What I need to know is, did a fellow named Ted DeWitt stop by the herd, and if he did, what'd he say?"

Monty and Bronco looked at each other.

Monty said, "Why don't you grab your plate. We'll get something to eat, and then we can have a little powwow."

Jack got his food, returned to his seat, and waited while everyone settled down. He had caught the look between Monty and Bronco, leaving him with an ominous feeling deep in the pit of his stomach. He didn't know why, but it was there, gnawing at him. It was gnawing hard enough to almost, but not quite, prevent him from finishing his steak. The cowhands were all talking to each other, but Monty and Bronco were quiet.

Monty turned to Jack, shoved his hat back, and cleared his throat. Lines of worry coursed across his forehead. "We met DeWitt. He came up on us about two weeks out of Ellsworth. There's been a lot happen, but I'll fill you in on the other stuff later. DeWitt, he rides in, nice and friendly like. He's all apologetic and says he's got some bad news. Says the Mould gang killed you."

Bronco whipped his hat against his leg. "I ain't never believed that so and so, and I said it." He shoved Monty in the shoulder. "I said so, didn't I?"

Monty nodded. "He did. He called DeWitt every name in the book, and a few extras. I figured the man would draw on him, but he didn't. He just stood there with this sad face, shaking his head like he was so sorry to be bringing such bad news."

Bronco burst out again. "I should've killed him right there. He comes ridin' in so big and proper on yore horse. I should've gut-shot him and stomped him. I shoulda—"

Monty turned to his friend. "That's enough, Bronco. Why don't you get us some more coffee."

Muttering, Bronco grabbed the cups and moved to the fire.

Monty turned back to continue, but Jack broke in. "He has Smokey?"

Monty nodded.

"What about Stonewall?"

A little grin drifted across Monty's wind-worn face. "We kinda forgot to tell him Stonewall was yours. That mule's out with the remuda right now. We were bringing him back. Between you and me, I figured to give him to Buster." He stared into the fire for a moment, then shrugged and cleared his throat.

"You were saying," Jack prompted.

"Oh, yeah. Well, that day, DeWitt kept asking me questions about the herd. Finally, as night was coming on, I asked him what business was it of his." Monty pulled a piece of paper out of his vest pocket. "He hands me this."

Jack looked it over, then looked at Monty. "I never wrote this."

Monty shook his head. "DeWitt swore you wrote this on your deathbed in Denton, and it was signed by you and witnessed."

Jack looked at his signature. It was close. It wasn't his, but it was close enough to fool most people.

"Can I keep it?"

"Sure. It's done its damage now."

Jack examined the little slip of paper that robbed him of all of his investment and time. He stood and walked to the shadows, standing, thinking, then returned and sat by Monty again. "What'd you sell the herd for?"

Monty shook his head. "That's another story. We had good luck all the way, crossings, water, weather, Indians. We had no problem, unlike Bryant and Jorgensen. I worked for Carson Bryant for a long time, and he's never had the trouble he had on this drive. He was leading the drives, number one into Ellsworth for the season. That means big money."

Bronco pitched in, "I'm off the man, but he was always good to us, and his was a good job. He just seemed to kinda turn this year, but even he didn't deserve the drive *he* had."

Monty, a little irritation showing at the edge of his eyes, looked over at his friend. When Bronco was finished, he turned back to Jack. "You remember they were driving a big herd, near three thousand head. First thing, as he's crossing the Brazos, he's hit with a flash flood that kills close to a thousand head. He was lucky it was at the end of their crossing, but in the long run, it didn't matter anyway. Next, he lost several hundred head crossing the Red. Got 'em into quicksand and couldn't get 'em out."

Bronco leaned forward, interrupting again. "That ain't all, he lost two boys tryin' to get them danged cattle out of the bog, and Carson knows the Red. Shoot, he showed us where to never cross, and that was one of the spots." Bronco shook his head. "He just ain't right in the head." Bronco glanced at Monty, held his hands up, and leaned back. "Alright, alright, I'll keep my mouth shut."

When Bronco leaned back, Jack glanced around the encampment. No one was eating. An occasional sip of coffee was taken, but all of the cowhands, including the trail boss Bradley Ruff, were listening intently.

Monty began again. "Then the Indians hit 'em. One of the hands I talked to said they were Kiowa. Ended up killing another cowhand and scattering cattle across a good bit of Oklahoma territory, most of which they never got back. Other tribes were waiting and were quick to make off with 'em.

"Next they git hit by tornadoes. Not just one, but three. I talked to one of the boys, and he said it looked like it was hailing steers. They was flying through the air, getting driven through with broken limbs, dropped, and broken in rocky washes. We came along a couple of weeks later, and it was a butchered mess."

Bronco couldn't resist. He leaned forward, whipped his hat at

Jack with every sentence. "That drive was cursed, right from the start. I'm mighty thankful we wasn't with it. Most of the remainder of them cowhands quit, and those are good boys. They was just played out, done in, finished."

Monty just shook his head and stayed quiet until his friend stopped talking. He turned to him. "You through."

Bronco leaned back, glared at Monty, yanked his hat down over his forehead, and crossed his arms. "I'm through."

Monty turned back to Jack. "Bottom line is, they finished the drive with seven hundred worn-out, scrawny cattle. The buyers gave Carson ten dollars a head, and I saw those steers. They gave him better than a good deal. It'll take a long time to put any meat on those bodies."

Jack stared back at Monty. *If I were superstitious,* he thought, *I'd have to agree with Bronco. It sure sounds like the drive was cursed.* "So how'd we do?"

"Luck smiled on us." Monty winced as soon as the words were out of his mouth. He shook his head and cleared his throat. His voice sounded more gruff than usual. "Sorry, Jack. You know what I mean, the herd, it smiled on the herd. It sure didn't smile on you."

Jack waved his hand. "No offense. Go ahead."

"We were the third herd to get in. The one between Carson and us was about our size, a thousand head, so they didn't pull the price down at all. Plus their cattle weren't in as good a shape as ours." Seeing Jack growing impatient, Monty hurried. "We got thirty-five dollars a head. Your part of that was fourteen thousand." Monty shook his head and shrugged. "We tried not to pay DeWitt, but he took it to an Ellsworth court, and they said his paper was legal. They made us pay him your money and give him your horses and equipment, all except Stonewall, who they didn't know about."

Jack sat silent. *Quite a story,* he thought. *All of it. Carson Bryant, Ted DeWitt. Not only did Bryant's luck turn bad, but so has mine. In all the battles I've fought, all the marshaling I've done, not once have I ever been hit by a bullet. But as a civilian, I've been shot twice, smashed in the back of the head with a rifle butt, and had my livelihood stolen. Is someone telling me what I should be doing for a living?*

"Jack? Jack?"

He heard it faintly at first, then his name intruded on his thoughts. He looked up at Monty.

"What's your plans?"

Jack smiled, but there was no humor in the smile. His gray eyes glinted red from the reflected, cavorting flames of the fire. "I'm headed to Ellsworth, boys, and if you're a mind, I'd like Monty, Bronco, and Buster to hang around with me."

There were moans and complaints from the rest of the hands. Every man wanted to stay and help Jack get his property back. Plus, he was certain they all wanted to see DeWitt get his just due.

Jack stood. "Thanks. I mean that. I certainly can't stop you from riding back to Ellsworth. It's a free country, but you've got family and friends waiting on you back home." He held his hands up at the cheering to quiet the men. "But here's the rules. No one, and I mean no one, confronts DeWitt. There's a way to do this, and we're going to do it legally. Does everyone understand?"

Several of the men had a different idea of their roles, but they at last agreed. "Good, here's what's going to happen. I'll find the judge and show him the difference between the forged signature and my signature. Once we have ownership of the cattle straightened out, I'm finding DeWitt, and I'm getting Smokey, my gear, and my money back, and maybe a little bit of justice."

22

Just before sundown, they rode into Ellsworth, Kansas.
Jack had seen similar towns. This was a wild end-of-track, end-of-trail town, but not end of sin. The wide dirt street was lined with saloons, some built with cedar planking, others large dirt- and mud-splattered tents, and all capped with wooden false fronts. Hammers crashed, and men yelled as construction continued up and down the street and would until darkness fell. Men and money waited, anxious to fill the buildings with card tables and roulette wheels or supplies ready to fly off shelves into the hands of demanding purchasers. The false fronts varied from the red of new cedar to the faded, worn dull gray produced by time, wind, and weather.

It wasn't dark yet, but pianos banged continuously from one end of main street to the other. Men's shouts and women's harsh laughter could be heard from inside each of the saloons. Tough-looking painted women in a variety of undress sat in front of several of the establishments, calling coarse invitations to the passing drovers.

A drunk cowboy, who looked to be no more than seventeen, staggered across the street in front of them. He waved, stumbled, fell into the dusty street on top of a pile of horse apples, pushed himself up, and disappeared, brushing off his vest, behind a set of swinging batwing doors.

Monty, dulled to the view, pointed toward a slim building jammed between a saloon and a general store. "The sheriff's office. His name's Cedrik Whitstone. He's a good man. Does his best to keep the peace, and does a pretty fine job most of the time. It's hard to maintain any kind of law in a place like this."

The four of them pulled up at the hitching rail. *I'm glad Monty was able to persuade most of the men to head home,* Jack thought. He swung down from Pepper's back, looped the reins on the hitching rail, and went into the sheriff's office. Monty followed close behind.

Sheriff Whitstone, a man of average build, dark hair, and a thick mustache that wrapped around his lips and connected to an equally thick goatee of several inches, was bent over the desk. He held a pencil in his right hand, working steadily on a document. He looked up at the sound of boots, spurs, and men, but remained silent.

"Evening, Sheriff Whitstone," Jack said, straightening after passing through the door.

"Good evening, sir. I fear you have me at a loss." The sheriff nodded, acknowledging Monty and Bronco. To them he said, "Thought your business was concluded, and you were headed back to Texas?"

"So did we," Monty replied.

Jack pulled the forged document from his pocket and handed it to the sheriff. "I'm Jack Sage, Sheriff. As you will see from this supposed last will and testament, I am dead, but prior to my death, I was able to sign over everything I owned to Ted DeWitt."

Sheriff Whitstone's dark eyes measured Jack as he took the document. His head lowered, and he slowly scanned the writing. Finished, he looked up with a wry grin. "Mr. Sage, for a dead man, you take up a lot of space."

"Yes, sir, I do."

Monty spoke up. "Sheriff Whitstone, we"—he waved his hand to encompass his companions—"can witness to the fact that this here is truly Jack Sage."

The sheriff kept his eyes on Jack. "I suppose you're askin' me if I know if this feller is here, and will I arrest him?"

Jack shook his head. "No, sir, I am not. I am informing you of this infraction of the law and would like your consent to allow me to skin my own cat."

"Any shooting involved?"

Jack shook his head. "Only if he starts it. Though I would dearly love to break him into little pieces, I do not plan to. All I want is what is left of my property. If you were kind enough to go along with us, it might deter any action on his part."

The sheriff rose from behind his desk. "I know about this case. In fact, the judge ruled it was legal. Therefore, he must first see it and agree. Once we've done that, I'll take you to Mr. DeWitt's location." Monty opened the door, and the sheriff led the way, Jack close behind.

Jack's nose wrinkled at the smell of beef cooking when they passed a restaurant, but at the next moment they were passing the smell of unwashed bodies, liquor, and stale beer. Before reaching the door of the next saloon, a man flew through the batwings, followed by his hat and, "I don't want to see you in here again!" The man rolled across the boardwalk into the street, turned, saw Sheriff Whitstone, sheepishly nodded, and moved on.

"Busy town," Jack said.

"You ain't seen anything. Wait until about ten o'clock tonight. My jail will be full of drunks, maybe a thief or two, and definitely a couple of scrappers, but hopefully no one gets shot." With his last statement, he gave Jack a pointed look.

"Sheriff, I have no plans for shooting anyone. Like I said, the only way I draw is if someone else does first."

"Good enough." He indicated a narrow building between two

saloons. "Here's Judge Spiegel's office." They turned and walked in.

The man behind the desk surprised Jack. He had expected an average-sized white-haired gentleman, along in years. Judge Spiegel was none of these. He was young. Why, he didn't look thirty years old. His black, pencil mustache fit him well and was neatly trimmed. The man was at least six feet tall with wide shoulders and a deep chest. His inquisitive smile rode well on his broad honest face. Black hair was trimmed perfectly to the edge of his ears and off his collar. He looked more like a junior to mid-rank army officer than a judge.

"Morning, Cedrik, gentlemen, what can I do for you?"

The sheriff stepped forward and handed Jack's will to Judge Spiegel.

He read it quickly. "Yes, I recognize this. I've already ruled on it."

"You sure have, Judge," Sheriff Whitstone replied. He turned to Jack, who filled the small room, leaving little space for the others. "I'd like you to meet Jack Sage, in the flesh."

The only indication of surprise from the judge was his head recoiling slightly. He looked at Jack, reread the will, and looked back up at him. "You certainly don't look dead, Mr. Sage. Can you prove you are Jack Sage?"

"Judge Spiegel, the sheriff knows my friends, and they know me and will attest I am indeed Jack Sage."

The judge turned to Monty, Bronco, and Buster. "Is this true?"

Three answers blended into their quick response. "Yes, Judge Spiegel, I can attest to it," "Danged tootin', Judge," and, "Yes, sir."

The judge smiled at Buster. "Thank you, gentlemen." His eyes stayed on Buster. "You're a little young to be on the trail, aren't you?"

"Yes, sir, I'm fourteen, my name's Buster Massey, and I'm from Texas. Mr. Sage, here—" he thumbed toward Jack "—promised my mom he would keep an eye on me if I could go on the drive. I'm good with horses."

Judge Spiegel nodded. "I see. Being good with horses is an excellent talent to have."

Buster flushed as red as a Texas sunset after a dust storm and mumbled, "Yes, sir."

The judge turned back to Jack. "Mr. Sage, would you be willing to give me a sample of your signature?"

Jack nodded and stepped forward while at the same time the judge slid paper, pen, and ink to the edge of the desk for him. Jack bent to sign the blank sheet of paper, and the judge looked up at Monty, Bronco, and Buster. "I want you men to know that I do not distrust your word. I fully believe what you are saying. However, this signature Mr. Sage is giving me will be kept in our records to provide evidence for what I am about to rule."

The three men nodded their understanding.

The judge let the ink dry for a few moments, picked it up, and compared the two. "Yes, there are distinct differences that any layman could pick out if he had the two signatures together." He looked up at Jack. "Thank you, Mr. Sage. I am sorry I previously ruled against you. This appeared to be a legal document. I suspect Mr. DeWitt, if that's his real name, had an accomplice." He shook his head. "But that is beside the point. I need to correct the injustice." He straightened in his chair. "I hereby rule that the previous ruling is void and terminated at this time. Mr. Sage, you are free to recover all properties of worth and value that are yours, including horses, tack, weapons, and money, and whatsoever else there may be involved." He tilted his head slightly and said, "Preferably without gunplay. Do I make myself clear?"

Before Jack could say anything, the sheriff spoke up. "I've already made that clear, Your Honor, and Mr. Sage is completely agreeable, with the exception he reserves the right to defend himself."

The judge nodded. "All right, good. Now, is there anything else, gentlemen?"

Jack stepped forward and extended his hand. "Judge Spiegel, I want to thank you. I've known other judges who were less inclined to reverse their rulings."

He stood and took Jack's hand. "As have I, Mr. Sage. Good luck in your recovery efforts. I hope DeWitt hasn't gambled all of your hard-earned income away."

"Thanks."

The men exited the office. Jack noticed the judge was back at work before they were out the door. *I'd like to know more about him. You don't see that many young judges in this country.*

"This way," Sheriff Whitstone said and turned east. "He's been losing your money at Joe Brennan's saloon."

The words drove deep into Jack, awakening his anger. This man he had befriended had tried to kill him and take everything he had. When he thought of DeWitt, he felt cold, deep-in-the-belly anger, and reminded himself, *Keep yourself under control. The man may deserve dying, but you're not an executioner.*

Jack turned to the youngest member of their party. "Buster, go get the horses watered."

Buster's excited grin jerked from his face like it was caught by the tip of a steer's long horn. "But—"

Jack was not in the mood for a discussion with a fourteen-year-old. His voice was hard. "No buts, boy. Do what I say."

Buster, without another word, marched, shoulders slumped, toward the horses.

"Kinda hard on him," Monty said.

"No time for coddling. He's got to learn he's in a man's world, and when the boss gives him an order, he moves without argument. Learning that just might save his life one day."

The sheriff pointed diagonally across the street. "Brennan's."

The men turned and strode across the wide, dusty street,

dodging wagons and riders making their way to various destinations. Almost as one, four hands dropped to their holsters, removing the leather thong holding each weapon in its holster, and each of those same four hands moved the revolver to ensure it was loose and ready.

Jack, his long strides outdistancing the others, stepped onto the boardwalk. "I'm going in first, Sheriff."

Whitstone nodded. "Go ahead. Just remember our deal."

Jack nodded in return and pushed the door open. Joe Brennan's was a busy place. Smoke filled the room, filtering through the light in waves from the fire of the flickering lamps hanging from the ceiling and along the walls. *They all smell and sound the same,* Jack thought. *Tangiers, Paris, Galveston, or Ellsworth, all the same.*

The smell of sawdust, deep across the floor, mixed with the odor of crowded men, liquor, and the perfume of painted ladies, filled the gambling hall. The smell didn't bother him. He had been around sweaty, unwashed men almost his entire life. It was just another smell. But of all of the senses, the one that wore him down the quickest was the sound or din of these places. Men yelled, women laughed, others talked louder trying to be heard above the yelling and laughter, glasses clinked and buckets banged, along with the incessant piano.

One thing Jack had never appreciated was music. He could never make sense of it. Instruments, either blaring or screeching, quickly wore on his nerves. He had tried opera, once, in Paris, never again. He could find no delight in hearing the nightingales sing from the stage. For to him, it was akin to the squeal of a stuck pig.

With the advantage of his height, he was easily able to pick DeWitt out from the crowd. The man was sweating, whether from excitement or the press of people, Jack knew not. His normally relaxed, friendly smile had a tense, pasted-on look to it as he bent over the roulette wheel. *Oh no,* Jack thought, *roulette wheels are notorious for being rigged.* He turned to ask the sheriff a question, but the press of people had separated them.

He moved quickly, shoving cowhands from his path, hearing exclamations of protest, but ignoring them. He had to get to that wheel before DeWitt lost any more of his money. It was as if the crowd knew his purpose and closed in to protect the killer. They multiplied, tightened, body against body. He shoved one of the dance-hall girls from in front of him, and she yelled and cursed him, which got the attention of a cowhand, who reached out to grab Jack's arm.

The sheriff had powered his way through the crowd to return to Jack's side and shook his head at the drover. The man hesitated, evidently weighing his options, and stepped back, disappearing into the crowd.

Jack broke through the press of people. The wheel was spinning, and the ball was sailing around its course. As he stepped into the open space, he heard the dealer say, "No more bets," and his head jerked to the table. DeWitt had no chips or money in front of him. He could feel his coldness deepening. All of his investment, what little there was, was sitting on this table. He followed the killer's eyes to the single number seventeen. *A single number,* he thought. *He picked the one bet with the highest odds of him losing.* He worked to control himself as the wheel spun and the ball raced around in circles, gradually slowing, its momentum dying. His eyes were glued to the ball. His entire financial future, thanks to a thief and a killer, was riding on that one little ball, and the odds were so high against him it felt like he might not be able to take a breath.

The ball dropped. It bounced and landed—on seventeen.

Hangers-on and saloon girls crowded around DeWitt, slapping him on the back, congratulating him. He could see him eating it up. Jack looked at the dealer. The man was as stunned as he was. The dealer said something to an assistant, who immediately ran toward an office. Then Jack heard DeWitt yell at the dealer, "How much?"

When the dealer said nothing, the crowd started to get belligerent. "You're gonna pay him, ain't you?" came from one of the observers.

Another said, "Texas boys hang cheaters."

The dealer quickly figured and cleared his throat. "Folks, this gentleman has won himself seventeen thousand, three hundred, and forty-two dollars."

Jack heard the sheriff comment, "Joe's not gonna be happy about this one."

At the announcement, silence fell over the crowd. Each person was thinking what it would be like for someone to give them seventeen thousand, three hundred, and forty-two dollars.

In the silence, Jack's deep voice rolled across the floor and bumped against Ted DeWitt's euphoria. "Hello, Ted."

The killer had raised a glass to his lips. Cooly, he tossed off the liquor and turned to Jack. "How're you doing, Jack?"

"Better than when you left me in those Texas briars."

The crowd got the gist of what was going on and moved rapidly away from the two men, opening a wide space between them.

Jack could see DeWitt trying to figure his way out of this problem. The man's light green eyes rapidly shifted from side to side, as if looking, hoping for an answer, an exit.

"I tried to save you, Jack."

"We'll talk about that in a moment. What about the Mould boy? The one who had dropped his gun. With all those tears in his eyes, he couldn't have hit anything. Why'd you shoot him?"

DeWitt's head jerked from left to right, like his eyes had previously done, but he could find no hope of escape. All those faces who, moments before, had been friendly and happy for him were now staring at him with hard disapproval. "Why, Jack, when I bent over to check on you, he went for his gun. I did what I had to do."

Jack stared at the man. Sweat covered DeWitt's face. His shirt was soaked. He looked like a man staring death in the face and not liking the prospect.

"Ted?" Jack said softly.

In almost the same tone, DeWitt replied, "Yeah, Jack?"

"You're a liar."

DeWitt held his hands up in front of him, palms toward Jack. "I'm not gonna fight you, Jack. You're too big. You'd kill me."

Jack nodded. "I would, Ted. Tell me, how much of my money do you have left?"

After shuffling his feet, he nodded to the roulette table. "That's it, Jack. I kinda lost most of it." And then he brightened. "But I won it all back for you and more." He grinned and nodded his head.

Jack had had enough. He knew if he drew this out any further, he might beat this killer to a pulp. "Alright, Ted, pull your weapon, nice and easy, and lay it on the table, then slide it to the end."

Jack watched the frightened man remove his revolver with his opposite hand, using his thumb and forefinger, and slide it to the end of the table.

"Now, I want you to stick your hands in the air just as high as you can reach."

DeWitt's hands shot up, at which point Jack turned slightly toward the dealer. "That money is mine. Jack Sage. Count it out and bag it up. I'll be back for it."

Realizing he was responsible for Mr. Brennan's money, the dealer began to protest. "Now wait just a minute. You can't march in here and claim another man's money."

Sheriff Whitstone stepped forward. "Dennis, make no mistake, this is completely legal. We just came from Judge

Spiegel's office. This DeWitt was playing with Jack Sage's money, so do like he says."

The tall dealer's long face got longer. "Mr. Brennan won't like this."

"No, I reckon he won't, but we all have to do things we don't like."

Someone shouted, "Look out. He's got a gun!"

23

Jack's peripheral vision had already registered the movement. A sleeve gun. There was no way to beat one of those unless you caught it before it came out of the sleeve, and that wasn't happening here. He spun and drew.

It didn't make sense. DeWitt was in Kansas. The man had a good chance of never being extradited to Texas. All he had to do was wait it out, and in a few days he would be out of jail and a free man, but he was drawing a gun. *Fear,* Jack thought, even as his .36-caliber Remington was clearing the holster. *Fear, guilt, and distrust. He judges me by his code. He doesn't believe anyone can be different from him.*

Jack watched as the sleeve gun extended and filled DeWitt's hand. The man's face was contorted, lips drawn up, exposing even white teeth in a terrible grimace. His brow wrinkled diagonally and way too deep for a younger man, like someone had made multiple slashes with a saber across it. Jack's draw continued while he stared directly into DeWitt's pale-green eyes. They were like Ruff's cowhand had said, spooky, and now wide and evil. He saw the muzzle of the revolver in DeWitt's hand explode in fire, and the black ball exit the flame. It was coming straight for him, but he had no time to watch. He fired. The little Remington hardly moved in his big hand, and instantly a spray of blood leaped from DeWitt's Adam's apple.

His eyes were still locked on DeWitt's, whose had grown larger in surprise and pain. Before he could cock his weapon and fire again, there was an explosion, and DeWitt jerked to the right. Another blast on top of the last one and the man swung to the left, with blood spurting from each wound. Then the slam of a big .44 drove the killer back against the roulette table, with a huge spray of blood exiting from his chest.

Jack never fired again. It wasn't necessary. The four rounds had destroyed the man. He watched DeWitt look down at his chest, then those pale-green eyes faded even more, rolled back into his head, and he fell forward. Jack looked to his left and right. On his left, Whitstone stood with a smoking .44 Colt, while to his right, Monty and Bronco had their .44s out and still leveled, smoke drifting up from the muzzle of each weapon. The bitter eye-burning sting from the black powder filled the roulette area.

A high-pitched scream broke through his consciousness, and he realized he had been hearing it since DeWitt had fired. He turned to see one of the saloon girls holding her neck, a shallow graze cut across her smooth white skin. Relieved, Jack thought, *She'll live and have a story to tell.* He looked around. No one else was down, only DeWitt. *A miracle,* he thought, *as crowded as this saloon is.*

He turned to the sheriff. "Thought you didn't want any shooting?"

Sheriff Whitstone gave Jack a lopsided grin. "Got a bad habit. When somebody shoots at me, I shoot back."

Jack looked over at Monty and Bronco. "Looks like a few other folks suffer from that same problem."

A large, well-dressed man walked up to the sheriff and

glanced nonchalantly at DeWitt's body. "Cedrik, can you tell me what the blue blazes is going on here?"

"I can, but let's move into your office. It'll be better that way." He motioned Jack, Monty, and Bronco to follow.

Brennan had seated himself in a large cushioned chair behind his desk and listened to Sheriff Whitstone's story. When the sheriff was finished, he leaned forward, placed his elbows on the highly polished oak desk, and steepled his fingers. "So DeWitt was playing with stolen money. That means the bet was no good."

"Joe," the sheriff said, "don't start thinking like that. Don't go tryin' to wriggle out of payin' your debts." He pointed at Jack. "This here fella as good as staked DeWitt, so he should get whatever would have been DeWitt's winnings. You know if he'd lost, you wouldn't of hesitated to keep the money."

Brennan looked at Jack. "You have anything to say?"

Jack shrugged. "You look like an honest man to me. I figure you'll come to the correct decision once all the excitement cools down."

Brennan looked Jack over. "You were just in a gunfight. You don't look too excited."

"Not my first one."

"You also don't look like a typical cowhand."

Jack thought for a second, then looked the owner in the eye. "Mr. Brennan, you know there's no such thing as a typical cowhand. Are you talking about a young fella who goes to college in New York and decides to come west for adventure, or maybe a businessman from New Orleans who's tired of the city's hassle? He might be an Irishman from County Cork or a Frenchman from Paris. Not every slow-talking, easygoing man toting a six-gun out here spent his growing life behind a cow or a plow. This country is a melting pot of adventurers, the poor and the wealthy. Each one is searching, in their own way, for their own kind of pot of gold, their own freedom. To answer your question, I fit perfectly into that group, so I must be a typical cowhand."

Brennan had kept his eye on Jack, taking in every word. "You a politician?"

At that, Jack laughed. "No, your question just hit me funny, so let me ask you a question. Are you ready to come to a correct decision?"

Brennan reached to the edge of his desk and lifted the top of a box of cigars. He leaned forward and pushed the box toward the sheriff. Whitstone picked one up, rolled it between his fingers, and then ran it lengthwise under his nose.

"Much obliged."

He then offered it to Monty and Bronco. Both deferred, as did Jack when he was offered one. Brennan closed the box and went about preparing his cigar. As he worked, he talked. "Mr. Sage, in my business, I meet all sorts of men. Some I like and trust, some I don't." He stopped and lit his cigar, holding the flaming match close. Rotating the cigar slowly, he drew air through the tight-wound leaves, causing the cut end to suck the flame into it with each draw. Satisfied, he shook the match out, felt it, and tossed it into an ashtray. Then he took a deep draw, held it for a moment while examining the cigar, exhaled the smoke, and waved his hand, as if he were waving the smoke away. "That's beside the point. Yes, I will be paying you the seventeen thousand, three hundred and forty-two dollars." Brennan stood and walked to his office door, opened it, and called, "Dennis."

The dealer appeared with a small, heavy canvas bag. Brennan took it, nodded to him, closed the door, shook the bag, and turned to Jack. The clink of gold sounded from the bag.

Brennan wasn't as tall as Jack, few people were. But he was thick, with powerful-looking biceps bulging through the sleeves of his dark brown, knee-length frock coat. He walked to Jack and handed him the bag, motioning toward the desk. "You're free to count it."

"As I said, I have determined you're an honest man. That won't be necessary. Thank you."

Brennan extended his hand. "It's been a pleasure meeting you. If you're ever looking for a job, you'll have one here. I need good men I can trust."

Jack smiled. "I thank you. If I do make it back, I'll stop by, not for a job, but for the opportunity to buy you a drink." The two men shook hands.

Jack looked at Monty and Bronco. "We need to be on our way. Buster's probably wondering what happened with all the shooting."

The sheriff rose, puffed on his cigar, and said, "See you later, Joe."

Brennan nodded, and the four men trooped from the office into the bedlam of the saloon. It was back to normal. DeWitt's body was gone. Sawdust had been dumped over the floor where he had bled out, and the roulette wheel was spinning. Laughing saloon girls hung on drunken cowhands. It was as if DeWitt had never existed.

The sheriff leaned toward Jack. "Just another day in Sin City." They marched out the door.

The dark night was lit by the flickering light coursing across the main street from the saloons and businesses still open. Once outside, the sheriff turned to Jack. "Staying or leaving?"

"Heading back, Sheriff. We'll stay the night, get a good supper and breakfast, and start out in the morning."

"Mr. Sage, I've heard about your marshalin' down in Texas. I need a good man to help keep this place under control. My deputies do an alright job, but they don't have your expertise."

Jack suppressed a grin. "Sheriff, I appreciate your offer, but I might have a girl waiting for me back in Texas. I've got to go find out."

The sheriff nodded. "Understand. Good luck to you." Jack

watched the man turn and stride down the boardwalk. The thought passed through his mind, *Good luck to you, Sheriff. This is a tough town to rein in.*

Bronco's belly let out a low grumble, and Jack chuckled. "Sounds like you're about ready to wrap yourself around a feedbag."

"Danged tootin'. Why don't we get the horses stashed, grab the kid, and I know just the place." They started for Buster. He could just barely be seen in the dim light of the street. "Reckon that boy'll be mighty relieved. He puts a heap of store in you."

Before Jack could respond, Bronco continued, "Now what's this about a girl in Texas? You ain't said anything about her."

Jack rolled his eyes. "You'll hear about her in good time. We've got a long ride back to Texas."

∽

THEY PULLED up to the hitching rail at Chisholm's Trading Post five days after leaving Ellsworth. The weather was still hot, but Jack was enjoying this ride much more than his previous race. They were taking it slow, and his leg wasn't bothering him at all. He glanced at the treeline not far away, another river. By his count, it should be the North Fork of the Canadian. That was where he had been ambushed, at least somewhere along this river. *Wish I'd known about this trading post,* he thought.

The post looked much like any other. It was log built—solid, and bigger than he would expect. In front, a large oak provided shade for four occupied rough-hewn chairs. The men in them appeared to be all white, although it was difficult to tell, as dirty as they were. They were as rough-cut as the chairs they sat in.

Jack gave them a quick once-over and determined they could mean trouble for someone, but hopefully not for them. All four had scruffy beards that hadn't been cut or trimmed in ages. Dirty flop hats battled unsuccessfully at covering dirty heads and shaggy hair. Their boots appeared to have never seen care. He swung down from Smokey and glanced at Buster, who was riding Dusty. The big palomino and the boy had really bonded. It had almost gotten ridiculous, to where the animal was a nuisance, following Buster right into the campfire area. Jack had made Buster stake Dusty well away from the camp, ensuring he stayed with the other animals.

His eyes fell on Stonewall. He hadn't realized how much he had missed that old mule. Evidently a lot more than Stonewall had missed him, for he couldn't stay away from Smokey. DeWitt's theft of Smokey had been tough on the mule and maybe Smokey, too. He seemed glad to have Stonewall around.

The men made sure there was enough free reins to allow the horses to drink, loosened the cinches, and walked inside the post. Buster slipped his rifle from the scabbard and carried it with him. An Indian man stood behind the counter. "Howdy, William," Monty said, upon entering the post.

"Monty," the man replied, "Bronco."

"William, this here is Jack Sage. He's a partner, and you might be seeing him again. He's a good friend of both Bronco and myself."

The man nodded to Jack. "Nice to meet you, Jack. You from Texas?"

"A pleasure," Jack responded. "I am now." He looked around the trading post. It was well supplied. "Nice place you have here."

"Pa built it. You may have heard of him, Jesse Chisholm? Built another farther south. It's still open, too."

Jack nodded. "I have." Remembering Buster, Jack said, "This is Buster."

The man nodded. "Nice to meet you, boy."

"You too, sir," Buster replied.

Monty nodded toward the door and the oak tree. "Nice bunch you've got sitting under your oak."

William shook his head. "Not much. Outlaws, part of the Haley gang. They don't bother me because I'm Cherokee. They know if they try anything with me, my family will have them stretched out like beaver hides in no time. A word of warning, they like to rob trail bosses who are headed back to Texas with money. That's why they sit around, scouting."

Monty grinned. "Figured. They look like a worthless bunch. They jump us, they may disappear. The law have any problem with that?"

William shook his head. "No problem."

Bronco spoke up. "You got any of that fine venison stew around here?"

"Sit. Stew, fresh beans, onions, and tomatoes straight from the garden, cornbread, and some fine peach pie Julia whipped up today."

"Umm," Bronco said. "You done made my mouth water like a flash-floodin' river." He grabbed Buster by the shoulder and pulled him toward a long table with a bench on each side. "Come on, boy, I know you're as hungry as me."

Buster grinned back at his friend. "Yes, sir, I'm mighty hungry."

The four of them sat at the same table, side by side facing the door, all handguns ready. Jack pulled his Stetson from his head and knocked Buster's hat off. The boy grinned at him and laid it on the bench next to his rifle. They had no sooner seated themselves than an attractive woman, along with a girl about Buster's age, came out with food. They brought big bowls of stew, a heaping platter of cornbread, fresh onions and bright red tomatoes cut up on a plate, and a big bowl of red beans.

"Howdy, Julia," Monty said.

"Mr. Huff, it is good to see you again. I heard about what happened to Mr. Bryant's herd. It is such a shame."

Bronco butted in. "Hi there, Julia. I swear you get prettier every time I see you."

She grinned at him and pushed a strand of hair behind her left ear before grabbing the spoon from the beans and shaking it at him. "Bronco, I'm surprised some husband hasn't shut that flirty mouth of yours by now."

Bronco put his thumbs behind his vest armholes and shoved his wide chest out. "I'm too tough." He quickly glanced at William. "Course, that don't apply to you, there, William."

The Cherokee grinned back. "I know, Bronco. If I thought you were serious, I'd have to put together a scalping party for you."

Bronco grinned at his friend and ran his hand through his thick hair. "Now, you wouldn't want to separate me from my lovely locks, would you?"

William appeared to be seriously examining Bronco's hair. "That's some mighty fine hair. It'd look real good on some brave's belt."

Bronco looked back at Julia and whispered in a loud voice, "He ain't serious. Don't you forget me."

She rolled her eyes and with the girl, who had been steadily watching Buster, whose face had turned a magnificent red, departed back to the kitchen.

Monty, between mouthfuls of beans, stew, and cornbread, said, "That mouth of yours is gonna get you in big trouble sometime, and I won't be there to bail you out."

"Pshaw. I've bailed you out so many times, you'll never catch up."

With the last comment, the men fell to their food, laying waste with a vengeance.

Finally Jack straightened. "Whew, that was good."

William, who had been watching, said, "More?"

Jack shook his head. "Not for me, but I could go for a piece of pie."

"Me too," Buster joined in. Monty and Bronco agreed.

Moments later, Julia and the girl were back carrying two pieces of pie each. Julia also had a medium-sized pitcher filled with fresh cream. The girl set the peach pie in front of Buster and smiled at him. He frowned back and said, "Thanks." She giggled and followed Julia. The interaction did not go unnoticed at the table.

Bronco spoke up. "Looks like she's sweet on you, boy."

"Aww, that ain't so," Buster said, eyebrows pulled together in a frown and voice full of disgust.

Bronco winked at Jack. "I'm the one in this bunch who knows those kinds of things, and I surely think she is."

To hide his face from the others, Buster bent way over his huge chunk of pie and sliced a piece with his fork. He put it into his mouth, and Jack could see the boy relishing the taste. He watched as Buster tried to reach for the cream pitcher without raising his head to look, but he couldn't quite make it. He lifted his head, and there was Bronco's toothy wide grin, thick mustache and all, staring at him. He grabbed the pitcher, poured, and set it back down, without making a comment, and went back to eating.

As Jack took his first bite of pie, shadows fell across the table. The four men, from the chairs outside, strolled into the trading post, their leader chewing on a long piece of bluestem. They leaned against the counter. The one with the bluestem coughed and took it from his mouth. "Give us a drink, William."

William set four glasses on the counter and pulled a bottle from beneath. He poured a shot in each one. "That'll be two bits."

The man who had ordered frowned and picked up his glass.

Jack was surprised at the speed with which William moved. One moment he was facing the four men with a bottle in his hand. The next, the bottle was gone, and he held a short-barreled shotgun, obviously shortened with a hacksaw. Its big muzzles swung from right to left, covering all four.

When the Cherokee spoke, his voice was low, conversational. "Two bits."

At the sudden appearance of the shotgun, the four men took

a step back from the bar. Their hands rose waist high, palms forward, as if they were trying to push the gaping muzzle away. The spokesman said, "We wuz only funnin' you."

Jack rose, stepped to the bar, and tossed a quarter on it. "On me, William."

24

The man gave an appraising look at Jack, one dirty eyebrow raised. "Why, thanks, big feller." He turned back to the bar, smirked at William, and along with his friends, tossed the drink back with one swig. "Ahh, mighty good."

William had stowed the shotgun and was going about his business, but Jack could see he was alert and ready for anything.

Jack slapped the spokesman on the back. "You boys want another?"

"Why, shore, mister. That's mighty big of you." The man laughed and elbowed his nearest companion. "You hear that, Cooter? Big, from this here big feller. Funny, huh?"

Jack grinned at the man's humorless joke. "That's real funny, my friend, but I'm not too keen on buying drinks for folks I don't know. What's you boys' names?"

The talkative one began. "Feller on the end is Jeff, then Blade, Cooter, and I'm Tom Mason, but the boy's call me Sarge." The man puffed his chest out. "I fought in the war."

"Did you? Which side?"

Sarge frowned and jerked his head back. "Whatcha mean,

which side? They was only one, the South. Why, I could tell you—"

The man's mouth stopped running when he saw the five-dollar gold piece Jack had shoved toward William. "Give these boys all they want. They deserve it. Sarge fought in the war."

Four heads nodded in unison, and four sets of eyes followed the bottle as William began to pour. Jack glanced back toward Monty and Bronco. Both men gave an almost imperceptible nod.

In less than twenty minutes all four were slurring their speech and staggering drunk. Sarge turned dulled eyes toward Jack, eyebrow raised again. Jack tossed another quarter on the bar.

"Why don't you fellas have one more for the trail."

William solemnly poured them another drink. The men had to concentrate in order to move the glass from the bar to their mouth without spilling any of their precious liquor, but each was successful in his own way. A few drops were spilled, but most found its way down greedy throats.

Sarge, his head lolling from side to side, held onto the bar with his left hand and turned unfocused eyes toward Jack. His turn was just far enough to allow him to see the big fist headed for his chin, but all he could do was observe the arrival. He dropped like a rock. Monty and Bronco had each moved up behind Jeff and Cooter, sending those two to join Sarge in a pile on the dirt floor.

Blade was a different matter. He was drunk, but he still maintained a few of his faculties, though his speed was significantly slower. His hand jumped to the back of his neck, gripped a long Arkansas toothpick, and yanked it from the scabbard hanging between his shoulder blades. Before he could make up his mind what to do with it, Jack hit him, accomplishing the same result as the others. The knife fell straight, sticking into the dirt floor, and Blade collapsed on top of his friends.

Jack glanced to Monty. "Figured we might have a better chance if we reduced this gang's number by four."

Bronco, hands on his hips, looked at the four unkempt killers lying in a pile. "If we was smart, we'd drag 'em out to that big tree and stretch them dirty necks."

William peered over the bar. "Nobody'd miss them, and they don't buy much."

"Tempting as it is," Jack said, "this is their lucky day." He glanced up at William, who had been joined by Julia, the girl, and two Indians, each at least six feet tall. "Can we expect any problem from these four?"

William shook his head. "No. They're just low-ranking soldiers for Haley. When Haley's gone, they'll move along to somewhere or someone else. My friends here"—he nodded to the two men who had magically appeared—"will haul them off and put them where they won't be bothering anyone for a while."

Jack looked at the large, solemn men. "I don't want them killed just for being a nuisance. They may deserve it, but not today."

William shook his head. "They won't be harmed." He paused before continuing, "I should say they won't have any permanent harm come to them."

Jack nodded. "Good. Need some help?"

The bigger of the two men shook his head. "No." He stepped forward and grabbed Sarge and Jeff by the collar and dragged them out the door. The other Indian did the same with Cooter and Blade after he picked up Blade's knife and shoved it into his waistband. A few minutes later the sound of horses trotting away from the trading post came through the open door.

Jack followed Monty and Bronco back to the table and sat next to Buster, who was laying his rifle alongside his hat. He winked at the boy, who grinned back and took another bite of pie. Jack savored the creamy, sweet-tart peach flavor and swallowed. "William, we need some information. You said you knew where

Haley's gang will be waiting for us. How much do you know about them?"

"Just about everything. They talk openly when they're here. Knox Haley runs roughshod over every traveler who comes through these parts."

"Without those four—" Jack nodded toward the door "—how many men does he have?"

"He's tight with his money, so he don't keep many men around. Right now, he has four more with him, total of five including himself. Since he lost his brother, he's gotten real mean, even to the men who work for him. He's a dangerous man. The only person he ever did any good for was Chester, his brother."

Julia and the girl brought coffee, filling each man's cup. They both smiled at Buster.

Jack nodded his thanks to Julia, took a sip of the bitter brew, and asked, "Is there a way to dry-gulch the dry-gulchers?"

William's mouth turned up at the corners. "I thought you'd never ask."

~

THE FOUR TURNED back west after crossing south of the North Fork of the Canadian River. Following the map William had drawn on the dirt floor of the trading post, they had circled east, well north of the river. Once far enough east, they'd turned south, crossed the river, and were circling in behind Haley's gang. The hills, bluffs, and trees gave them plenty of cover.

Monty, riding next to Jack, leaned near him, speaking in a low voice. "You know, we could have ridden on out of this country. They'd never caught us."

"Yeah, but what happens to the next travelers who come along? We have a chance here to put these killers out of business." Jack turned and looked at Monty. "If you didn't think this was a good idea, why didn't you say something back at the post? It's your life too."

Monty grinned at him. "What you're doin' is fine with me. I'm just pointin' out that you've got a wide streak of puttin' the other feller's needs over yores."

Jack frowned. "I wasn't putting anyone else's needs over mine when I went after DeWitt."

"Sure you was. Course, he did steal yore horse and money, but he killed that boy in cold blood. You was after justice for that young feller. Just pointin' out, Jack, you've got lawman blood in yore veins. You might get yourself a ranch, but I'll tell you right now, you'll never be satisfied unless you're a-helpin' people."

Jack shook his head. "I respect you, Monty, but what you're saying is crazy."

The late afternoon was split with two shots, not far ahead, then silence.

Bronco shoved his hat back and scratched his head. "Now what do you suppose they're doing? If they set up an ambush for us, why would they be shooting if we ain't there?"

Jack swung down and pointed to the rocky, oak-strewn ridge ahead. Opening his saddlebags, he pulled out his field glasses. "The river's just on the other side of the ridge, right, Monty?"

Both Monty and Bronco nodded.

"I'll slip to the top of the ridge and see if I can see what's going on." He tossed his reins to Buster. "Hang on to Smokey for me. I'll be right back."

He slipped up the slope of the ridge, dodging small boulders and broken rocks. A scrubby oak with low-hanging limbs was anchored along the backbone of the ridgeline. Beneath the crest, he laid his hat on the ground, eased forward as close as he could without being seen, stretched prone, and crawled the last few feet, shoving his head past the limbs. The tragedy was playing out before him.

An older man was on his back. Jack put the glasses on him.

The man was bleeding from a shoulder wound, and one of the bushwhackers was kicking him in that shoulder. Two other men, Jack guessed the trail boss and another hand, were being beaten. All five members of the gang were standing round, either watching or taking part. Their horses were nowhere in sight. He saw where the trail traveled up out of the river, past the bandits, and disappeared around the base of the ridge he was on. *We can circle around from that direction, and they'll never hear us or see us until we're on top of them.*

He slid off the crest and down to his hat, got to his feet, and ran to his waiting companions. "Looks like they've got a trail boss and a couple of his men. One of them's been shot and is down. All three are being beaten by Haley's gang, and all five of the gang are right there in the bottom." He turned to Buster. "You bring the extra horses with us until we hit the trail. It's not far. When we get there, I want you to hold up and keep the horses together and quiet. Can you do that?"

Buster gave a sharp nod. "Yes, sir."

"Good. Keep your rifle ready in case any of them come up the trail. You know what to do."

"Yes, sir."

He turned to Monty and Bronco. "When we hit the trail, we'll walk the horses as quietly as possible until we're close. Then we'll charge right at 'em. I don't have to tell you they're killers. Be ready."

Bronco grinned. "Let's go."

The four of them rode toward the end of the ridge. It was no more than four hundred yards, so they were there quickly. Jack nodded to Buster, who gathered the horses while he, Monty, and Bronco continued around the ridge and onto the trail. Jack made sure the Remington in his holster was loose and the other was ready behind his waistband. He checked his Winchester, loose in the scabbard, ready.

They had ridden only a short distance when they heard the

sounds of blows, cursing, and shouts. "Where's that blasted money?" Then more sounds of blows. When they cleared the base of the ridgeline, the oaks thinned, and the panorama fell away before them.

It was a lovely glade surrounding the river crossing and moving out from the river. Tall oak, elm, and willow stood along the waterway, with a natural trail for the river crossing. Shallow water gurgled over the rocks in the river, inviting to the traveler. The trees stood like sentinels on each side of the trail until they gave way to the open grassy area, which traveled to the base of the ridge.

They were no more than forty yards from the killers when they broke into the open. Jack, with Monty to his left, and Bronco his right, yelled, "Now!" and kicked Smokey in the flanks. The horse leaped forward. Jack's word was followed by two bloodcurdling rebel yells that, even now, sent chills up Jack's spine. During the war, he had been on the receiving end of more than one of those charges.

Haley's gang spun from their victims, shock quickly followed by fear.

They were on them in an instant. Jack watched one of the men bring his .44 to bear on Monty, and shot down into the man's face, immediately swinging to another, who fell before he could pull the trigger.

Blasts of gunfire hammered his ears. Smoke filled the glade. Blood smell blended with the acrid smell of burned gunpowder.

A man grabbed at his leg. He leaned over, shoving the muzzle of the revolver into the man's neck, and pulled the trigger. The hand gripping his leg jerked and was gone.

He saw another man running for the treeline and wheeled Smokey after him. In two long leaps the big horse reached him, knocking the outlaw sprawling to the ground.

It was over.

So like other battles, Jack thought, swinging down to grab the bandit. *Bedlam, smoke, blood, noise, confusion, and then silence except for the groans of the wounded.*

Jack jerked the man to his feet. He was larger than average, with a flat nose that had long ago been smashed and mean little eyes. The man was dazed from being knocked flying by Smokey. Jack yanked a .44 Colt and a knife from the man's belt and looked over to Monty and Bronco.

Bronco saw him looking and waved. "We're all right, and we got 'em all. Three are dead, with two still kickin', countin' the one you got."

Jack shoved the man toward the injured cowhands.

The older-looking man, with blood covering his head, extended his hand. "Mighty glad you fellers showed up. Name's Birch Grover, trail boss of what's left of this outfit. Old feller on the ground is Kit Jeffers." He pointed to the cowhand still standing, with blood covering his shirt and vest. "That there's Ray Sadler."

Grover wiped blood from his forehead. "Good thing you came when you did. The feller you caught was just pulling out that pig-sticker"—he pointed to the knife in Jack's hand—"said he was gonna skin us alive, one at a time, until we gave up the money we got for the cattle."

Jack spun the big man around so he could look him in the eyes. "Is that right?"

The man stared at Jack, fists clinched, and eyes pulled tight, seeming to hurl hate at him. "I ain't got nothin' to say to you."

"What's your name?"

The man lowered his head and spit near Jack's feet, then raised it and continued to glare at him.

Jack ignored him, turned and yelled for Buster.

Monty had squatted next to Kit Jeffers and was examining the man's wound while Bronco kept an eye on the remaining outlaw.

Moments later, the boy and horses trotted into the glade.

To Grover, Jack said, "You know this bunch?"

He shook his head. "Nope. Never seen 'em before." He tossed a thumb over his shoulder toward the river crossing. "We rode up out of the river, and they blasted us."

All the while Grover talked, Monty worked on the wounded man.

"They shot Kit, then dragged him out of his saddle and started beatin' on him. Did the same thing to us. We was surprised and outnumbered." He bent closer to the wounded cowhand and spoke to Monty. "Is he going to make it?"

Monty had the man's shirt off and was closely examining the wound. "I suspect he'll be fine. I'm gonna have to clean this thing out, but after that, he oughta recover fine."

Jack turned to the outlaw Bronco was holding. "Your name."

The man tried to carry off the attitude of the other. He stuck his chest out and said, "Ain't none of yore business."

Jack slapped him with the flat of his hand. He'd seen this kind of bravado many times before. This man would crumble like dried mud. The slap sounded like a gunshot in the glade.

The man staggered two steps back. His hand flew to his cheek, which had instantly turned a deep crimson. His eyes darted from Jack to the other outlaw, who was glaring at him.

Jack took one long step, closing the distance, and drew back, this time with a thick, hard fist.

"Wait, wait! My name's Harvey Shine." He continued to rub his cheek.

Jack nodded his acceptance of Shine's statement, stopped, and lowered his fist. He jerked a thumb toward the other outlaw. "Who's he?"

Shine's nervous eyes bounced back and forth between Jack and the remaining outlaw, who continued to glare at him. "Why, he's the leader of our gang. He's Knox Haley."

Haley made as if to move toward Shine, but stopped when Jack locked him in his stony gaze. "So you're Knox Haley?"

Haley didn't flinch at Jack's stare. "What's it to you?"

Jack started looking around at the trees. "I like to know a man's name before I hang him."

As tough as he was, Haley paused at the statement, licked his lips, and rubbed his chin. "You ain't the law."

"I'm as close as you're ever going to get to a lawman, Haley. By the way, you shouldn't have taught your brother to ambush people at night. A body could get killed doing that."

Haley's jaws locked, and the muscles stood out like cords. "You killed my brother?"

"Wouldn't have if he hadn't tried to kill me."

"You'd be Jack Sage?" He looked Jack up and down. "Of course you are. There ain't nobody else around your size."

Jack ignored him, turning to Shine. "Where are your horses?"

Shine raised his stubble-covered chin to point at an elm thicket a short distance up the creek. "On the other side of that thicket."

"Buster, why don't you go get their horses."

The boy turned the big palomino toward the thicket, crossed the glade, disappeared into the thicket, and moments later reappeared with five horses.

He herded them toward the other bunch. Once he had them all together, he said, "These are some fine horses, Jack. I thought outlaws always had scrubs."

Jack shook his head. "Naw. They've got to have the best they can find so they can escape law-abiding folks like ourselves who can't afford that kind of stock." He turned to Bronco. "Why don't you find a couple of piggin' strings so we can tie these fellows' hands behind them."

25

Grover and Sadler had recovered their guns, and when Bronco dropped his back into his holster, they pulled theirs. The metallic click of hammers being cocked filled the glade. Both Shine and Haley eyed the guns. Sweat coursed down their faces.

Bronco pulled two piggin' strings from one of the saddles and yanked first Shine's and then Haley's hands behind their backs and tied them. Jack watched the two men. They both knew they were about to meet their maker, and their nerve was starting to break. He looked Shine over closely. Beneath the scraggly beard and dirty clothes, he wasn't much more than a kid. He couldn't be over twenty-two. *I wonder what led him on this path,* Jack thought. *He's surely regretting it now.*

Haley was definitely the tougher of the two, but his unease was beginning to show. His tough outer shell was melting away in sweat running down his face.

Jack looked at the young Shine. "How old are you, boy?"

"Mister, if this is September, I'll be twenty-one next month."

"How'd you get into this line of work?"

The boy shrugged. "I was from St. Louis, and I had no pa. Ma did her best, but we never had much food. I started out stealing food from markets. Then Ma died of consumption. It just kinda come natural."

Jack turned to Grover and Sadler. Jeffers was still out on the ground. They were the ones who had been injured by these men. "What do you think? Should he hang?"

Grover looked at Jeffers, then Sadler. "I'm not much for hangin' boys unless there ain't no question. How about you, Ray?"

Sadler looked at the young man, then back to Grover. "I'll tell you, boss, I'm torn. He was with 'em when they shot Kit, and I didn't hear him trying to stop anyone when Haley there was talking about skinning us alive." He scuffed at a rock with his boot, thought for a long moment, and scratched at a patch of dried blood on his cheek. "You been around a lot longer than I have, so you've got way more smarts than me. You want to turn him loose, I'll go along with it. I'm not sure I like it, but I'll go along with it."

Jack looked at Bronco and Monty. They both nodded, then he looked up at Buster astride Dusty. "What do you think, Buster?"

The boy's gray eyes widened in surprise. "You're askin' me, Jack? Shoot, I'm a kid. I don't know."

"You're part of this crew. You've been with us all the way. You get a say. Speak up."

Jack watched the boy as his mind went over the problem. It wasn't just the idea of keeping a man alive, it was also what he would do with his life if he received a reprieve, and nobody had that answer. A fella had to go with his knowledge and his heart. For if Shine was released, if his life was saved, would he go on to take the life of someone in the future who would have no part in the decision that might change their life?

Jack waited.

Finally, Buster said, "Turn him loose."

"How'd you come by that decision, Buster?"

The boy, still in the saddle, leaned forward, placing both hands on the saddle horn. "Well, Jack, I figger he's young enough to learn. Ain't no guarantee he will, but he's guaranteed not to if we hang him."

"Good thinking." He nodded to Bronco, who stepped over and untied Shine's hands.

The young man stood there rubbing his wrists, not quite comprehending what had happened. He looked around to every man in the group except for Knox Haley. "Thanks. I swear I'll never—"

"Hold up," Jack said. "You're not in any position to be making promises. I'm not sure I'd believe anything you said right now, anyway. Just think about what happened and what good men, even those you were about to harm, did for you. Hopefully you'll straighten out your life. Now get on your horse and ride. Ride long and far from here. Start a new and *honest* life." He turned to Bronco. "Check his horse for weapons. He gets no guns."

The boy looked like he was about to say something, thought better of it, and marched to his horse. Bronco walked along with him, stopped him when he reached the animal, and pulled his rifle from its boot. Then he went through the boy's saddlebags, finding another .36 Remington Navy. He shoved it behind his belt and motioned to Shine, who stepped up and swung onto his horse. He sat looking at each man, as if memorizing their faces, gave a nod, and rode south, down the trail. They watched until he disappeared.

"You gonna let me go?" Haley asked in his gravelly voice.

Jack grabbed him by the arm. "Which is your horse?"

"It don't matter."

"You're right." He half pulled and half supported the killer to a buckskin and helped him mount the animal. Jack was torn. He had always enforced the law. Hanging a man without a trial was against everything he stood for, but there was no judge or jury in the heart of Indian Territory. Still torn, he released his hold on the killer.

Haley had no sooner hit the saddle before he slammed the spurs into the bay's flanks. The surprised animal leaped once and then raced for the edge of the clearing. A .44 exploded in the glade, and Haley tilted, then fell from the saddle. His left boot slipped through and locked in the stirrup. His arms spread, hands grasping, but found nothing but air as his back struck the ground. The bay kicked at the lopsided weight attached to him, missed and dashed into the trees. Haley's body swung and slammed against one trunk and then another until disappearing after the animal. Moments later, splashing could be heard as the horse raced into the river.

Jack turned to see Birch Grover standing with a smoking .44-caliber Colt New Army revolver.

"I couldn't let him get away."

Jack nodded and looked around the grove. The acrid cloud of gun smoke settled over him. It was a smell he was used to. Truth be told, it was a smell he liked. His thoughts drifted to Kathryn Grace O'Donnell, her golden blonde hair and lovely blue eyes. She deserved a man who would come home every night to love her and protect her, a man she didn't have to constantly worry over. He couldn't be that man. He couldn't replace her happiness with worry, and he mustn't think of himself. He'd had his one love, and he would be satisfied with her memories.

This country needed him. It was experiencing growing pains. Justice was pushing its way west, but his type was still needed, hard men to stand up against evil like the Knox Haley gang, the Mould gang, and Ted DeWitt. *Monty called it,* Jack thought. *He nailed it down. I need to help and protect people, and I'm good at it. I'll see Buster home safely, and there'll be another town or families who need help. I'll find them, or they'll find me.*

Jack walked across the glade to Smokey and swung into the saddle. "I'll go find Haley. If we don't free that horse, wolves will have him tonight. Back shortly." He felt a weight lift, a decision made. Thanks to Monty, after all these years, he knew his mission.

Jack patted Smokey on the neck, clucked, and the grulla moved north, content to follow its master's command.

AUTHOR'S NOTE

I hope you've enjoyed reading *Without The Star,* the second book in the Jack Sage Western Series.

Thanks for reading my books. It is a true privilege to be able to share these stories with you.

At the age of eighty-one, I have seen many changes take place through my lifetime. I grew up in a simpler time. On Saturdays, several of us (eight, nine, and ten year old boys) would ride our bicycles to the only theater in town for the morning matinee. Cartoons, serials, usually Wild Bill Elliott, Tom Mix, or the Rocket Man, would fill the screen while we filled our bellies with candy, ice cream, popcorn, coke, grapette, or orange soda. Ten cents got us into the theater, and with a quarter we could eat more than we should. With fifty cents we could make ourselves and our friends sick.

But the thing that sticks with me about the movies and serials I saw, were there were good guys and bad guys, and it was always easy to determine the difference. So with the main features starring Roy Rogers or Gene Autry, how could kids go wrong. We'd spend our entire morning at the movie, then jump on our bikes and peddle home. Our parents probably looked forward to those Saturday mornings to have a few hours for themselves. It was a different time.

Thanks for letting me reminisce and, once again, for reading my books.

If you have any comments, what you like or what you don't, please let me know. You can email me at: Don@DonaldLRobertson.com, or fill in the contact form on my website.

www.DonaldLRobertson.com

I'm looking forward to hearing from you.

BOOKS
A Jack Sage Western Series
STRANGER WITH A STAR
WITHOUT THE STAR
RETURN OF THE STAR

Logan Mountain Man Series
(Prequel to Logan Family Series)

SOUL OF A MOUNTAIN MAN
TRIALS OF A MOUNTAIN MAN
METTLE OF A MOUNTAIN MAN

Logan Family Series

LOGAN'S WORD
THE SAVAGE VALLEY
CALLUM'S MISSION
FORGOTTEN SEASON
TROUBLED SEASON
TORTURED SEASON

Clay Barlow - Texas Ranger Justice Series

FORTY-FOUR CALIBER JUSTICE
LAW AND JUSTICE
LONESOME JUSTICE

NOVELLAS AND SHORT STORIES

RUSTLERS IN THE SAGE
BECAUSE OF A DOG
THE OLD RANGER

Printed in Great Britain
by Amazon

52798181R00148